Me

A Book of Remembrance

Me

A Book of Remembrance

Onoto Watanna

MINT EDITIONS

Me: A Book of Remembrance was first published in 1915.

This edition published by Mint Editions 2021.

ISBN 9781513271576 | E-ISBN 9781513276571

Published by Mint Editions®

minteditionbooks.com

Publishing Director: Jennifer Newens
Design & Production: Rachel Lopez Metzger
Project Manager: Micaela Clark
Typesetting: Westchester Publishing Services

Contents

I

It was a cold, blizzardy day in the month of March when I left Quebec, and my weeping, shivering relatives made an anxious, melancholy group about my departing train. I myself cried a bit, with my face pressed against the window; but I was seventeen, my heart was light, and I had not been happy at home.

My father was an artist, and we were very poor. My mother had been a tight-rope dancer in her early youth. She was an excitable, temperamental creature from whose life all romance had been squeezed by the torturing experience of bearing sixteen children. Moreover, she was a native of a far-distant land, and I do not think she ever got over the feeling of being a stranger in Canada.

Time was when my father, a young and ardent adventurer (an English-Irishman) had wandered far and wide over the face of the earth. The son of rich parents, he had sojourned in China and Japan and India in the days when few white men ventured into the Orient. But that was long ago.

This story is frankly of myself, and I mention these few facts merely in the possibility of their proving of some psychological interest later; also they may explain why it was possible for a parent to allow a young girl of seventeen to leave her home with exactly ten dollars in her purse (I do not think my father knew just how much money I did have) to start upon a voyage to the West Indies!

In any event, the fact remains that I had overruled my father's weak and absentminded objections and my mother's exclamatory ones, and I had accepted a position in Jamaica, West Indies, to work for a little local newspaper called *The Lantern*.

It all came about through my having written at the age of sixteen a crude, but exciting, story which a kindly friend, the editor of a Quebec weekly paper, actually accepted and published.

I had always secretly believed there were the strains of genius somewhere hidden in me; I had always lived in a little dream world of my own, wherein, beautiful and courted, I moved among the elect of the earth. Now I had given vivid proof of some unusual power! I walked on air. The world was rose-colored; nay, it was golden.

With my story in my hand, I went to the office of a family friend. I had expected to be smiled upon and approved, but also lectured and advised. My friend, however, regarded me speculatively.

"I wonder," said he, "whether *you* couldn't take the place of a girl out in Jamaica who is anxious to return to Canada, but is under contract to remain there for three years."

The West Indies! I *had* heard of the land somewhere, probably in my school geography. I think it was associated in my mind in some way with the fairy-stories I read. Nevertheless, with the alacrity and assurance of youth I cried out that *of course* I would go.

"It's a long way off," said my friend, dubiously, "and you are very young."

I assured him earnestly that I should grow, and as for the distance, I airily dismissed that objection as something too trivial to consider. Was I not the daughter of a man who had been back and forth to China no fewer than eighteen times, and that during the perilous period of the Tai-ping Rebellion? Had not my father made journeys from the Orient in the old-fashioned sailing-vessels, being at sea a hundred-odd days at a time? What could not his daughter do?

Whatever impression I made upon this agent of the West Indian newspaper must have been fairly good, for he said he would write immediately to Mr. Campbell, the owner of *The Lantern*, who, by the way, was also a Canadian, and recommend me.

I am not much of a hand at keeping secrets, but I did not tell my parents. I had been studying shorthand for some time, and now I plunged into that harder than ever, for the position was one in which I could utilize stenography.

It was less than two weeks later when our friend came to the house to report that the West Indian editor had cabled for me to be sent at once.

I was the fifth girl in our family to leave home. I suppose my father and mother had become sadly accustomed to the departing of the older children to try their fortunes in more promising cities than Quebec; but I was the first to leave home for a land as distant as the West Indies, though two of my sisters had gone to the United States. Still, there remained a hungry, crushing brood of little ones younger than I. With what fierce joy did I not now look forward to getting away at last from that same noisy, tormenting brood, for whom it had been my particular and detested task to care! So my father and mother put no obstacle in the way of my going. I remember passionately threatening to "run away" if they did.

My clothes were thick and woolen. I wore a red knitted toque, with a tassel that wagged against my cheek. My coat was rough and hopelessly

Canadian. My dress a shapeless bag belted in at the waist. I was not beautiful to look at, but I had a bright, eager face, black and shining eyes, and black and shining hair. My cheeks were as red as a Canadian apple. I was a little thing, and, like my mother, foreign-looking. I think I had the most acute, inquiring, and eager mind of any girl of my age in the world.

A man on the train who had promised my father to see me as far as my boat did so. When we arrived in New York he took me there in a carriage—the first carriage in which I had ever ridden in my life!

I had a letter to the captain, in whose special charge I was to be, that my Jamaica employer had written. So I climbed on board the *Atlas*. It was about six in the morning, and there were not many people about—just a few sailors washing the decks. I saw, however, a round-faced man in a white cap, who smiled at me broadly. I decided that he was the captain. So I went up to him and presented my letter, addressing him as "Captain Hollowell." He held his sides and laughed at me, and another man—this one was young and blond and very good-looking; at least so he seemed to the eyes of seventeen—came over to inquire the cause of the merriment. Greatly to my mortification, I learned from the new arrival that the man I had spoken to was not the captain, but the cook. He himself was Mr. Marsden, the purser, and he was prepared to take care of me until Captain Hollowell arrived.

The boat would not sail for two hours, so I told Mr. Marsden that I guessed I'd take a walk in New York. He advised me strenuously not to, saying that I might "get lost." I scorned his suggestion. What, *I* get lost? I laughed at the idea. So I went for my "walk in New York."

I kept to one street, the one at the end of which my boat lay. It was an ugly, dirty, noisy street,—noisy even at that early hour,—for horrible-looking trucks rattled over the cobblestoned road, and there were scores of people hurrying in every direction. Of the streets of New York I had heard strange, wonderful, and beautiful tales; but as I trotted along, I confess I was deeply disappointed and astonished. I think I was on Canal Street, or another of the streets of lower New York.

I was not going to leave the United States, however, without dropping a bit of my ten dollars behind me. So I found a store, in which I bought some postcards, a lace collar, and some ribbon—pink. When I returned to the boat I possessed, instead of ten dollars, just seven. However, this seemed a considerable sum to me, and I assured myself that on the boat itself, of course, one could not spend money.

I was standing by the rail watching the crowds on the wharf below. Every one on board was saying good-by to some one else, and people were waving and calling to one another. Everybody seemed happy and excited and gay. I felt suddenly very little and forlorn. I alone had no one to bid me good-by, to wave to me, and to bring me flowers. I deeply pitied myself, and I suppose my eyes were full of tears when I turned away from the rail as the boat pulled out.

The blond young purser was watching me, and now he came up cheerfully and began to talk, pointing out things to me in the harbor as the boat moved along. He had such nice blue eyes and shining white teeth, and his smile was quite the most winning that I had ever seen. Moreover, he wore a most attractive uniform. I forgot my temporary woes. He brought me his "own special" deck chair,—at least he said it was his,—and soon I was comfortably ensconced in it, my feet wrapped about with a warm rug produced from somewhere—also his. I felt a sense of being under his personal charge. A good part of the morning he managed to remain near me, and when he did go off among the other passengers, he took the trouble to explain to me that it was to attend to his duties.

I decided that he must have fallen in love with me. The thought delightfully warmed me. True, nobody had ever been in love with me before. I was the Ugly Duckling of an otherwise astonishingly good-looking family. Still, I was sure I recognized the true signs of love (had I not in dreams and fancies already been the heroine in a hundred princely romances?), and I forthwith began to wonder what life as the wife of a sailor might be like.

At dinner-time, however, he delivered me, with one of his charming smiles, to a portly and important personage who proved to be the real captain. My place at table was to be at his right side. He was a red-faced, jovial, mighty-voiced Scotchman. He called me a "puir little lassie" as soon as he looked at me. He explained that my West Indian employer (also a Scotch-Canadian) was his particular friend, and that he had promised to take personal care of me upon the voyage. He hoped Marsden, in his place, had looked after me properly, as he had been especially assigned by him to do. I, with a stifling lump of hurt vanity and pride in my throat, admitted that he had.

Then he was *not* in love with me, after all!

I felt cruelly unhappy as I stole out on deck after dinner. I disdained to look for that special deck chair my sailor had said I could have all for my own, and instead I sat down in the first one at hand.

Ugh! how miserable I felt! I suppose, said I to myself, that it was I who was the one to fall in love, fool that I was! But I had no idea one felt so wretched even when in love. Besides, with all my warm Canadian clothes, I felt chilly and shivery.

A hateful, sharp-nosed little man came poking around me. He looked at me with his eyes snapping, and coughed and rumbled in his throat as if getting ready to say something disagreeable to me. I turned my back toward him, pulled the rug about my feet, closed my eyes, and pretended to go to sleep. Then he said:

"Say, excuse me, but you've got my chair and rug."

I sat up. I was about to retort that "first come, first served" should be the rule, when out on deck came my friend Marsden. In a twinkling he appeared to take in the situation, for he strode quickly over to me, and, much to my indignation, took me by the arm and helped me to rise, saying that my chair was "over here."

I was about to reply in as haughty and rebuking a tone as I could command when I was suddenly seized with a most frightful surge of nausea. With my good-looking blond sailor still holding me by the arm, and murmuring something that sounded both laughing and soothing, I fled over to the side of the boat.

II

For four days I never left my state-room. "A sea-voyage is an inch of hell," says an old proverb of my mother's land, and to this proverb I most heartily assented.

An American girl occupied the "bunk" over mine, and shared with me the diminutive state-room. She was even sicker than I, and being sisters in great misery, a sweet sympathy grew up between us, so that under her direction I chewed and sucked on the sourest of lemons, and under mine she swallowed lumps of ice, a suggestion made by my father.

On the second day I had recovered somewhat, and so was able to wait upon and assist her a bit. Also, I found in her a patient and silent listener (Heaven knows she could not be otherwise, penned up as she was in that narrow bunk), and I told her all about the glorious plans and schemes I had made for my famous future; also I brought forth from my bag numerous poems and stories, and these I poured into her deaf ears in a voluble stream as she lay shaking and moaning in her bunk.

It had been growing steadily warmer—so warm, indeed, that I felt about the room to ascertain whether there were some heating-pipes running through it.

On the fourth day my new friend sat up in her bunk and passionately went "on strike." She said:

"Say, I wish you'd quit reading me all that stuff. I know it's lovely, but I've got a headache, and honestly I can't for the life of me take an interest in your poems and stories."

Deeply hurt, I folded my manuscripts. She leaned out of her berth and caught at my arm.

"Don't be angry," she said. "I didn't mean to hurt you."

I retorted with dignity that I was not in the slightest degree hurt. Also I quoted a proverb about casting one's pearls before swine, which sent her into such a peal of laughter that I think it effectually cured her of her lingering remnants of seasickness. She jumped out of her bunk, squeezed me about the waist, and said:

"You're the funniest girl I've ever met—a whole vaudeville act." She added, however, that she liked me, and as she had her arm about me, I came down from my high horse, and averred that her affection was reciprocated. She then told me her name and learned mine. She was bookkeeper in a large department store. Her health had been bad, and she had been saving for a long time for this trip to the West Indies.

We decided that we were now well enough to go on deck. As I dressed, I saw her watching me with a rather wondering and curious expression. My navy-blue serge dress was new, and although it was a shapeless article, the color at least was becoming, and with the collar purchased in New York, I felt that I looked very well. I asked her what she thought of my dress. She said evasively:

"Did you make it yourself?"

I said:

"No; mama did."

"Oh," said she.

I didn't just like the sound of that "Oh," so I asked her aggressively if she didn't think my dress was nice. She answered:

"I think you've got the prettiest hair of any girl I ever knew."

My hair *did* look attractive, and I was otherwise quite satisfied with my appearance. What is more, I was too polite to let her know what I thought of *her* appearance. Although it was March, she, poor thing, had put on a flimsy little muslin dress. Of course it was suffocatingly hot in our close little state-room, but, still, that seemed an absurd dress to wear on a boat. I offered to lend her a knitted woolen scarf that mama had made me to throw over her shoulders, but she shook her head, and we went up on deck.

To my unutterable surprise, I found a metamorphosis had taken place on deck during my four days' absence. Every one appeared to be dressed in thin white clothes; even the officers were all in white duck. Moreover, the very atmosphere had changed. It was as warm and sultry as midsummer, and people were sipping iced drinks and fanning themselves!

Slowly it dawned upon me that we were sailing toward a tropical land. In a hazy sort of way I had known that the West Indies was a warm country, but I had not given the matter much thought. My father, who had been all over the world, had left my outfitting to mama and me (we had so little with which to buy the few extra things mama, who was more of a child than I, got me!), and I had come away with clothes fit for a land which often registered as low as twenty-four degrees below zero!

My clothes scorched me; so did my burning shame. I felt that every one's eyes were bent upon me.

Both Captain Hollowell and Mr. Marsden greeted me cordially, expressing delight at seeing me again, but although the captain said (in a big, booming voice that every one on deck could hear) that I looked like a nice, blooming peony, I sensitively fancied I detected a laugh beneath his words.

Tragedies should be measured according to their effects. Trifles prick us in youth as sharply as the things that ought to count. I sensitively suffered in my pride as much from the humiliation of wearing my heavy woolen clothes as I physically did from the burden of their weight and heat. I was sure that I presented a ridiculous and hideous spectacle. I felt that every one was laughing at me. It was insufferable; it was torture.

As soon as I could get away from that joking captain, who *would* keep patting me on the head, and that purser, who was always smiling and showing his white teeth, I ran down to my room, which I had hoped to see as little of as possible for the rest of the voyage.

I sat down on the only chair and began to cry. The ugly little room, with its one miserable window, seemed a wretched, intolerable prison. I could hear the soughing of the waves outside, and a wide streak of blue sky was visible through my port-hole window. The moving of the boat and the thud of the machinery brought home to me strongly the fact that I was being carried resistlessly farther and farther away from the only home I had ever known, and which, alas! I had yearned to leave.

It was unbearably hot, and I took off my woolen dress. I felt that I would never go on deck again; yet how was I going to endure it down here in this little hole? I was thinking miserably about that when my room-mate came back.

"Well, here you are!" she exclaimed. "I've been looking for you everywhere! Now what's the matter?"

"N-nothing," I said; but despite myself the sob would come.

"You poor kid!" she said. "I know what's the matter with you. I don't know what your folks were thinking of when they sent you off to the West Indies in Canadian clothes. Are they all as simple as you there? But now don't you worry. Here, I've got six pretty nice-looking shirt-waists, besides my dresses, and you're welcome to any of them you want. You're just about my size. I'm thirty-four."

"Thirty-four!" I exclaimed, astonished even in the midst of my grief. "Why, I thought you were only about twenty."

"Bust! Bust!" she cried, laughing, and got her waists out and told me to try them on. I gave her a kiss, a big one, I was so delighted; but

I insisted that I could not borrow her waists. I would, however, buy some of them if she would sell them.

She said that was all right, and she sold me three of them at a dollar-fifty each. They fitted me finely. I never felt happier in my life than when I put on one of those American-made shirt-waists. They were made sailor-fashion, with wide turnover collars and elbow sleeves; with a red silk tie in front, and with my blue cloth skirt, I really did look astonishingly nice, and, anyway, cool and neat. The fact that I now possessed only two dollars and fifty cents in the world gave me not the slightest worry, and when I ran out of my room, humming, and up the stairs and bang into the arms of Captain Hollowell, he did not say this time that I looked like a peony, but that, "By George!" I looked like a nice Canadian rose.

III

"D o you know," said my room-mate on the night before we reached Jamaica, "that that four-fifty you paid me for those waists just about covers my tips."

"Tips?" I repeated innocently. "What are tips?"

She gave me a long, amazed look, her mouth wide-open.

"Good heavens!" at last she said, "where *have* you lived all of your life?"

"In Quebec," I said honestly.

"And you never heard of tips—people giving tips to waiters and servants?"

I grew uncomfortably red under her amused and amazed glance. In the seven days of that voyage my own extraordinary ignorance had been daily brought home to me. I now said lamely:

"Well, we had only one servant that I can ever remember, a woman named Sung-Sung whom papa brought from China; but she was more like one of our family, a sort of slave. We never gave her tips, or whatever you call it."

Did I not know, pursued my American friend, that people gave extra money—that is, "tips"—to waiters at restaurants and hotels when they got through eating a meal?

I told her crossly and truthfully that I had never been in a hotel or restaurant in all my life. She threw up her hands, and pronounced me a vast object of pity. She then fully enlightened me as to the exact meaning of the word "tips," and left me to calculate painfully upon a bit of paper the division of two dollars and fifty cents among five people; to wit, stewardesses, cabin boys, waiters, etc.

I didn't tell her that that was the last of my money—that two-fifty. However, I did not expend any thought upon the subject of what was to become of me when I arrived in Jamaica *sans* a single cent.

We brought our bags and belongings out on deck before the boat docked next day. Every one was crowded against the rails, watching the approaching land.

A crowd seemed to be swarming on the wharves, awaiting our boat. As we came nearer, I was amazed to find that this crowd was made up almost entirely of negroes. We have few negroes in Canada, and I had seen only one in all my life. I remember an older sister had shown him to me in church—he was pure black—and told me he was the "Bogy man," and that he'd probably come around to see me that night. I was six. I never took my eyes once from his face during the service, and I have never forgotten that face.

It was, therefore, with a genuine thrill of excitement and fear that I looked down upon that vast sea of upturned black and brown faces. Never will I forget that first impression of Jamaica. Everywhere I looked were negroes—men and women and children, some half naked, some with bright handkerchiefs knotted about their heads, some gaudily attired, some dressed in immaculate white duck, just like the people on the boat.

People were saying good-by, and many had already gone down the gang-plank. Several women asked me for my address, and said they did not want to lose me. I told them I did not know just where I was going. I expected Mr. Campbell to meet me.

As Mr. Campbell had not come on board, however, and as Captain Hollowell and Mr. Marsden seemed to have forgotten my existence in the great rush of arrival, I, too, at last descended the gang-plank. I found myself one of that miscellaneous throng of colored and white people.

A number of white men and women were hurrying about meeting and welcoming expected passengers, who were soon disposed of in various vehicles. Soon not one of the boat's passengers remained, even my room-mate being one of a party that climbed aboard a bus marked, "The Crystal Springs Hotel."

I was alone on that Jamaica wharf, and no one had come to claim me!

It was getting toward evening, and the sky in the west was as red as blood. I sat down on my bag and waited. Most of the people left on the dock were laborers who were engaged in unloading the ship's cargo. Women with heavy loads on their heads, their hands on their shaking hips, and chattering in a high singsong dialect (I didn't recognize it for English at first!), passed me. Some of them looked at me curiously, and one, a terrifying, pock-marked crone, said something to me that I could not understand.

I saw the sun slipping down in the sky, but it was still as bright and clear as mid-day. Sitting alone on that Jamaica wharf, I scarcely saw the shadows deepening as I looked out across the Caribbean Sea, which shone like a jewel under the fading light. I forgot my surroundings and my anxiety at the failure of my employer to meet me; I felt no fear, just a vague sort of enchantment and interest in this new land I had discovered.

But I started up screaming when I felt a hand on my shoulder, and looking up in the steadily deepening twilight, I saw a smiling face approach my own, and the face was black!

I fled toward the boat, crying out wildly:

"Captain Hollowell! O Captain Hollowell!"

I left my little bag behind me. Fear lent wings to my feet, and I kept crying out to Captain Hollowell as I ran up that gang-plank, mercifully still down. At the end of it was my dear blond purser, and right into his arms unhesitatingly I ran. He kept saying: "Well! well! well!" and he took me to Captain Hollowell, who swore dreadfully when he learned that Mr. Campbell had not met me. Then my purser went to the dock wharf to get my bag, and to "skin the hide off that damned black baboon" who had frightened me.

I ate dinner with Captain Hollowell and the officers of the *Atlas* that night, the last remaining passenger on the boat. After dinner, accompanied by the captain and the purser, I was taken by carriage to the office of *The Lantern*.

I don't know what Captain Hollowell said to Mr. Campbell before I was finally called in, for I had been left in the outer office. Their voices were loud and angry, and I thought they were quarreling. I devoutly hoped it was not over me. I was tired and sleepy. In fact, when Captain Hollowell motioned to me to come in, I remember rubbing my eyes, and he put his arm about me and told me not to cry.

In a dingy office, with papers and books scattered about in the most bewildering disorder, at a long desk-table, likewise piled with books and journals and papers, sat an old man who looked exactly like the pictures of Ibsen. He was sitting all crumpled up, as it were, in a big arm-chair; but as I came forward he sat up straight. He stared at me so long, and with such an expression of amazement, that I became uneasy and embarrassed. I remember holding on tight to Captain Hollowell's sleeve on one side and Mr. Marsden's on the other. And then at last a single sentence came from the lips of my employer. It came explosively, despairingly:

"My God!" said the owner of *The Lantern*.

It seems that our Quebec friend had been assigned to obtain for *The Lantern* a mature and experienced journalist. Mr. Campbell had expected a woman of the then approved, if feared, type of bluestocking, and behold a baby had been dropped into his lap!

The captain and Marsden had departed. I sat alone with that old man who looked like Ibsen, and who stared at me as if I were some freak of nature. He had his elbows upon his desk, and his chin propped up in the cup of his hands. He began to ask me questions, after he had literally stared me down and out of countenance, and I sat there before him, twisting my handkerchief in my hand.

"How old are you?"

"Seventeen. I mean—I'm going on eighteen." Eighteen was, in fact, eleven months off.

"Have you ever worked before?"

"I've written things."

After a silent moment, during which he glared at me more angrily than ever, he demanded:

"What have you written?"

"Poetry," I said, and stopped because he said again in that lost voice, "My God!"

"What else?"

"I had a story published in *The Star*," I said. "I've got it here, if you'd like to see it."

He made a motion of emphatic dissent.

"What else have you done?"

"I taught myself shorthand," I said, "and I can take dictation as fast as you can talk."

He looked frankly skeptical and in no wise impressed.

"How can you do that if you've had no experience as a stenographer?"

"I got a shorthand book," I said eagerly. "It's not at all hard to teach yourself after you learn the rudiments. My sister showed me that. She's secretary to the Premier of Canada. As soon as I had learned shorthand, I acquired practice and speed by going to church and prayer-meetings and taking down sermons."

After a moment he said grudgingly:

"Not a bad idea." And then added, "What do you think you are going to do here?"

"Write for your paper," I said as conciliatingly as I could.

"What?" he inquired curiously.

"Why—anything—poetry—"

He waved his hand in such a dismissing manner that I got up, though it was my poetry, not I, he wished to be rid of just then. I went nearer to him.

"I know you don't want me," I said, "and I don't want to stay. I'm sorry I came. I wouldn't if I had known that this was a hot, beastly old country where nearly everybody is black. If you'll just get me back to the boat, I know Captain Hollowell will let me go back with him, even if I haven't the money for my fare."

"What about the money I paid for you to come here?" he snarled. "Think I'm going to lose that?"

I did not answer him. I felt enervated, homesick, miserable, and tired. He got up presently, limped over to another table,—he was lame,—poured a glass of water, brought it to me with a big fan, and said gruffly, "Sit!"

The act, I don't know why, touched me. In a dim way I began to appreciate his position. He was a lame old man running a fiery, two-sheet little newspaper in this tropical land far from his native Canada. There was no staff, and, indeed, none of the ordinary appurtenances of a newspaper office. He employed only one able assistant, and as he could not get such a person in Jamaica and could not afford to pay a man's salary, being very loyal to Canada, he had been accustomed to send there for bright and expert young women reporters to do virtually all the work of running his newspaper. Newspaper women are not plentiful in Canada. The fare to Jamaica is, or was then, about $55. Mr. Campbell must have turned all these things over in his mind as he looked at this latest product of his native land, a green, green girl of seventeen, whose promise that she would "look older next day," when her "hair was done up," carried little reassurance as to her intelligence or ability.

He did a lot of "cussing" of our common friend in Canada. Finally he said that he would take me over to the Myrtle Bank Hotel, where accommodations had been arranged for me, and we could talk the matter over in the morning.

While he was getting his stick and hat, the latter a green-lined helmet, I couldn't resist looking at some of his books. He caught me doing this, and asked me gruffly if I had ever read anything. I said:

"Yes, Dickens, George Eliot, and Sir Walter Scott; and I've read Huxley and Darwin, and lots of books on astronomy to my father, who is very fond of that subject." As he made no comment, nor seemed at all impressed by my erudition, I added proudly: "My father's an Oxford man, and a descendant of the family of Sir Isaac Newton."

There was some legend to this effect in our family. In fact, the greatness of my father's people had been a sort of fairy-story with us all, and we knew that it was his marriage with mama that had cut him off from his kindred. My Jamaica employer, however, showed no interest in my distinguished ancestry. He took me roughly by the arm, and half leaning upon, half leading me, hobbled with me out into the dark street.

It was about nine o'clock. As we approached the hotel, which was only a short distance from the office of *The Lantern*, it pleased me as a happy omen that somewhere within those fragrant, moonlit gardens a band began to play most beautifully.

Mr. Campbell took me to the room of the girl whose place I was to take, and who was also from Quebec. She had already gone to bed, but she rose to let me in. Mr. Campbell merely knocked hard on the door and said:

"Here's Miss Ascough. You should have met her," and angrily shoved me in, so it seemed to me.

Miss Foster, her hair screwed up in curl-papers, after looking at me only a moment, said in a tired, complaining voice, like that of a sick person, that I had better get to bed right away; and then she got into bed, and turned her face to the wall. I tried to draw her out a bit while undressing, but to all my questions she returned monosyllabic answers. I put out the light, and crept into bed beside her. The last thing she said to me, and very irritably, was:

"Keep to your own side of the bed."

I slept fairly well, considering the oppressiveness of the heat, but I awoke once when something buzzed against my face.

"What's that?" I cried, sitting up in bed.

She murmured crossly:

"Oh, for heaven's sake lie down! I haven't slept a wink for a century. You'll have to get used to Jamaica bugs and scorpions. They ought to have screens in the windows!"

After that I slept with the sheet over my head.

IV

I was awakened at six the following morning. A strange, singsong voice called into the room:

"Marnin', missee! Heah's your coffee."

I found Miss Foster up and dressed. She was sitting at a table drinking coffee. She put up the shade and let the light in. Then she came over to the bed, where the maid had set the tray. I was looking at what I supposed to be my breakfast. It consisted of a cup of black coffee and a single piece of dry toast.

"You'd better drink your coffee," said Miss Foster, wearily. "It will sustain you for a while."

I got a good look at her, standing by my bed. The yellowness of her skin startled me, and I wondered whether it could be possible that she, too, was "colored." Then I remembered that she was from my home. Moreover, her eyes were a pale blue, and her hair a light, nondescript brown. She had a peevish expression, even now while she made an effort at friendliness. She sat down on the side of my bed, and while I drank my coffee and nibbled my piece of toast she told me a few things about the country.

Jamaica, she said, was the beastliest country on the face of the earth. Though for a few months its climate was tolerable, the rest of the year it was almost unbearable. What with the crushing heat and the dirty, drizzling rain that followed, and fell without ceasing for months at a time, all ambition, all strength, all hope were slowly knocked out of one. There were a score of fevers, each one as bad as the others. She was suffering from one now. That was why she was going home. She was young, so she said, but she felt like an old woman. She pitied me, she declared, for what was before me, and said Campbell had no right to bring healthy young girls from Canada without first telling them what they were coming up against.

I put in here that perhaps I should fare better. I said:

"I'm almost abnormally healthy and strong, you know, even if I look thin. I'm the wiry kind."

She sniffed at that, and then said, with a shrug:

"Oh, well, maybe you will escape. I'm sure I wish you better luck than mine. But one thing's certain: you'll lose that Canadian complexion of yours all right."

My duties, she said, would be explained to me by Mr. Campbell himself, though she was going to stay over a day or two to help break me in. My salary would be ten dollars a week and free board and lodging at the Myrtle Bank Hotel. I told her of the slighting reception I had received at the hands of Mr. Campbell, and she said:

"Oh, well, he's a crank. You couldn't please him, no matter what you did." Then she added: "I don't see, anyhow, why he objected to you. Brains aren't so much needed in a position like this as legs and a constitution of iron."

As the day advanced, the heat encroached. Miss Foster sat fanning herself languidly by the window, looking out with a far-away expression. I told her about my clothes, and how mortified I was to find them so different from those of the others on the boat. She said:

"You can have all my clothes, if you want. They won't do for Canada."

That suggested a brilliant solution of my problem of how I was to secure immediately suitable clothes for Jamaica. I suggested that as she was going to Canada, she could have mine, and I would take hers. The proposition seemed to give her a sort of grim amusement. She looked over my clothes. She took the woolen underwear and heavy, hand-knitted stockings (that Sung-Sung had made for an older brother, and which had descended to me after two sisters had had them!), two woolen skirts, my heavy overcoat, and several other pieces.

She gave me a number of white muslin dresses,—they seemed lovely to me,—an evening gown with a real low neck, cotton underwear, hose, etc.

I put my hair up for the first time that morning. As I curled it a bit, this was not difficult to do. I simply rolled it up at the back and held the chignon in place with four bone hair-pins that she gave me. I put on one of her white muslin dresses but it was so long for me that we had to make a wide tuck in it. Then I wore a wide Leghorn hat, the only trimming of which was a piece of cream-colored mull twisted like a scarf about the crown.

I asked Miss Foster if I looked all right, and was suitably dressed, and she said grudgingly:

"Yes, you'll do. You're quite pretty. You'd better look out."

Asked to explain, she merely shrugged her shoulders and said:

"There's only a handful of white women here, you know. We don't count the tourists. You'll have all you can do to hold the men here at arm's-length."

This last prospect by no means bothered me. I had the most decided and instinctive liking for the opposite sex.

The hotel was beautiful, built somewhat in the Spanish style, with a great inner court, and an arcade that ran under the building. Long verandas ran out like piers on each side of the court, which was part of the wonderful garden that extended to the shores of the Caribbean.

The first thing I saw as we came out from our room upon one of the long-pier verandas was an enormous bird. It was sitting on the branch of a fantastic and incredibly tall tree that was all trunk, and then burst into great fan-like foliage at the top. Subsequently I learned that this was a cocoanut tree.

The proprietor of the hotel, who was dark, smiling, and deferential, came up to be introduced to me, and I said, meaning to pay a compliment to his country:

"You have fine-looking birds here."

He looked at me sharply and then snickered, as if he thought I were joking about something.

"That's a scavenger," he said. "There are hundreds, thousands of them here in Jamaica. Glad you like them."

I thought it an ugly name for a bird, but I said:

"It's a very interesting bird, I think."

Miss Foster pulled me along and said sharply that the birds were vultures. They called them scavengers in Jamaica because they really acted as such. Every bit of dirt and filth and refuse, she declared with disgust, was thrown into the streets, and devoured shortly by the scavengers. If a horse or animal died or was killed, it was put into the street. Within a few minutes it had completely disappeared, the scavengers having descended like flies upon its body. She darkly hinted, moreover, that many a human corpse had met a similar fate. I acquired a shuddering horror for that "interesting bird" then and there, I can tell you, and I thought of the unscreened windows, and asked Miss Foster if they ever had been known to touch living things. She shrugged her shoulders, which was not reassuring.

Miss Foster took me into the hotel's great dining-room, which was like a pleasant open conservatory, with great palms and plants everywhere. There we had breakfast, for it seems coffee and toast were just an appetizer. I never became used to Jamaica cooking. It was mushy, hot, and sweet.

After breakfast we reported at *The Lantern*, where Mr. Campbell, looking even fiercer in the day, impatiently awaited us. He wished Miss

Foster to take me directly out to Government House and teach me my duties there, as the Legislative Council was then in session. He mumbled off a lot of instructions to Miss Foster, ignoring me completely. His apparent contempt for me, and his evident belief that there was no good to be expected from me, whetted my desire to prove to him that I was not such a fool as I looked, or, rather, as he seemed to think I looked. I listened intently to everything he said to Miss Foster, but even so I received only a confused medley of "Bills—attorney-general—Representative So and So—Hon. Mr. So and So," etc.

I carried away with me, however, one vivid instruction, and that was that it was absolutely necessary for *The Lantern* to have the good-will of the Hon. Mr. Burbank, whom we must support in everything. It seemed, according to Mr. Campbell, that there was some newspaper libel law that was being pressed in the House that, if passed, would bring the Jamaica press down to a pusillanimous condition.

Mr. Burbank was to fight this bill for the newspapers. He was, in fact, our representative and champion. *The Lantern*, in return, was prepared to support him in other measures that he was fathering. Miss Foster and I were to remember to treat him with more than common attention. I did not know, of course, that this meant in our newspaper references to him, and I made a fervent vow personally to win the favor of said Burbank.

We got into a splendid little equipage, upholstered in tan cloth and with a large tan umbrella top, which was lined with green.

We drove for several miles through a country remarkable for its beautiful scenery. It was a land of color. It was like a land of perpetual spring—a spring that was ever green. I saw not a single shade that was dull. Even the trunks of the gigantic trees seemed to have a warm tone. The flowers were startlingly bright—yellow, scarlet, and purple.

We passed many country people along the road. They moved with a sort of languid, swinging amble, as if they dragged, not lifted, their flat feet. Women carried on their heads enormous bundles and sometimes trays. How they balanced them so firmly was always a mystery to me, especially as most of them either had their hands on their hips, or, more extraordinary, carried or led children, and even ran at times. Asses, loaded on each side with produce, ambled along as draggingly as the natives.

Miss Foster made only three or four remarks during the entire journey. These are her remarks. They are curious taken altogether:

"This carriage belongs to Mr. Burbank. He supplies all the vehicles, by the way, for the press."

"Those are the botanical gardens. Jamaica has Mr. Burbank to thank for their present excellent condition. Remember that."

"We are going by the Burbank plantation now. He has a place in Kingston, too, and a summer home in the mountains."

"If we beat that newspaper libel law, you'll have a chance to write all the funny things and rhymes you want about the mean sneaks who are trying to push it through."

Even during the long drive through the green country I had been insensibly affected by the ever-growing heat. In the long chamber of Government House, where the session was to be held, there seemed not a breath of air stirring. It was insufferably hot, though the place was virtually empty when we arrived. I had a shuddering notion of what it would be like when full.

Miss Foster was hustling about, getting "papers" and "literature" of various kinds, and as the legislators arrived, she chatted with some of them. She had left me to my own devices, and I did not know what to do with myself. I was much embarrassed, as every one who passed into the place took a look at me. We were the only two girls in the House.

There was a long table in the middle of the room, at which the members of Parliament and the elected members had their seats, and there was a smaller table at one side for the press. I had remained by the door, awaiting Miss Foster's instructions. The room was rapidly beginning to fill. A file of black soldiers spread themselves about the room, standing very fine and erect against the walls. At the council table, on one side, were the Parliament members, Englishmen, every one of whom wore the conventional monocle. On the other side were the elected members, who were, without an exception, colored men. I was musing over this when a very large, stout, and handsome personage (he was a personage!) entered ponderously, followed by several younger men. Every one in the room rose, and until he took his seat (in a big chair on a little elevated platform at the end of the room) they remained standing. This was his Excellency Sir Henry Drake, the Governor-General of Jamaica. The House was now in session.

By this time I experienced a natural anxiety to know what was to become of me. Surely I was not supposed to stand there by the door. Glancing across at the press table, I presently saw Miss Foster among the reporters. She was half standing, and beckoning to me to join her.

Confused and embarrassed, I passed along at the back of one end of the council table, and was proceeding in the direction of the press table, when suddenly the room reverberated with loud cries from the soldiers of, "Order! order! order!"

I hesitated only a moment, ignorant of the fact that that call was directed against me, and, as I paused, I looked directly into the purpling face of the Governor of Jamaica. He had put on his monocle. His face was long and preternaturally solemn, but there was a queer, twisted smile about his mouth, and I swear that he winked at me through that monocle, which fell into his hand. I proceeded to my seat, red as a beet.

"Great guns!" whispered Miss Foster, dragging me down beside her, "you walked in *front* of the governor! You should have gone behind his chair. What will Mr. Campbell say when he knows you were called to order the first day! A fine reflection on *The Lantern*!" She added the last sentence almost bitterly.

What went on at that session I never in the world could have told. It was all like an incomprehensible dream. Black men, the elected members, rose, and long and eloquently talked in regard to some bill. White men (government) rose and languidly responded, sometimes with a sort of drawling good humor, sometimes satirically. I began to feel the effect of the oppressive atmosphere in a way I had not yet experienced. An unconquerable impulse to lay my head down upon the table and go to sleep seized upon me, and I could scarcely keep my eyes open. At last my head did fall back against the chair; my eyes closed. I did not exactly faint, but I succumbed slightly to the heat. I heard a voice whispering at my ear, for the proceedings went on, as if it were a common thing for a woman to faint in Government House.

"Drink this!" said the voice, and I opened my eyes and looked up into a fair, boyish face that was bending over mine. I drank that cool Jamaica kola, and recovered myself sufficiently to sit up again. Said my new friend:

"It'll be cooler soon. You'll get used to the climate, and if I were you, I wouldn't try to do *any* work to-day."

I said:

"I've got to *learn*. Miss Foster sails to-morrow, and after that—"

"I'll show you after that," he said, and smiled reassuringly.

At one there was an adjournment for luncheon. I then became the center of interest, and was introduced by Miss Foster to the members of the press. Jamaica boasted three papers beside ours, and there were representatives at the Parliament's sessions from other West Indian islands. I was also introduced to several of the members, both black and white.

I went to luncheon with Miss Foster and two members of Parliament (white) and three reporters, one of them the young man who had given me the kola, and whose name was Verley Marchmont. He was an Englishman, the younger son in a poor, but titled, family. We had luncheon at a little inn hard by, and while there I made three engagements for the week. With one of the men I was to go to a polo match (Jamaica had a native regiment whose officers were English), with another I was to attend a ball in a lighthouse, and young Marchmont, who was only about eighteen, was to call upon me that evening.

At the end of the afternoon session, which was not quite so wearing, as it had grown cooler, I was introduced by Miss Foster to the governor's secretary, Lord George Fitzpatrick, who had been smiling at me from behind the governor's back most of the day. By him I was introduced to the governor, who seemed to regard me as a more or less funny curiosity, if I am to judge from his humorous expression. Lord George also introduced me to other government members, and he asked me if I liked candies. I said I did. He asked me if I played golf or rode horseback. I said I didn't, but I could learn, and he said he was a great teacher.

By this time I thought I had met every one connected with the House, when suddenly I heard some one—I think it was one of the reporters—call out:

"Oh, all right, Mr. Burbank. I'll see to it."

Miss Foster was drawing me along toward the door. It was time to go. Our carriage was waiting for us. As we were going out, I asked her whether I had yet met Mr. Burbank, and she said she supposed so.

"I don't remember meeting him," I persisted, "and I want very specially to meet Mr. Burbank."

On the steps below us a man somewhat dudishly attired in immaculate white duck, and wearing a green-lined helmet, turned around and looked up at us. His face was almost pure black. His nose was large and somewhat hooked. I have subsequently learned that he was partly Hebrew. He had an enormous mouth, and teeth thickly set with gold. He wore gold-rimmed glasses with a chain, and these and his fine clothes gave a touch of distinction to his appearance. At least it made him stand out from the average colored man. As I spoke, I saw him look at me with a curious expression; then smiling, he held out his big hand.

"I am the Hon. Mr. Burbank," he said.

I was startled to find that this man I had been planning to cultivate was black. I do not know why, but as I looked down into that ingratiating face, I was filled with a sudden panic of almost instinctive fear, and although he held out his hand to me, I did not take it. For that I was severely lectured by Miss Foster all the way back. She reminded me that I could not afford to snub so powerful a Jamaican as Burbank, and that if I had the slightest feeling of race prejudice, I had better either kill it at once or clear out of Jamaica. She said that socially there was absolutely no difference between the white and colored people in Jamaica.

As a matter of fact, I had literally never even heard the expression "race prejudice" before, and I was as far from feeling it as any person in the world. It must be remembered that in Canada we do not encounter the problem of race. One color there is as good as another. Certainly people of Indian extraction are well thought of and esteemed, and my own mother was a foreigner. What should I, a girl who had never before been outside Quebec, and whose experience had been within the narrow confines of home and a small circle, know of race prejudice?

Vaguely I had a feeling that all men were equal as men. I do not believe it was in me to turn from a man merely because of his race, so long as he himself was not personally repugnant to me. I myself was dark and foreign-looking, but the blond type I adored. In all my most fanciful imaginings and dreams I had always been golden-haired and blue-eyed.

V

I got on better with Mr. Campbell after Miss Foster went. He told me it was necessary for us to keep on the right side of Mr. Burbank, who was one of the greatest magnates and philanthropists of Jamaica, but he took occasion to contradict some of Miss Foster's statements. It was not true, he said, that there was no social distinction between black and white in Jamaica. That was the general opinion of tourists in Jamaica, who saw only the surface of things, but as a matter of fact, though the richest people and planters were of colored blood; though they were invited to all the governor's parties and the various official functions; though they were in vast evidence at polo and cricket matches; though many of them were talented and cultivated, nevertheless, there was a fine line drawn between them and the native white people who counted for anything. This he wished me to bear in mind, so that while I should always act in such a way as never in the slightest to hurt or offend the feelings of the colored element, whose good-will was essential to *The Lantern*, I must retain my dignity and stoop to no familiarity which would bring me and *The Lantern* into disrepute with the white element, whose good-will was equally essential.

I think in less than a week my employer began grudgingly to approve of me; in about two weeks we were friends. His eyes no longer glared at me through his thick glasses. Once when I timidly proffered one of my "poems," those same fierce eyes actually beamed upon me. What is more, he published the poem!

Of course it was chiefly my work that won me favor with Mr. Campbell. I came back every day from Government House with accurate and intelligent reports of the debates. I wonder what Mr. Campbell would have said to me had he known that nearly all my first reports were written for me by young Verley Marchmont of *The Daily Call*, *The Lantern's* deadliest rival! For the life of me, I never could grasp the details of the debates clearly enough to report them coherently, and so young Marchmont obligingly "helped" me. However, these debates were only a part of my work, though at this time they constituted the chief of my duties.

For a young person in a hot country I was kept extremely busy. Even after my day's work was over I had to bustle about the hotel and dig up society notes and stories, or I had to attend meetings, functions, and parties of various kinds.

One morning after I had been on *The Lantern* about a week, Mr. Campbell handed me a list of my duties as an employee of *The Lantern*. Perhaps you would like to know exactly what they were:

1. To attend and report the debates of the Legislative Council when in session.
2. To report City Council proceedings.
3. To report court cases of interest to the public.
4. To keep posted on all matters of interest to Great Britain and Jamaica.
5. To make calls upon and interview at intervals His Excellency the Governor-General, the Colonial Secretary, the Commander of the Forces, the Attorney-General, and other Government officials.
6. To interview elected members when matters of interest demand it.
7. To interview prominent Americans or those who are conspicuous on account of great wealth.
8. To report political speeches.
9. To report races, cricket matches, polo, etc.
10. To represent *The Lantern* at social functions.
11. To visit stores, factories, etc., and to write a weekly advertising column.
12. To prepare semi-weekly a bright and entertaining woman's column, into which must be skilfully woven the names of Jamaica's society women.
13. To review books and answer correspondence.
14. To correct proof in the absence of the proofreader.
15. To edit the entire paper when sickness or absence of the editor prevents him from attending.

Mr. Campbell watched my face keenly as I read that list, and finally, when I made no comment, he prompted me with a gruff, "Well?" To which I replied, with a smile:

"I think what you want, Mr. Campbell, is a mental and physical acrobat."

"Do I understand from that," he thundered, "that you cannot perform these necessary duties?"

"On the contrary," I returned coolly, "I think that I can perform them all, one at a time; but you have left out one important item."

"Well, what?"

"Poetry," I said.

My answer tickled him immensely, and he burst into loud laughter.

"Got any about you?" he demanded. "I believe you have it secreted all over you."

I said:

"I've none of my own this morning, but here's a fine little verse I wish you'd top our editorial page with," and I handed him the following:

> *For the cause that lacks assistance;*
> *For the wrong that needs resistance;*
> *For the future in the distance,*
> *And the good that we can do!*

With such a motto, we felt called upon to be pugnacious and virtuous, and all of that session of Parliament our little sheet kept up a peppery fight for the rights of the people.

Mr. Campbell said that I looked strong and impudent enough to do anything, and when I retorted that I was not the least bit impudent, but, on the contrary, a dreamer, he said crossly:

"If that's the case, you'll be incompetent."

But I was a dreamer, and I was not incompetent.

It was all very well, however, to joke with Mr. Campbell about these duties. They were pretty hard just the same, and I was kept rushing from morning till night. There was always a pile of work waiting me upon my return from Government House, and I could see that Mr. Campbell intended gradually to shift the major part of the work entirely upon me.

The unaccustomed climate, the intense heat, and the work, which I really loved—all contributed to make me very tired by evening, when my duties were by no means ended.

Miss Foster's warning that I should have to keep the men at arm's-length occasionally recurred to me, but I dare say she exaggerated the matter. It is true that considerable attention was directed at me when I first came to Jamaica, and I received no end of flowers and candies and other little gifts; but my work was so exacting and ceaseless that it occupied all of my time. I could do little more than pause a moment or two to exchange a word or joke with this or that man who sought flirtations with me. I was always in a hurry. Rushing along through the hotel lobby or parlors or verandas, I scarcely had time to get more than a confused impression of various faces.

There was a ball nearly every night, and I always had to attend, for a little while, anyway; but I did not exactly mingle with the guests. I never danced, though lots of men asked me. I would get my list of guests and the description of the women's dresses, etc., write my column, and despatch it by boy to *The Lantern*, and I would go to bed while the music was still throbbing through the hotel. Often the guests were dancing till dawn.

Now I come to Dr. Manning. He was the one man in the hotel who persistently sought me and endeavored to make love to me. He was an American, one of a yachting party cruising in the Caribbean. I was not attracted to him at all, and as far as I could, I avoided him; but I could not come out upon the verandas or appear anywhere about the hotel without his seeming to arise from somewhere, and come with his flattering smiles and jokes. His hair was gray, and he had a pointed, grizzled beard. He was tall, and carried himself like a German officer.

He was always begging me to go to places with him, for walks, drives, or boat-trips, etc., and finally I did accept an invitation to walk with him in the botanical gardens, which adjoined, and were almost part of our own grounds.

That evening was a lovely one, with a great moon overhead, and the sea like a vast glittering sheet of quicksilver. The Marine Band was playing. People were dancing in the ball-room and on the verandas and out in a large pagoda in the gardens. Down along the sanded paths we passed numerous couples strolling, the bare shoulders of the women gleaming like ivory under the moonlight. The farther we strolled from the hotel, the darker grew the paths. Across the white backs of many of the women a black sleeve was passed. Insensibly I felt that in the darkness my companion was trying to see my face, and note the effect upon me of these "spooners." But he was not the first man I had walked with in the Jamaica moonlight. Verley Marchmont and I had spent a few brief hours from our labors in the gardens of the hotel.

Dr. Manning kept pressing nearer to me. Officiously and continuously, he would take my arm, and finally he put his about my waist. I tried to pull it away, but he held me firmly. Then I said:

"There are lots of people all around us, you know. If you don't take your arm down, I shall scream for help."

He took his arm down.

After a space, during which we walked along in silence, I not exactly angry, but irritated, he began to reproach me, accusing me of disliking him. He said he noticed that I was friendly with every one else, but that when he approached me my face always stiffened. He asked if I disliked him, and I replied that I did not, but that other men did not look at or speak to me as he did. He laughed unbelievingly at that, and exclaimed:

"Come, now, are you trying to make me believe that the young men who come to see you do not make love to you?"

I said thoughtfully:

"Well, only one or two come to see me, and—no—none of them has yet. I suppose it's because I'm always so busy; and then I'm not pretty and rich like the other girls here."

"You are pretty," he declared, "and far more interesting than any other girl in the hotel. I think you exceedingly captivating."

For that compliment I was truly grateful, and I thanked him for saying it. Then he said:

"Let me kiss you just once, won't you?" Again he put his arm about me, and this time I had to struggle considerably to release myself. When he let me go, he said almost testily:

"Don't make such a fuss. I'm not going to force you," and then after a moment, "By the way, why do you object to being kissed?" just as if it were unusual for a girl to object to that.

"I'll tell you why," I said tremulously, for it is impossible for a young girl to be unmoved when a man tries to kiss her, "because I want to be in love with the first man who kisses me."

"And you cannot care for me?"

I shook my head.

"Why?"

"Because you are an old man," I blurted out.

He stopped in the path, and I could feel him bristling with amazement and anger. Somewhat of a fop in dress, he had always carried himself in the gay manner of a man much younger than he probably was. His voice was very nasty:

"What?"

I repeated what I had said:

"You are an old man."

"What on earth makes you think that?" he demanded.

"Because your hair is gray," I stammered, "and because you look at least forty."

At that he broke into a loud chuckle.

"And you think forty old?"

I nodded. For a long moment he was silent, and then suddenly he took my arm, and we moved briskly down the path. We came to one of the piers, and he assisted me up the little stone steps. In silence we went out to the end of the pier. There was a little rustic inclosure at the end, covered with ivy from some sort of tree that seemed to grow out of the water. We sat down for a while and looked out across the sea. Everything was very dark and still. Presently he said:

"What would you do if I were to take you into my arms by force now?"

"I would scream," I said childishly.

"That wouldn't do you much good, for I could easily overpower you. You see, there is not a soul anywhere near us here."

I experienced a moment's fear, and stood up, when he said in a kind and humorous way:

"Sit down, child; I'm not going to touch you. I merely said that to see what you would do. As a matter of fact, I want to be your friend, your very particular friend, and I am not going to jeopardize my chances by doing something that would make you hate me. Do sit down."

Then as I obeyed, he asked me to tell him all about myself. It was not that I either trusted or liked him, but I was very lonely, and something in the quiet beauty of our surroundings affected me, I suppose. So long as he did not make love to me, I found him rather attractive. So I told him what there was to tell of my simple history up to this time, and of my ambitions.

He said a girl like me deserved a better fate than to be shut up in this country; that in a few weeks the hot season would set in, and then I would probably find life unbearable, and surely have some fever. He advised me very earnestly, therefore, not to remain here, but suggested that I go to America. There, he said, I would soon succeed, and probably become both famous and rich. His description of America quickened my fancy, and I told him I should love to go there, but, unfortunately, even if I could get away from this position, and managed to pay my fare to America, I did not know what I would do after arriving there virtually penniless.

When I said that, he turned and took both my hands impulsively and in a nice fatherly way in his, and said:

"Why, look here, little girl, what's the matter with your coming to work for me? I have a huge practice, and will need a secretary upon my return. Now, what do you say?"

I said:

"I say, 'Thank you,' and I'll remember."

At the hotel he bade me good night rather perfunctorily for a man who had recently tried to kiss a girl, but I lay awake some time thinking about what he had said to me.

I suppose every girl tosses over in her mind the thought of that first kiss that shall come to her. In imagination, at least, I had already been kissed many many times, but the ones who had kissed me were not men or boys. They were strange and bewildering heroes, princes, kings, knights, and great nobles. Now, here was a real man who had wanted to kiss me. I experienced no aversion to him at the thought; only a cool sort of wonder and a flattering sense of pride.

VI

It was a cruel coincidence that the dreadful thing that befell me next day should have followed at a time when my young mind was thus dreamily engrossed.

The day had been a hard one, and I know not why, but I could not concentrate my mind upon the proceedings. I felt inexpressibly stupid, and the voices of the legislators droned meaninglessly in my ears. As I could not follow the debates intelligently, I decided that I would stay a while after the council had adjourned, borrow one of the reporters' notes, and patch up my own from them.

So, with a glass of kola at my elbow, and Verley Marchmont's notes before me, I sat at work in the empty chamber after every one, I supposed, had gone, though I heard the attendants and janitors of the place at work in the gallery above. Young Marchmont waited for me outside.

A quiet had settled down over the place, and for a time I scribbled away upon my pad. I do not know how long I had worked—not more than ten or fifteen minutes—when I felt some one come up behind me, and a voice that I recognized from having heard it often in the House during the session said:

"May I speak to you a moment, Miss Ascough?"

I looked up, surprised, but not alarmed. Mr. Burbank was standing by my chair. There was something in his expression that made me move my chair back a little, and I began gathering up my papers rapidly. I said politely, however:

"Certainly, Mr. Burbank. What can *The Lantern* do for you?"

I sat facing the table, but I had moved around so that my shoulder was turned toward him. In the little silence that followed I felt his breath against my ear as he leaned on the table and propped his chin upon his hand, so that his face came fairly close to mine. Before he spoke I had shrunk farther back in my chair.

He said, with a laugh that was an odd mixture of embarrassment and assurance:

"I want nothing of *The Lantern*, but I do want something of you. I want to ask you to—er—marry me. God! how I love you!"

If some one had struck me hard and suddenly upon the head, I could not have experienced a greater shock than the words of that negro gave me. All through the dreaming days of my young girlhood one lovely moment had stood out like a golden beam in my imagination—my first proposal. Perhaps all girls do not think of this; but *I* did, who lived upon my fancies. How many gods and heroes had I not created who had whispered to me that magical question? And now out of that shining, beautiful throng of imaginary suitors, what was this that had come? A great black man, the "bogy man" of my childhood days!

Had I been older, perhaps I might have managed that situation in some way. I might even have spoken gently to him; he believed he was honoring me. But youth revolts like some whipped thing before stings like this, and I—I was so hurt, so terribly wounded, that I remember I gasped out a single sob of rage. Covering my face with my hands, I stood up. Then something happened that for a moment robbed me of all my physical and mental powers.

Suddenly I felt myself seized in a pair of powerful arms. A face came against my own, and lips were pressed hard upon mine.

I screamed like one gone mad. I fought for my freedom from his arms like a possessed person. Then blindly, with blood and fire before my eyes and burning in my heart, I fled from that terrible chamber. I think I banged both my head and hands against the door, for later I found that my forehead and hands were swollen and bruised. Out into the street I rushed.

I heard Verley Marchmont call to me. I saw him like a blur rise up in my path, but behind him I fancied was that other—that great *animal* who had kissed me.

On and on I ran, my first impulse being to escape from something dreadful that was pursuing me. I remember I had both my hands over my mouth. I felt that it was unclean, and that rivers and rivers could not wash away that stain that was on me.

I think it was Marchmont's jerking hold upon my arm that brought me to a sense of partial awakening.

"Miss Ascough, what is the matter? What is the matter?" he was saying.

I looked up at him, and I started to speak, to tell him what had happened to me, and then suddenly I knew it was something I could tell no one. It loomed up in my child's imagination as something filthy.

"I can't tell you," I said.

"Did something frighten you? What is it, dear?"

I remember, in all my pain and excitement, that he called me "dear," that fair-haired young Englishman; and like a child unexpectedly comforted, it brought the sobs stranglingly to my throat.

"Come and get into the carriage, then," he said. "You are ill. Your hands and face are burning. I'm afraid you have fever. You'd better get home as quickly as possible."

The driver of our carriage, who had followed, drew up beside us; but even as I turned to step into the carriage, suddenly I remembered what Miss Foster had said that first day:

"This carriage is owned by Mr. Burbank. He supplies all the carriages for the press."

"I can't ride in *that*!" I cried.

"You've got to," said Marchmont. "It's the last one left except Mr. Burbank's own."

"I'm going to walk home," I said.

I was slowly recovering a certain degree of self-possession. Nevertheless, my temples were throbbing; my head ached splittingly. I was not crying, but gasping sobs kept seizing me, such as attack children after a tempestuous storm of tears.

"You can't possibly walk home," declared Marchmont. "It is at least four and a half miles, if not more."

"I am going to walk just the same," I said. "I would rather die than ride in that carriage."

He said something to the driver. The latter started up his horses, and drove slowly down the road. Then Marchmont took my arm, and we started.

That interminable walk in the fearful Jamaica heat and sun recurs sometimes to me still, like a hectic breath of hateful remembrance. The penetrating sun beat its hot breath down upon our backs. The sand beneath our feet seemed like living coals, and even when we got into the cooler paths of the wooded country, the closeness and oppressive heaviness of the atmosphere stifled and crushed me.

At intervals the driver of that Burbank carriage would draw up beside us on the road, and Marchmont would entreat me to get in; but always I refused, and a strength came to me with each refusal.

Once he said:

"If you would let me, I could carry you."

I looked up at his anxious young face. His clothes were thicker than mine, and he had a number of books under his arm. He must have been suffering from the heat even as I was, but he was ready to sacrifice himself for what he must have thought was a sick whim on my part. He was nothing but a boy, very little older than I; but he was of that plugging English type which sticks at a task until it is accomplished. The thought of his carrying me made me laugh hysterically, and he, thinking I was feeling better, again urged me to get into the carriage, but in vain.

We met many country people on the road, and he bought from one a huge native umbrella. This he hoisted over my head; I think it did relieve us somewhat. But the whole of me, even to my fingers, now seemed to be tingling and aching. There was a buzzing and ringing in my head. I was thirsty. We stopped at a wayside spring, and an old woman lent me her tin cup for a drink. Marchmont gave her a coin, and she said in a high, whining voice:

"Give me another tuppence, Marster, and I'll tell missee a secret."

He gave her the coin, and then she said:

"Missee got the fever. She better stand off'n dat ground."

"For God's sake!" he said to me, "let me put you in the carriage!"

"You would not want to, if you knew," I said, and my voice sounded in my own ears as if it came from some distance.

On and on we tramped. Never were there five such miles as those.

Many a time since I have walked far greater distances. I have covered five and six miles of links, carrying my own golf-clubs. I've climbed up and down hills and valleys, five, ten, and more miles, and arrived at my destination merely healthily tired and hungry.

But five miles under a West Indian sun, in a land where even the worms and insects seemed to wither and dry in the sand!

It was about four-forty when we left Government House; it was seven when we reached the hotel. I was staggering as we at last passed under the great arcade of the Myrtle Bank. Though my eyes were endowed with sight, I saw nothing but a blurred confusion of shadows and shapes.

Mr. Marchmont and another man—I think the manager of the hotel—took me to my room, and some one—I suppose the maid—put me to bed. I dropped into a heavy sleep, or, rather, stupor, almost immediately.

The following day a maid told me that every one in the hotel was talking about me and the sick condition in which I had returned to the hotel, walking! Every one believed I was down with some bad fever and had lost my mind, and there was talk of quarantining me somewhere until my case was properly diagnosed. I sent a boy for Mr. Campbell.

He came over at once. Grumbling and muttering something under his breath, he stumped into my room, and when he saw I was not sick in bed, as report had made me, he seemed to become angry rather than pleased. He cleared his throat, ran his hand through his hair till it stood up straight on his head, and glared at me savagely.

"What's the matter with you?" he demanded. "Why did you not report at the office last evening? Are you sick or is this some prank? What's this I've been hearing about you and that young cub of *The Call*?"

"I don't know what you've been hearing," I said, "but I want to tell you that I'm not going to stay here any longer. I'm going home."

"What do you mean by that?" he shouted at me.

"You asked me what happened to me?" I said excitedly. "I'll tell you."

And I did. When I was through, and sat sobbingly picking and twisting my handkerchief in my hands, he said explosively:

"Why in the name of common sense did you remain behind in that place?"

"I told you I wanted to go over my notes. I had not been able to report intelligently the proceedings, as I felt ill."

"Don't you know better than to stay alone in *any* building where there are likely to be black men?"

No, I did not know better than that.

And now began a heated quarrel and duel between us. I wanted to leave Jamaica at once, and this old Scotchman desired to keep me there. I had become a valuable asset to *The Lantern*. But I was determined to go. After Mr. Campbell left I sought out Dr. Manning. He had offered to help me if I went to America. To America, then, I would go.

Dr. Manning watched my face narrowly as I talked to him. I told him of the experience I had had, and he said:

"Now, you see, I warned you that this was no place for a girl like you."

"I know it isn't," I said eagerly, "and so I'm going to leave. I want to take the first boat that sails from Jamaica. One leaves for Boston next Friday, and I can get passage on that. I want to know whether you meant what you said the other night about giving me a position after I get there."

"I certainly did," he replied. "I live in Richmond, and when you get to Boston, telegraph me, and I will arrange for you to come right on. I myself am leaving to-night. Have you enough money?"

I said I had, though I had only my fare and a little over.

"Well," he said, "if you need more when you reach Boston, telegraph me, and I'll see that you get it at once."

"This relieves me of much anxiety," I said. "And I'm sure I don't know how to thank you."

He stood up, took my hand, and said:

"Perhaps you won't thank me when you see what a hard-worked little secretary you are to be."

Then he smiled again in a very fatherly way, patted my hand, and wished me good-by.

I now felt extremely happy and excited. Assured of a position in America, I felt stronger and more resolved. I put on my hat and went over to *The Lantern* office. After another quarrel with Mr. Campbell, I emerged triumphant. He released me from my contract.

That evening Verley Marchmont called upon me, and of course I had to tell him I was leaving Jamaica, a piece of information that greatly disheartened him. We were on one of the large verandas of the hotel. The great Caribbean Sea was below us, and above, in that marvelous, tropical sky, a sublime moon looked down upon us.

"Nora," said Verley, "I think I know what happened to you yesterday in Government House, and if I were sure that I was right, I'd go straight out and half kill that black hound."

I said nothing, but I felt the tears running down my face, so sweet was it to feel that this fine young Englishman cared. He came over and knelt down beside my chair, like a boy, and he took one of my hands in his. All the time he talked to me he never let go my hand.

"Did that nigger insult you?" he asked.

I said:

"He asked me to marry him."

Verley snorted.

"Anything else?"

A lump came up stranglingly in my throat.

"He—kissed—me!" The words came with difficulty.

"Damn him!" cried young Verley Marchmont, clenching his hands.

There was a long silence between us after that. He had been kneeling all this time by my chair, and at last he said:

"I don't blame you for leaving this accursed hole, and I wish I were going with you. I wish I were not so desperately poor. Hang it all!" he added, with a poor little laugh. "I don't get much more than you do."

"I don't care anything about money," I said. "I like people for themselves."

"Do you like me, Nora?" He had never called me Nora till this night.

I nodded, and he kissed my hand.

"Well, some day then I'll go to America, too, and I'll find you, wherever you may be."

I said chokingly, for although I was not in love with this boy, still I liked him tremendously, and I was sentimental:

"I don't believe we'll ever meet again. We're just 'Little ships passing in the night.'"

Marchmont was the only person to see me off. He called for me at the hotel, arranged all the details of the moving of my baggage, and then got a hack and took me to the boat. He had a large basket with him, which I noticed he carried very carefully. When we went to my state-room, he set it down on a chair, and said with his bright, boyish laugh:

"Here's a companion for you. Every time you hear him, I want you to think of me."

I heard him almost immediately; a high, questioning bark came out that package of mystery. I was delighted. A dear little dog—fox terrier, the whitest, prettiest dog I had ever seen. Never before in my life had I had a pet of any kind; never have I had one since. I lifted up this darling soft little dog—he was nothing but a puppy—and as I caressed him, he joyfully licked my face and hands. Marchmont said he was a fine little thoroughbred of a certain West Indian breed. His name, he said, was to be "Verley," after my poor big "dog" that I was leaving behind.

"Are you pleased with him?" he asked.

"I'm crazy about him," I replied.

"Don't you think I deserve some reward, then?" he demanded softly.

I said:

"What do you want?"

"This," he said, and, stooping, kissed me.

I like to think always that that was my first real kiss.

VII

The trip home was uneventful, and, on account of Verley, spent for the most part in my state-room. The minute I left the room he would start to whine and bark so piercingly and piteously that of course I got into trouble, and was obliged either to take him with me or stay with him.

I used to eat my meals with Verley cuddled in my lap, thrusting up his funny, inquiring little nose, and eating the morsels I surreptitiously gave him from my plate, much to the disgust of some of the passengers and the amusement of others.

Once they tried to take Verley from me,—some of the ship's people,—but I went to the captain, a friend of Captain Hollowell, about whom I talked, and I pleaded so fervently and made such promises that when I reached the tearful stage he relented, and let me keep my little dog.

I had an address of a Boston lodging-house, given me by a woman guest of the Myrtle Bank. A cab took me to this place, and I was fortunate in securing a little hall room for three dollars a week. There was a dining-room in the basement of a house next door where for three dollars and fifty cents I could get meal-tickets enough for a week. My landlady made no objection to Verley, but she warned me that if the other lodgers objected, or if Verley made any noise, I'd have to get rid of him. She gave me a large wooden box with straw in it. This was to be his bed. I didn't dare tell her that Verley slept with me. He used to press up as closely to my back as it was possible to get, and with his fore paws and his nose resting against my neck, he slept finely. So did I. I kept him as clean as fresh snow. I had tar soap, and I scrubbed him every day in warm water, and I also combed his little white coat. If I found one flea on him, I killed it.

The first day I went into the dining-room next door with little Verley at my heels, every one turned round and looked at him, he was such a pretty, tiny little fellow, and so friendly and clean. The men whistled and snapped their fingers at him. He ran about from table to table, making friends with every one, and being fed by every one.

I was given a seat at a table where there was just one other girl. Now here occurred one of the coincidences in my life that seem almost stranger than fiction. The girl at the table was reading a newspaper when I sat down, and I did not like to look at her at once; but presently

I became aware that she had lowered her paper, and then I glanced up. An exclamation escaped us simultaneously, and we jumped to our feet.

"Nora!" she screamed.

"Marion!" I cried.

She was one of my older sisters!

As soon as we recognized each other, we burst out hysterically laughing and crying. Excited words of explanation came tumbling from our lips.

"What are you doing here?"

"What are you?"

"Why aren't you in Jamaica?"

"Why aren't you in Quebec?"

I soon explained to Marion how I came to be in Boston, and then, crying and eating at the same time, she told me of her adventures. They were less exciting, but more romantic, than mine. She had left Quebec on account of an unhappy love-affair. She had quarreled with the young man to whom she was engaged, and "to teach him a lesson, and because, anyway, I hate him," she had run away. She had been in Boston only one day longer than I. She said she had been looking for work for two days, but only one kind had been offered her thus far. I asked her what that was. Her eyes filled with tears, and she said bitterly, that of an artist's model.

Marion could paint well, and papa had taught her considerably. It was her ambition, of course, to be an artist. In Quebec she had actually had pupils, and made a fair living teaching children to draw and paint on china. But here in Boston she stood little chance of getting work like that. Nevertheless, she had gone the rounds of the studios, hoping to find something to do as assistant and pupil. Nearly every artist she had approached, however, had offered to engage her as a model.

Marion was an unusually pretty girl of about twenty-two, with an almost perfect figure, large, luminous eyes, which, though fringed with black lashes, were a golden-yellow in color; hair, black, long, and glossy; small and charmingly shaped hands and feet; and a perfectly radiant complexion. In fact, she had all the qualities desirable in a model. I did not wonder that the artists of Boston wanted to paint her. I urged her to do the work, but poor Marion felt as if her best dreams were about to be shattered. She, who had cherished the hope of being an artist, shrank from the thought of being merely a model. However, she had scarcely any money. She said she would not mind posing in costume; but only one of the artists had asked her to do that, a man who wanted to use her in "Oriental studies."

In her peregrinations among the studios she had come across other girls who were making a profession of posing, and one of them had taken her to a large art school, so that she could see exactly what the work was. This girl, Marion said, simply stripped herself "stark naked," and then went on before a large roomful of men and women. Marion was horrified and ashamed, but her friend, a French girl, had laughed and said:

"Que voulez-vous? It ees nutting."

She told Marion that she had felt just as she did at first; that all models experienced shame and embarrassment the first time. The plunge was a hard thing; and to brace the girl up for the ordeal, the model was accustomed to take a drink of whisky before going on. After that it was easy. Marion was advised to do this.

"Just tek wan good dreenk," said the French girl; "then you get liddle stupid. After zat it doan' matter."

Marion remarked hysterically that whisky might not make *her* stupid. She might be disposed to be hilarious, and in that event what would the scandalized class do?

However, Marion was hopeful, and she expected to get the costume work with the artist mentioned before.

As for me, just as I advised Marion to take this easy work that was offered her, so she most strenuously advised me not to waste my time looking for work in Boston, but to go on to Richmond, where a real position awaited me.

It is curious how natural it is for poor girls to slip along the path of least resistance. We wanted to help each other, and yet each advised the other to do something that upon more mature thought might have been inadvisable; for both courses held pitfalls of which neither of us was aware. However, we seized what was nearest to our hand.

Marion got the work to pose in Oriental studies next day, and I, who had telegraphed Dr. Manning, received by telegraph order money for my fare. I at once set out for Richmond, and I did not see my sister again for nearly five years. I left her crying at the station.

VIII

They would not let me keep my little dog with me on the train, although I had smuggled him into my Pullman in a piece of hand baggage; but in the morning he betrayed us. Naughty, excitable, lonely little Verley! The conductor's heart, unlike that sea-captain's, was made of stone. Verley was banished to the baggage-car. However, I went with him, and I spent all of that day with my dog among the baggage, not even leaving him to get something to eat; for I had brought sandwiches.

There were a number of other dogs there besides Verley, and they kept up an incessant barking. One of the trainmen got me a box to sit on, and I took my little pet on my lap. The trainmen were very kind to me. They told me they'd feed Verley well and see that he got plenty of water; but I would not leave him. I said I thought it was shameful of that conductor to make me keep my little dog there. The men assured me it was one of the rules of the road, and that they could make no exception in my case. They pointed out several other dogs, remarkable and savage-looking hounds, which belonged to a multi-millionaire, so they said, and I could see for myself that even he was obliged to have them travel this way.

While the men were reassuring me, a very tall man came into the car and went over to these hounds. They were making the most deafening noises. They were tied, of course, but kept leaping out on their chains, and I was afraid they would break loose, and perhaps attack and rend my little Verley.

The tall man gave some instructions to a man who seemed to be in charge of the hounds, and after patting the dogs' heads and scratching their ears, he started to leave the car, when he chanced to see me, and stopped to look at Verley.

Before I even saw his face there was something about his personality that affected me strangely, for though I had been talking freely with the men in the baggage-car, I suddenly felt unconscionably shy. He had a curious, drawling voice that I have since learned to know as Southern. He said:

"Is that your little dog?"

I nodded, and looked up at him.

I saw a man of between thirty-five and forty. (I have since learned he was forty-one.) His face was clean-shaven, and while not exactly wrinkled, was lined on the forehead and about the mouth. It was lean and rather haggard-looking. His lips were thin, and his steel-gray eyes were, I think, the weariest and bitterest eyes I have ever seen, though when he smiled I felt strangely drawn to him, even that first time. He was dressed in a light gray suit, and it looked well on him, as his hair at the temples was of the same color. As my glance met his curious smile, I remember that, embarrassed and blushing, I dropped my eyes to his hands, and found that they impressed me almost as much as his face. It is strange how one may be so moved by another at the first meeting! At once I had a feeling, a sort of subtle premonition, you might call it, that this man was to loom large in my life for all the rest of my days.

Stooping down, he patted Verley as he lay on my lap, but as he did so, he kept looking at me with a half-teasing, half-searching glance. I felt flustered, embarrassed, ashamed, and angry with myself for feeling so much confusion.

"What's your dog's name?" he asked.

He was opening and shutting his hand over Verley's mouth. The dog was licking his hand as if he liked him.

"Verley," I replied.

"Verley! That's a pretty name. Who's he named for?"

"The young Englishman who gave him to me," I said.

"I see!"

He laughed as if I had confided something to him. I said ingenuously:

"He's a real thoroughbred," and that caused him to smile again.

He had turned Verley over on my lap, and was dancing his fingers over the dog's gaping mouth, but he still kept looking at me, with, I thought, a half-interested, half-amused expression.

"He's a fine little fellow," he said. "Where is he going?"

"To Richmond."

"To Richmond!"

That seemed greatly to surprise him, and he asked why I was going to that city, and if I knew any one there. I said that I knew Dr. Manning; that I had met him in the West Indies, and he had promised me a position as his secretary.

By this time he had let Verley alone, and was staring at me hard. After a moment he said:

"Do you know Dr. Manning well?"

"No; but he has been kind enough to offer me the position," I replied. He seemed to turn this over in his mind, and then he said:

"Put your little dog back in his box, and suppose you come along and have dinner with me."

I did not even think of refusing. Heedless of the frantic cries of my poor little dog, I followed this stranger into the dining-car.

I don't know what we ate. I do know it was the first time I had ever had clams. I did not like them at all, and asked him what they were. He seemed highly amused. He had a way of smiling reluctantly. It was just as if one stirred or interested him against his will, and a moment after his face would somehow resume its curiously tired expression. Also I had something to drink,—I don't know what,—and it came before dinner in a very little glass. Needless to say, it affected me almost immediately, though I only took two mouthfuls, and then made such a face that again he laughed, and told me I'd better let it alone.

It may have been because I was lonely and eager for some one I could talk to, but I think it was simply that I fell under the impelling fascination of this man from the first. Anyhow, I found myself telling him all of my poor little history: where I had come from; the penniless condition in which I had arrived in Jamaica; my work there; the people I had met; and then, yes, I told *him* that very first day I met him, of that horrible experience I had had in the Government House.

While I talked to him, he kept studying me in a musing sort of way, and his face, which perhaps might have been called a hard or cold one, softened rather beautifully, I thought, as he looked at me. He did not say a word as I talked, but when I came to my experience with Burbank, he leaned across the table and watched me, almost excitedly. When I was through, he said softly:

"Down South we lynch a nigger for less than that," and one of his long hands, lying on the table, clenched.

Although we were now through dinner, and I had finished my story, he made no move to leave the table, but sat there watching me and smoking, with neither of us saying anything. Finally I thought to myself:

"I suppose he is thinking of me as Mr. Campbell and Sir Henry Drake and other people have—as something queer and amusing, and perhaps he is laughing inside at me." I regretted that I had told him about myself one minute, and the next I was glad that I had. Then suddenly I had an eloquent desire to prove to him that really there was a great deal more to me than he supposed. Down in my heart there was the deep-rooted conviction, which nothing in the world could shake, that I was one of the exceptional human beings of the world, that I was destined to do things worth while. People were going to hear of *me* some day. I was not one of the commonplace creatures of the earth, and I intended to prove that vividly to the world. But at that particular moment my one desire was to prove it to this man, this stranger with the brooding, weary face. So at last, awkwardly and timidly, and blushing to my temples and ears, and daring scarcely to look at him, I said:

"If you like, I'll read you one of my poems."

The gravity of his face softened. He started to smile, and then he said very gravely:

"So you write poetry, do you?"

I nodded.

"Go ahead," he said.

I dipped into my pocket-book, and brought forth my last effusion. As I read, he brought his hand to his face, shading it in such a way that I could not see it, and when I had finished, he was silent for so long that I did not know whether I had made an impression upon him or whether he was amused, as most people were when I read my poems to them. I tremblingly folded my paper and replaced it in my bag; then I waited for him to speak. After a while he took his hand down. His face was still grave, but away back in his eyes there was the kindliest gleam of interest. I felt happy and warmed by that look. Then he said something that sent my heart thudding down low again.

"Wouldn't you like to go to school?" said he.

"I did go to school," I said.

"Well, I mean to—er—school to prepare you for college."

The question hurt me. It was a visible criticism of my precious poem. Had that, then, revealed my pathetic condition of ignorance? I said roughly, for I felt like crying:

"Of course college is out of the question for me. I have to earn my living; but I expect to acquire an education gradually. One can educate herself by reading and thinking. My father often said that, and he's a college man—an Oxford graduate."

"That's true," said the man rather hurriedly, and as if he regretted what he had just said, and wished to dismiss the subject abruptly: "Now

I'm going to take you back to your seat. We'll be in Richmond very shortly now."

We got up, but he stopped a minute, and took a card from his pocket. He wrote something on it, and then gave it to me.

"There, little girl, is my name and address," he said. "If there ever comes a time when you—er—need help of any kind, will you promise to come to me?"

I nodded, and then he gave me a big, warm smile.

When I was quite alone, and sure no one was watching me, I took out his card and examined it. "Roger Avery Hamilton" was his name. Judge of my surprise, when I found the address he had written under his name was in the very city to which I was going—Richmond!

I arrived about eight-thirty that evening. Dr. Manning was at the train to meet me. He greeted me rather formally, I thought, for a man who had been so pronounced in his attentions in Jamaica.

As he was helping me into his carriage, Mr. Hamilton passed us, with other men.

"You forgot your dog," he said to me, smiling, and handed me a basket, in which, apparently, he had put my Verley. I had indeed forgotten my poor little dog! I thanked Mr. Hamilton, and he lifted his hat, and bade us good night.

Dr. Manning turned around sharply and looked after him. They had exchanged nods.

"How did you get acquainted with that chap?" he asked me. I was now in the carriage, and was settling Verley in his basket at my feet.

"Why, he spoke to me on the train," I said.

"Spoke to you on the train!" repeated the doctor, sharply. "Are you accustomed to make acquaintances in that way?"

My face burned with mortification, but I managed to stammer:

"No, I never spoke to any one before without an introduction."

He had climbed in now and was about to take up the reins when Verley, at our feet, let out a long, wailing cry.

"I'll have to throw that beast out, you know," he said unpleasantly.

"Oh, no! Please, please don't throw my little dog out!" I begged as he stooped down. "It's a beautiful little dog, a real thoroughbred. It's worth a lot of money."

My distress apparently moved him, for he sat up and patted me on the arm and said:

"It's all right, then. It's all right."

The doctor again began to question me about Mr. Hamilton, and I explained how he became interested in my dog; but I did not tell him about my dining with him.

"You ought to be more careful to whom you speak," he said. "For instance, this man in particular happens to be one of the fastest men in Richmond. He has a notorious reputation."

I felt very miserable when I heard that, especially when I recalled how I had talked intimately about myself to this man; and then suddenly I found myself disbelieving the doctor. I felt sure that he had slandered Mr. Hamilton, and my dislike for him deepened. I wished that I had not come to Richmond.

Dr. Manning's house was large and imposing. It stood at a corner on a very fine street. A black girl opened the door.

"You will meet Mrs. Manning in the morning," said the doctor to me, and then, turning to the girl: "'Mandy, this is Miss Ascough. She is coming to live with us here. Take her up to her room." To me he said, "*Good* night." With a perfunctory bow, he was turning away, when he seemed to recall something, and said: "By the way, 'Mandy, tell Toby to put the dog he'll find in the buggy in the stable."

I started to plead for Verley, but the doctor had disappeared into his office. A lump rose in my throat as I thought of my little dog, and again I wished that I had not come to this place. The doctor seemed a different man to the one I had known in the West Indies, and although I had resented his flattery of me there, the curt, authoritative tone he had used to me here hurt me as much.

Curiously enough, though I had not thought about the matter previously, nor had he told me, I was not surprised to find that he was married.

My room was on the top floor. It was a very large and pretty chamber, quite the best room I had ever had, for even the hotel room, which had seemed to me splendid, was bare and plain in comparison.

'Mandy was a round-faced, smiling, strong-looking girl of about eighteen. Her hair was screwed up into funny little braids that stuck up for all the world like rat-tails on her head. She had shiny black eyes, and big white teeth. She called me "chile," and said:

"I hopes you sleep well, honey chile."

She said her room was just across the hall, and if I wanted anything in the night, I was to call her.

My own room was very large, and it was mostly in shadow. Now, all my life I've had the most unreasonable and childish fear of "being in the dark alone." I seldom went to bed without looking under it, behind bureaus, doors, etc., and I experienced a slight sense of fear as 'Mandy was about to depart.

"Isn't there any one on this floor but us?" I asked.

"No; no one else sleeps up here, chile," said 'Mandy; "but Dr. Manning he hab he labriterry there, and some time he work all night."

The laboratory was apparently adjoining my room, and there was a door leading into it. I went over and tried it after 'Mandy went. It was locked.

I took my hair down, brushed and plaited it, and then I undressed and said my prayers (I still said them in those days), and got into bed. I was tired after the long journey, and I fell asleep at once.

I am a light sleeper, and the slightest stir or movement awakens me. That night I awoke suddenly, and the first thing I saw was a light that came into the room from the partly opened door of the doctor's laboratory, and standing in my room, by the doorway, was a man. I recognized him, though he was only a silhouette against the light.

The shock of the awakening, and the horrible realization that he was already crossing the room, held me for a moment spellbound. Then my powers returned to me, and just as I had fled from that negro in Jamaica, so now I ran from this white man.

My bed was close to the door that opened into the hall. That was pitch-dark, but I ran blindly across it, found 'Mandy's door, and by some merciful providence my hand grasped the knob. I called to her:

"'Mandy!"

She started up in bed, and I rushed to her.

"Wha' 's matter, chile?" she cried.

I was sobbing with fright and rage.

"I'm afraid," I told her.

"What you 'fraid of?"

"Oh, I don't know. I'm afraid to sleep alone," I said. "Please, please, let me stay with you."

"Ah'll come and sleep on the couch in your room," she said.

"No, no, I won't go back to that room."

"It ain't ha'nted, chile," declared 'Mandy.

"Oh, I know it isn't," I sobbed; "but, O 'Mandy, I'm afraid!"

IX

Next morning 'Mandy went back with me to my room. There was no one in it. For a moment the thought came to me that perhaps I had suffered from a nightmare. My clothes, everything, I found exactly as I had left them. I went over to the door opening from my room into the laboratory, and then I knew that I had not erred: the door was unlocked. I saw 'Mandy watching me, and I think she guessed the truth, for she said:

"You needn't be 'fraid no more, chile. I goin' to sleep with you every night now."

"No, 'Mandy," I said; "I can't stay here now. I've got to get away somehow."

"Dat's all right, chile," she said. "Jus' you tek you li'l' bag and slip out right now. No one's stirring in dis house yet. You won't be missed till after you sure am gone."

I was sitting on the side of the bed, feverishly turning the matter over in my mind.

"I wish I could do that," I said, "but I have no place to go, and I have no money."

'Mandy comforted me as best she could, and told me to wait till after breakfast, when I'd feel better; then I could talk to the doctor about it, and perhaps he'd give me some money; and if he wouldn't, said the colored girl, shrewdly, "you tell him you goin' ask his wife."

I felt I could not do that. I would have to find some other solution. One thing was certain, however, I could no more stay here than I could in Jamaica. There are times in my life when I have been whipped and scorched, and nothing has healed me save to get away quickly from the place where I have suffered. I felt like that in Jamaica. I felt like that now. There came another time in my life when I uprooted my whole being from a place I loved, and yet where it would have killed me to remain.

The doctor met me in the lower hall as I came down-stairs. His manner was affable and formal, and he said he would take me to his wife. I found myself unable to look him in the face, for I felt his glance would be hateful.

Mrs. Manning was in bed, propped up with pillows. At first glance she seemed an old woman. Her pale, parched face lay like a shadow among her pillows, and her fine, silvery hair was like an exquisite aureole. She had dark, restless, seeking eyes, and her expression was peevish, like that of a complaining child. As I came in, she raised herself to her elbow, and looked curiously at me and then at the doctor, who said:

"This is Miss Ascough, dear. She is to be my new secretary."

She put out a thin little hand, which I took impetuously in my own, and, I know not why, I suddenly wanted to cry again. There was something in her glance that hurt me. I had for her that same overwhelming pity that I had felt for Miss Foster in Jamaica—a pity such as one involuntarily feels toward one who is doomed. She murmured something, and I said, "Thank you," though I did not understand what she had said. Then the doctor shook up her pillows and settled her back very carefully among them, and he kissed her, and she clung to him. I realized that, incredible as it seemed, here where I had expected it least there was love.

After breakfast, which I had with the doctor, who read the morning paper throughout the meal, waited on by 'Mandy, he took me down to his offices, two large adjoining rooms on the ground floor, in one wing of the house. One room was used as a reception-room, the other as the doctor's own. Showing me through the offices, he had indicated the desk at which I was to sit in the reception-room before I summoned the courage to tell him I had decided to go. When I faltered this out, he turned clear around, and although an exclamation of astonishment escaped him, I knew that he was acting. I felt sure that he had been waiting for me to say something about the previous night.

"You certainly cannot realize what you are saying, Miss Ascough. Why should you leave a position before trying it?"

I looked steadily in his face now, and I was no longer afraid of him. I was only an ignorant girl of seventeen, and he was a man of the world past forty. I was friendless, had no money, and was in a strange country. He was a man of power, and, I suppose, even wealth. This was the city where he was respected and known. Nevertheless, I said to him:

"If I work for a man, I expect to be paid for my actual labor. That's a contract between us. After that, I have my personal rights, and no man can step over these without my consent."

They were pretty big words for a young girl, and I am proud of them even now. I can see myself as I faced that man defiantly, though I knew I had barely enough money in my purse upstairs to buy a few meals.

"I do not understand you," said the doctor, pulling at his beard. "I shall be obliged if you will make yourself clearer."

"I will, then," I said. "Last night you came into my room."

For a long time he did not say a word, but appeared to be considering the matter.

"I beg your pardon for that," he said at last, "but I think my explanation will satisfy you. I did not know that that room was the one my wife had assigned to you. I had been accustomed to occupy it myself when engaged at night upon laboratory work. I was as mortified as you when I discovered my unfortunate mistake last night, and I very much regret the distress it gave you."

No explanation could have been clearer than that, but looking at the man, I felt a deep-rooted conviction that he lied.

"Come now," he said cheerfully, "suppose we dismiss this painful subject. Let us both forget it." He held out his hand, with one of his "fatherly" smiles. I reluctantly let him take mine, and I did not know what to do or say. He took out his watch and looked at it.

"I have a number of calls to make before my noon hour," he said, "but I think I can spare an hour to explain your duties to you."

They were simple enough, and in other circumstances I should have liked such a position. I was to receive the patients, send out bills, and answer the correspondence, which was light. I had one other duty, and that he asked me to do now. There was something wrong with his eyes, and it was a strain upon them for him to read. So part of my work was to read to him an hour in the morning and one or two in the evening.

There was a long couch in the inner office, and after he had selected a book and brought it to me, he lay down on the couch, with a green shade over his eyes, and bade me proceed. The book was Rousseau's "Confessions."

In ordinary circumstances the book would have held my interest at once, but now I read it without the slightest sense of understanding, and the powerful sentences came forth from my lips, but passed through heedless ears. I had read only two chapters when he said that that would do for to-day. He asked me to bring from the top of his desk a glass in which was some fluid and an eye-dropper. He requested me to put two drops in each of his eyes.

As he was lying on his back on the couch, I had to lean over him to do this. I was so nervous that the glass shook in my hand. Judge of my horror when, in squeezing the little rubber bulb, the glass part fell off and dropped down upon his face.

I burst out crying, and before I knew it, he was sitting up on the couch and comforting me, with his arms about my waist. I freed myself and stood up. He said:

"There, there, you are a bit hysterical this morning. You'll feel better later."

He began moving about the office, collecting some things, and putting them into a little black bag. Toby knocked, and called that the buggy was ready. As the doctor was drawing on his gloves he said:

"Now, Miss Ascough, suppose you make an effort to—er accustom yourself to things as they are here. I'm really not such a bad sort as you imagine, and I will try to make you very comfortable and happy if you will let me."

I did not answer him. I sat there twisting my handkerchief in my hands, and feeling dully that I was truly the most miserable girl in the world. As the doctor was going out, he said:

"Do cheer up! Things are not nearly as bad as they seem."

Maybe they were not, but, nevertheless, the stubborn obsession persisted in my mind that I must somehow get away from that place. How I was going to do that without money or friends, I did not know. And if I did leave this place, where could I go?

I thought of writing home, and then, even in my distress, I thought of papa, absent-minded, impractical dreamer. Could I make him understand the situation I was in without telling him my actual experience? I felt a reluctance to tell my father or mother that. It's a fact that a young girl will often talk with strangers about things that she will hesitate to confide to her own parents. My parents were of the sort difficult to approach in such a matter. You see, I was one of many, and my father and mother were in a way even more helpless than their children. It was almost pathetic the way in which they looked to us, as we grew up, to take care of ourselves and them. Besides, it would take two days for a letter to reach my home, and another two days for the reply to reach me, and where could my poor father raise the money for my fare? No, I would not add to their distresses.

I went up to my room, after the doctor was gone, and I aimlessly counted my money. I had less than three dollars. I was putting it back into my bag, with the papers, trinkets, cards, and the other queer things that congregate in a girl's pocketbook, when Mr. Hamilton's card turned up on my lap.

I began to think of him. I sat there on the side of my bed in a sort of dreaming trance, recalling to my mind that charmed little journey in the company of this man. Every word he had said to me, the musing expression of his face, and his curious, grudging smile—I thought of all this. It was queer how in the midst of my trouble I could occupy my mind like this with thoughts of a stranger. I remembered that Dr. Manning had said he was a notorious man. I did not believe that. I thought of that kindly look of interest in his tired face when he had asked me if I wanted to go to school, and then electrically recurred to me his last words on the train when he had given to me his card,—that if I ever needed help, would I come to him?

I needed help now. I needed it more than any girl ever needed it before. Of that I felt truly convinced. This doctor was a villain. There was something bad and covetous about his very glance. I had felt that in Jamaica. It was impossible for me to remain alone with him in his house; for I should be virtually alone, since his wife was a paralytic.

Hurriedly I packed my things, shoving everything back into my suitcase, and then I put on my hat. In the doctor's office I found the telephone-book. I looked up the name of Hamilton. Yes, it was there. It seemed to me a miraculous thing that he really was there in that telephone-book and that he actually was in this city.

I called the number, and somebody, answering, asked whom I wished to speak to, and I said Mr. Roger Avery Hamilton.

"Who is it wants him?" I was asked.

"Just a friend," I replied.

"You will have to give your name. Mr. Hamilton is in a conference, and if it is not important, he cannot speak to you just now."

"It is important," I said. "He would want to speak to me, I know."

There was a long pause, and central asked me if I was through, and I said frantically:

"No, no; don't ring off."

Then a moment later I heard his voice, and even over the telephone it thrilled me so that I could have wept with relief and joy.

"Yes?"

"Mr. Hamilton, this is Miss Ascough."

"Miss Ascough?"

"Yes; I met you on the train coming from Boston."

"Oh, yes, the little girl with the dog," he said.

His voice, more than his words, warmed me with the thought that he had not forgotten me, and was even pleased to hear from me again.

"You said if I ever needed help—"

I broke off there, and he said slowly:

"I—see. Where are you?"

I told him.

"Can you leave there right away?"

I said I could, but that I did not know my way about the city.

He asked me to meet him in half an hour at the St. R—— Hotel, and directed me explicitly what car to take to get there, telling me to write it down. I was to have 'Mandy put me on this car, and I must be sure to tell the conductor to let me off at this hotel. The car stopped in front of it.

I wrote a note to Dr. Manning before going. I said I was sorry to leave in this way, but despite what he had said, I could not trust him. I added that I was so unhappy I had decided the best thing for me to do was to go at once. I left the note with 'Mandy, whom I kissed good-by, something I had never dreamed I could do, kiss a black girl! All the way on the car I was desperately afraid the conductor would not let me off at the right place, and I asked him so often that finally, in exasperation, he refused to answer me. When we at last reached there, he wrathfully shouted the name of the hotel into the car, though he did not need to cry, "Step lively!"

X

Mr. Hamilton was waiting for me outside the hotel. He gave my bag to a boy, who produced it later, and then took me to a corner of the drawing-room. Almost at once he said:

"I expected to hear from you, but not so soon."

"You were expecting?" I said. "Why?"

"Well," he said rather reluctantly, "I had a hunch you would not stay there long. Just what happened?"

I told him.

He kept tapping with his fingers on the table beside him and looking at me curiously. When I was through, he said:

"Well, we're a pretty bad lot, aren't we?"

I said earnestly:

"*You're* not!" which remark made him laugh in a rather mirthless sort of way, and he said:

"You don't know me, my child." Then, as if to change the subject: "But now, what do you want to do? Where do you want to go?"

"I'd like to go to some big city in America," I said. "I think, if I got a chance, I'd succeed as a poet or author."

"Oh, that's your idea, is it?" he asked half good-humoredly, half rather cynically. I nodded.

"Well, what big city have you decided upon?"

"I don't know. You see, I know very little about the States."

"How about New York or Chicago?"

"Which is the nearest to you?" I asked, timidly.

He laughed outright at that.

"Oh, so you expect to see *me*, do you?"

"I *want* to," I said. "You *will* come to see me, won't you?"

"We'll see about it," he said slowly. "Then it's Chicago? I have interests there." I nodded.

"And now," he went on, "how much money do you need?"

That question hurt me more than I suppose he would have believed. Certainly I would need money to go to Chicago, but I hated to think of taking any from him. I felt like a beggar. Young, poor, ignorant as I was, even then I had an acute feeling of reluctance to permit any sordid considerations to come between this man and me. I was so long in answering him that he said lightly:

"Well, how many thousands or millions of shekels do you suppose it will take to support a little poetess in Chicago?"

I said:

"You don't have to support poetesses if they are the right sort. All I want is enough money to carry me to Chicago. I'll get work of some kind then."

"Well, let's see," he said. "I'll get you your ticket, and then you'd better have, say, a hundred dollars to start with."

"No! no!" I cried out. "I couldn't use a whole hundred dollars."

"What?"

"I never had that much money in my life," I said. "I shouldn't know what to do with it."

He laughed shortly.

"You'll know all right," he said, "soon after you get to Chicago." Then he added almost bitterly, "You'll be writing to me for more within a week."

"Oh, Mr. Hamilton, I won't do that! I'll never take any more from you—honestly I won't."

"Nonsense!" he returned lightly. "And now come along. You have time for a bite of luncheon before your train leaves."

He ordered very carefully a meal for us, and took some time to decide whether I should have something to drink or not. He kept tapping the pencil on the waiter's pad and looking at me speculatively, and at last he said:

"No, I guess not this time."

So I got nothing to drink.

It was a fine luncheon, and for the first time I had soft-shell crabs; also for the first time I tasted, and liked, olives. Mr. Hamilton seemed to take a grim sort of pleasure in watching me eat. I don't know why, I'm sure, unless it was because I frankly did not know what most of the dishes were, and I was helplessly ignorant as to which was the right fork or knife to use for this or that dish. I think I ate my salad with my oyster-fork, and I am sure I used my meat-knife for my butter. All these intricate things have always bothered me, and they do still.

I suppose my eyes were still considerably swollen from the crying I had done, and, besides, I had slept very little after that awakening. Mr. Hamilton made me tell him all over again, and in minute detail, just what happened, and when I told him how I cried the rest of the night in 'Mandy's arms, he said:

"Yes, I can see you did," which made me say quickly, I was so anxious to look my best before him:

"I look a fright, I know."

Whereupon he slowly looked at me and said, with a suggestion of a smile:

"You look pretty good to me," and that compensated for everything.

He gave me the hundred dollars while we were in the dining-room, and advised me, with a slight smile, to hide it in "the usual place."

I asked innocently where that was.

"No one told you *that* yet?" he asked teasingly, and when I shook my head, he laughed and said:

"What a baby you are! Why, put it in your stocking, child."

I turned fiery red, not so much from modesty, but from mortification at my ignorance and his being forced to tell me. What is more, I *had* kept money there before, and I remember the girl on the boat going to Jamaica had, too; but I did not suppose men knew girls did such things.

On the way to the station, as he sat beside me in the carriage, I tried to thank him, and told him how much I appreciated what he was doing for me. I said that I supposed he had done good things like this for lots of other unfortunate girls like me (oh, I hoped that he had not!), and that I never could forget it.

He said lightly:

"Oh, yes, you will. They all do, you know."

From this I inferred that there were "other girls," and that depressed me so that I was tongue-tied for the rest of the journey.

We found, despite the hotel's telephoning, that it was impossible for me to get a lower berth. I am sure I didn't care whether I had a lower or upper. So, as he said he wanted me to have a comfortable journey, he had taken a little drawing-room for me. I didn't know what that meant till I got on the train. Then I saw I was to have a little car all to myself. The grandeur of this rather oppressed me; I do not know why. Nevertheless, it was an added proof of his kindness, and I stammered my thanks. He had come on the train with me, and was sitting in the seat opposite me, just as if he, too, were going. The nearer it approached the time for the train to leave, the sadder I felt. Perhaps, I thought, I should never see him again. Perhaps he looked upon me simply as a poor little beggar whom he had befriended.

It may be that some of my reflections were mirrored on my face, for he suddenly asked me what I was thinking about, and I told him.

"Nonsense!" he said. He had a way of dismissing things with "Nonsense!"

He got up and walked up and down the little aisle a moment, pulling at his lower lip in a way he had, and watching me all the time. I was huddled up on the seat, not exactly crying, but almost. Presently he said:

"Just as if it mattered whether you ever saw me again or not. After you've been in Chicago a while, you'll only think of me, perhaps, as a convenient old chap—a sort of bank to whom you can always apply for—" he paused before saying the word, and then brought it out hard—"money."

"Please don't think that of me!" I cried.

"I don't think it of you in particular, but of every one," he said. "Women are all alike. For that matter, men, too. Money is their god— money, *dirty* money! That's what men, and women, exist for. They marry for money. They live for it. Good God! they die for it! You can have a man's wife or anything else, but touch his money, his dirty money—" He threw out his hands expressively. He had been talking disjointedly, and as if the subject was one that fascinated him, and yet that he hated. "You see," he said, "I know what I am talking about, because that's about all any one has ever wanted of me—my money."

I made a little sound of protest. I was not crying, badly as I felt, but my face was burning, and I felt inexpressibly about that money of his that I, too, had taken. He went on in the jerking, bitter way he had been speaking:

"Just now you think that such things do not count. That's because you are so young. You'll change quickly enough; I predict that. I can read your fate in your young face. You love pretty things, and were made to have them. Why not? Some one is going to give them to you, just as Dr. Manning—and, for that matter, I myself—would have given them to you here in Richmond. I don't doubt in Chicago there will be many men who will jump at the chance."

He made a queer, shrugging gesture with his shoulders, and then swung around, looked at me hard, and as if almost he measured me. Then his face slightly softened, and he said:

"Don't look so cut up. I'm only judging you by the rest of your sex."

I said:

"I'm going to prove to you that I'm different. You will see."

He sat down opposite me again, and took one of my hands in his.

"How will you prove it, child?" he said.

"I'll never take another cent from you," I said, "and I'll give you back every dollar of this hundred you have lent me now."

"Nonsense!" he said, and flushed, as if he regretted what he had been saying.

"Anyway," I went on, "you're mistaken about me. I don't care so much about those things—pretty clothes and things like that. I like lots of other things better. *You*, for instance. I—I—like *you* better than all the money in the world."

"Nonsense!" he said again.

He still had my hand in his, and he had turned it over, and was looking at it. Presently he said:

"It's a sweet, pretty little hand, but it badly needs to be manicured."

"What's that?" I asked, and he laughed and set my hands back in my lap.

"Now I must be off. Send me your address as soon as you have one. Think of me a little, if you can."

Think of him! I knew that I was destined to think of nothing else. I told him so in a whisper, so that he had to bend down to hear me, but he merely laughed—that short unbelieving, reluctant laugh, and said again twice:

"Good-by, good-by."

I followed him as far as the door, and when he turned his back toward me, and I thought he could not see me, I kissed his sleeve; but he did see me,—in the long mirror on the door, I suppose,—and he jerked his arm roughly back and said brusquely:

"You mustn't do things like that!"

Then he went out, and the door shut hard between us.

I said to myself:

"I will die of starvation, I will sleep homeless in the streets, I will walk a thousand miles, if need be, in search of work, rather than take money from him again. Some one has hurt him through his money, and he believes we are all alike; but I will prove to him that I indeed am different."

A sense of appalling loneliness swept over me. If only a single person might have been there with me in my little car! If I had but the smallest companion! All of a sudden I remembered my little dog. My immediate impulse was to get directly off the train, and I rushed over to the door, and out upon the platform. He was down below, looking up at the window of my compartment; but he saw me as I came out on the platform and started to descend. At the same moment the train gave that first sort of shake which precedes the starting, and I was thrown back against the door. He called to me:

"Take care! Go back inside!"

The train was now moving, and I was holding to the iron bar.

"Oh, Mr. Hamilton," I cried, "I've forgotten Verley! I've forgotten my little dog!"

He kept walking by the train, and now, as its speed increased, he was forced to run. He put his hand to his mouth and called to me:

"I'll *bring* him to you, little girl. Don't you worry!"

Worry!

I went back to my seat, and all that afternoon I did not move. The shining country slipped by me, but I saw it not. I was like one plunged in a deep, golden dream. There was a pain in my heart, but it was an ecstatic one, and even as I cried softly, soundlessly, something within me sang a song that seemed immortal.

XI

I saw Chicago first through a late May rain—a mad, blowing, windy rain. The skies were overcast and gray. There was a pall like smoke over everything, and through the downpour, looking not fresh and clean from the descending streams, but dingy and sullen, as if unwillingly cleansed, the gigantic buildings shot up forbiddingly into the sky.

Such masses of humanity! I was one of a sweeping torrent of many, many atoms. People hurried this way and that way and every way. I rubbed my eyes, for the colossal city and this rushing, crushing mob, that pushed and elbowed, bewildered and amazed me.

I did not know what to do when I stepped off the train and into the great station. For a time I wandered aimlessly about the room, jostled and pushed by a tremendous crowd of people, who seemed to be pouring in from arriving trains. It must have been about eight in the morning.

All the seats in the waiting-room were taken, and after a while I sat down on my suitcase, and tried to plan out just what I should do.

I had a hundred dollars, a fabulous sum, it seemed to me. With it I presumed I could live wherever I chose, and in comparative luxury. But that hundred dollars was not mine, and I had a passionate determination to spend no more of it than I should actually need. I wanted to return it intact to the man who had given it to me.

As I had lain in my berth on the train I had vowed that he should not hear from me till I wrote to return his money. "Dirty money," he had called it, but to me anything that was his was beautiful. I planned the sort of letter I should write when I inclosed this money. By that time I should have secured a remarkable position. My stories and my poems would be bought by discerning editors, and I—ah me! the extravagant dreams of the youthful writer! What is there he is not going to accomplish in the world? What heights he will scale! But, then, what comfort, what sublime compensation for all the miserable realities of life, there is in being capable of such dreams! That alone is a divine gift of the gods, it seems to me.

But now I was no longer dreaming impossible dreams in my berth. I was sitting in that crowded Chicago railway station, and I was confronted with the problem of what to do and where to go.

It would of course be necessary for me to get a room the first thing; but I did not know just where I should look for that. I thought of going out into the street and looking for "furnished-room" signs, and then I thought of asking a policeman. I was debating the matter rather stupidly, I'm afraid, for the crowds distracted me, when a woman came up and spoke to me.

She had a plain, kind face and wore glasses. A large red badge, with gilt letters on it, was pinned on her breast.

"Are you waiting for some one?" she asked.

"No," I answered.

"A stranger?" was her next question.

"Yes."

"Just come to Chicago?"

"Yes. I just arrived."

"Ah, you have friends or relatives here?"

I told her I did not know any one in Chicago. What was I doing here, then, she asked me, and I replied that I expected to work. She asked at what, and I replied:

"As a journalist."

That brought a rather surprised smile. Then she wanted to know if I had arranged for a room somewhere, and I told her that that was just what I was sitting there thinking about—wondering where I ought to go.

"Well, I've just got you in time, then," she said, with a pleasant smile. "You come along with me. I'm an officer of the Young Women's Christian Association." She showed me her badge. "We'll take care of you there."

I went with her gladly, you may be sure. She led me out to the street and up to a large carriage, which had Y. W. C. A. in big letters on it. I was very fortunate.

Unlike New York's Y. W. C. A., which is in an ugly down-town street, Chicago's is on Michigan Avenue, one of its finest streets, and is a splendid building.

I was taken to the secretary of the association, a well-dressed young woman with a bleak, hard face. She looked me over sternly, and the first thing she said was:

"Where are your references?"

I took Mr. Campbell's letter of recommendation from my pocket-book, and handed it to her:

It was as follows:

To Whom it may Concern:
The bearer of this, Miss Nora Ascough, has been on the staff of *The Lantern* for some time now, but unfortunately the

tropical climate of Jamaica is not suited to her constitution. In the circumstances she has to leave a position for which her skill and competency eminently qualify her.

As a stenographer, amanuensis, and reporter I can give her the highest praise. She has for the entire session of the local legislature reported the proceedings with credit to herself and *The Lantern*, notwithstanding she was a stranger to her surroundings, the people, and local politics. These are qualities that can find no better recommendation. I confidently recommend her to any one requiring a skilled amanuensis and reporter.

I was justifiably proud of that reference, which Mr. Campbell had unexpectedly thrust upon me the day I left Jamaica. I broke down when I read it, for I felt I did not deserve it. The secretary of the Y. W. C. A., however, said in her unpleasant nasal voice as she turned it over almost contemptuously in her hand:

"Oh, this won't do at all. It isn't even an American reference, and we require a reference as to your *character* from some minister or doctor."

Now, on the way to the association the lady who had brought me had told me that this place was self-supporting, that the girls must remember they were not objects of charity; but, on the contrary, that they paid for everything they got, the idea of the association being to *make* no money from the girls, but simply to pay expenses. In that way the girls were enabled to board there at about half the price of a boarding-house. Under these circumstances I could not but inwardly resent the tone of this woman, and it seemed to me that these restrictions were unjust and preposterous. Of course I was not in a position to protest, so I turned to my friend who had brought me from the station.

"What shall I do?" I asked her.

"Can't you get a reference from your minister, dear?" she asked sympathetically. Why, yes, I thought I could. I'd write to Canon Evans, our old minister in Quebec. My friend leaned over the desk and whispered to the secretary, who appeared to be very busy, and irritated at being disturbed.

All public institutions, I here assert, should have as their employees only people who are courteous, pleasant, and kind. One of the greatest hardships of poverty is to be obliged to face the autocratic martinets who seem to guard the doorways of all such organizations. There is something detestable and offensive in the frozen, impatient, and often insulting manner of the women and men who occupy little positions of authority like this, and before whom poor working-girls—and, I suppose, men—must always go.

She looked up from her writing and snapped:

"You know our rules as well as I do, Miss Dutton."

"Well, but she says she can get a minister's reference in a few days," said my friend.

"Let her come here *then*," said the secretary as she blotted the page on which she was writing. How I hated her, the cat!

"But I want to get her settled right away," protested my friend.

How I loved her, the angel!

"Speak to Mrs. Dooley about it, then," snapped the secretary.

As it happened, Mrs. Dooley was close at hand. She was the matron or superintendent, and was a big splendid-looking woman, who moved ponderously, like a steam-roller. She gave one look at me only and said loudly and belligerently:

"Sure. Let her in!"

The secretary shrugged then, and took my name and address in Quebec. Then she made out a bill, saying:

"It's five dollars in advance."

I was greatly embarrassed to be obliged to admit that my money was in my stocking. Mrs. Dooley laughed at that, my friend looked pained, and the secretary pierced me with an icy glare. She said:

"Nice girls don't keep their money in places like that."

It was on the tip of my tongue to retort that I was not "nice," but I bit my tongue instead. My friend gave me the opportunity to remove my "roll," and I really think it made some impression on these officers of the Y. W. C. A., for the secretary said:

"If you can afford it, you can have a room to yourself for six a week."

I said:

"No, I can't. This money is not mine."

The elevator "boy" was a girl—a black girl.

We went up and up and up. My heart was in my mouth, for I had never been in an elevator before. Never had I been in a tall building before. We did not have one in Quebec when I was there. We got off at the top floor. Oh, me! how that height thrilled me, and, I think, frightened me a little! On the way to the room, my friend—though I had learned her name, I always like to refer to her as "my friend."

Ah, I wonder whether she is still looking for and picking up poor little homeless girls at railway stations!—said:

"You know, dear, we have to be careful about references and such things. Otherwise all sorts of undesirable girls would get in here."

"Well," I said, "I don't see why a girl who has a reference from a minister is any more desirable than one who has not."

"No, perhaps not," she said; "but then, you see, we have to use some sort of way of judging. We do this to protect our good girls. This is frankly a place for good girls, and we cannot admit girls who are not. By and by you'll appreciate that yourself. We'll be protecting you, don't you see?"

I didn't, but she was so sweet that I said I did.

XII

O h, such a splendid room! At least it seemed so to me, who had seen few fine rooms. It was so clean, even dainty. The walls and ceiling were pink calcimine, and some one had twisted pink tissue-paper over the electric lights. I didn't discover that till evening, and then I was delighted. No beautiful, costly lamps, with fascinating and ravishing shades, have ever moved me as my first taste of a shaded colored light in the Y. W. C. A. did.

Our home in Quebec had been bare of all these charming accessories, and although my father was an artist, poor fellow, I remember he used to paint in the kitchen, with us children all about him, because that was the only warm room in the house. In our poor home the rooms were primitive and bare. Papa used to say that bare rooms were more tolerable than rooms littered with "trash," and since we could not afford good things, it was better to have nothing in the place but things that had an actual utility. I think he was wrong. There are certain pretty little things that may be "trash," but they add to the attractiveness of a home.

Though papa was an artist, there were no pictures at all on our walls, as my older sisters used to take his paintings as fast as he made them, and go, like canvassers, from house to house and sell them for a few dollars. Yet my father, as a young man, had taken a gold medal at an exhibition at the Salon. Grandpapa, however, had insisted that no son of his should follow the "beggarly profession of an artist," and papa was despatched to the Far East, there to extend the trade of my grandfather, one of England's greatest merchant princes. When misfortune overtook my father later, and his own people turned against him, when the children began to arrive with startling rapidity, then my father turned to art as the means of securing for us a livelihood.

One of my sisters was known in Quebec as the "little lace girl." She sold from door to door the lace that she herself made. Marion followed in her steps with papa's paintings. Other sisters had left home, and some were married. I was the one who had to mind the children,—the little ones; they were still coming,—and I hated and abhorred the work. I remember once being punished in school because I wrote this in my school exercise:

"This is my conception of hell: a place full of howling, roaring, fighting, shouting children and babies. It is supreme torture to a sensitive soul to live in such a Bedlam. Give me the bellowings of a madhouse in preference. At least there I should not have to dress and soothe and whip and chide and wipe the noses of the crazy ones."

Ah, I wish I could have some charming memories of a lovely home! That's a great deal to have. It is sad to think of those we love as in poor surroundings.

I suppose there are people in the world who would smile at the thought of a girl's ecstatic enthusiasm over a piece of pink paper on an electric light in a room in the Chicago Y. W. C. A. Perhaps I myself am now almost snob enough to laugh and mock at my own former ingenuousness. That room, nevertheless, seemed genuinely charming to me. There were two snow-white beds, an oak bureau, oak chairs, oak table, a bright rug on the floor, and simple white curtains at the window. At home I slept in a room with four of my little brothers and sisters. I hate to think of that room. As fast as I picked up the scattering clothes, others seemed to accumulate. *Why* do children soil clothes so quickly!

There was even a homey look about my room in the Y. W. C. A., for there were several good prints on the wall, photographs on the mantel and the bureau, a bright toilet set on the bureau, and a work-basket on the table. From these personal things I speculated upon the nature of my room-mate to be, and I decided she was "nice." One thing was certain, she was exceedingly neat, for all her articles were arranged with almost old-maid primness. I determined to be less careless with my own possessions.

After unpacking my things, and hiding my money,—right back in my stocking, despite what the secretary had said!—I went down-stairs again, as I had been told a large reading-room, parlor, reception-rooms, etc., were on the ground floor.

The night before I had planned a definite campaign for work. I intended to go the rounds of the newspaper offices. I would present to the editors first my card, which Mr. Campbell had had specially printed for me, with the name of our paper in the corner, show Mr. Campbell's reference, and then leave a number of my own stories and poems. After that, I felt sure, one or all of the editors of Chicago would be won over. You perceive I had an excellent opinion of my ability at this time. I wish I had it now. It was more a conviction then—a conviction that I was destined to do something worth while as a writer.

In the reading-room, where there were a score of other girls, I found not only paper, pencils, pens, but all the newspapers and journals. Nearly all the girls were looking at the papers, scanning the advertising columns. I got an almanac,—we had one in Jamaica that was a never-failing reference-book to me,—and from it I obtained a list of all the Chicago papers, with the names of the proprietors and editors. I intended to see those editors and proprietors. It took me some time to make up this list, and by the time I was through it was the luncheon hour.

I followed a moving throng of girls into a great clean dining-room, with scores of long tables, covered with white cloths. There were all sorts of girls there, pretty girls, ugly girls, young girls, old girls, shabby girls, and richly dressed girls. In they came, all chatting and laughing and seeming so remarkably care-free and happy that I decided the Y. W. C. A. must be a great place, and there I would stay forever, or at any rate until I had won Mr. Hamilton.

You perceive now that I intended to court this man and, what is more, to win him, just as I intended to conquer Fate, and achieve fame in this city. How can I write thus lightly, when I felt so deeply then! Ah, well, the years have passed away, and we can look back with a gleam of humor on even our most sacred desires.

It was a decent, wholesome meal, that Y. W. C. A. luncheon. All the girls at my table seemed to know one another, and they joked and "swapped" stories about their "fellows" and "bosses," and told of certain adventures and compliments, etc. I attracted very little notice, though a girl next to me—she squinted—asked me my name. I suppose they were used to strangers among them. New girls came and went every day.

All the same, I did feel lonely. All these girls had positions and friends and beaux. I ardently hoped that I, too, would be working soon. A great many of them, however, were not working-girls at all, but students of one thing or another in Chicago who had taken advantage of the cheapness of the place for boarding purposes. By right they should not have been there, as the association was supposed to board only self-supporting girls. However, they got in upon one excuse or another, and I think the other girls were rather glad than otherwise to have them there. They were of course well dressed and well mannered, and they lifted the place a bit above the average working-girl's home. Curiously enough, there were few shop or factory girls there. Most of the girls were stenographers and bookkeepers.

When I went up to my room after luncheon, I found a girl washing her face in the basin. She looked up, with her face puffed out and the water dripping from it, and she sang out in all her dampness:

"Hello!"

She proved, of course, to be my room-mate. Her name was Estelle Mooney. She was not good-looking, but was very stylish and had a good figure. Then, her hair appeared such a wonderful fabric that really one could scarcely notice anything else about her. It was a mass of rolls and coils and puffs, and it was the most extraordinary shade of glittering gold that I have ever seen. I could not imagine how she ever did it up like that—till I saw her take it off! Well, that hair, false though it was, entirely dominated her face. It was stupendous, remarkable. However, it was the fashion at that time to wear one's hair piled gigantically upon one's head, and every one had switches and rolls and rats galore—every one except me. I had a lot of hair of my own. It came far down below my waist, and was pure black in color. It waved just enough to look well when done up. Canadian girls all have good heads of hair. I never saw an American girl with more than a handful. Still, they make it look so fine that it really does not matter—till they take it down or off.

My room-mate chewed gum constantly, and the back of our bureau was peppered with little dabs that she, by the way, told me to "please let alone." As if I'd have touched her old gum! I laughed at the idea then; I can still laugh at the remembrance.

Estelle was a character, and she talked so uniquely that for once in my life I listened, tongue-tied and secretly enchanted. Never had I heard such speech. With Estelle to room with, why had I not been born a female George Ade! But, then, I soon discovered that nearly all American girls (the working-girls at least) used slang fluently in their speech, and it did not take me long to acquire a choice vocabulary of my own.

Estelle had to return to her office by one, so she could snatch only a moment's conversation with me, and she talked with hair-pins in her mouth, and while sticking pins, bone knobs, and large rhinestone pins and combs into that brilliant mass of hair that dominated her. On top of this she finally set a great work of art, in the shape of an enormous hat. Its color scheme was striking, and set rakishly upon Estelle's head, it certainly did look "fetching" and stylish.

Now, this girl, with all her slang and gaudy attire, was earning fifteen dollars a week as a stenographer and type-writer. She not only supported herself in "ease and comfort," as she herself put it, but she contributed three dollars a week to her family—she hailed from Iowa, despite her name—and she saved two dollars a week. Also she was engaged. She showed me her ring. I envied her not so much for the ring as for the man. I should have loved to be engaged. She said if it wasn't for the fact that her "fellow" called every evening, she'd take me out with her that night; and perhaps if Albert didn't object too much, she would, anyhow. Albert must have objected, for she did not take me.

Albert worked in the same office as Estelle. He got twelve dollars a week; but Estelle planned that if they married, Albert, who was the next in line, would take her place. He was bound to rise steadily in the firm, according to Estelle. As they did not intend to marry for two or three years, she expected to have considerable saved by then, especially as Albert was also saving. I liked Estelle from the first, and she liked me. I always got on well with her, though she used to look at me suspiciously whenever she took a piece of gum from the back of the bureau, as if she wondered whether I had been at work upon it in her absence.

I don't know how I found my way about the city that afternoon, but I declare that there was not a single newspaper office in Chicago at which I did not call. I went in with high hopes, and I sent in my card to proprietor and editor, and coldly stared out of countenance the precocious office boys, patronizing, pert, pitying, impudent, or indifferent, who in every instance barred my way to the holy of holies within. In not one instance did I see a proprietor of a paper. No deeply impressed editor came rushing forth to bid me enter. In most of the offices I was turned away with the cruel and laconic message of the office boy of "Nothing doing."

In two cases "cub" reporters—I suppose they were that, for they looked very little older than the office boys—came out to see me, but although they paid flattering attention to the faltering recitation of my experiences as a reporter in Jamaica, West Indies, they, too, informed me there was "nothing doing," though they took my address. As far as that goes, so did the office boys. One of the reporters asked me if I'd like to go out to dinner with him some night. I said no; I was not looking for dinners, but for a position.

I was very tired when I reached "home." I went up to my room to think the matter over alone, for the reading-room and the halls were crowded with girls. Estelle, however, had returned from work. She had taken off all her puffs and rats, and looked so funny with nothing but her own hair that I wanted to laugh, but turned away, as I would not have hurt her feelings for worlds.

"Hello!" she cried as I came in. "Dead tired, ain't you?"

How *can* a firm employ a stenographer who says "ain't"?

She offered me a piece of gum—unchewed. I took it and disconsolately went to work.

"Got soaked in the eye, didn't you?" she inquired sympathetically.

I nodded. I knew what she meant by that.

"Well, you'll get next to something soon," said Estelle. "What's your line?"

I started to say "journalism." In Canada we never say "newspaper work." Journalism seems a politer and more dignified term. To Estelle I said, "I write," thinking that that would be clear; but it was not. She thought I meant I wrote letters by hand, and she said at once:

"Say, if I were you, I'd learn type-writing. You can clip off ten words on the machine to one you can write by hand, and it's dead easy to get a job as a type-writer. Gee! I don't see how you expect to get anything by writing! That's out of date now, girl. Say, where do you come from, anyhow?"

Unconsciously, Estelle had given me an idea. Why should I not learn type-writing? I was an expert at shorthand, and if I could teach myself that, I could also teach myself type-writing. If a girl like Estelle could get fifteen dollars a week for work like that, what could not I, with my superior education—

Heavens and earth! compared with Estelle I called myself "educated," I whose mind was a dismal abyss of appalling ignorance!

A type-writer, then, I determined to be. It was a come-down; but I felt sure I would not need to do it for long. Estelle generously offered to have a type-writer sent to our room (three dollars a month for a good machine), and she said she would show me how to use it. In a few weeks, she said, I would be ready for a position.

A few weeks! I intended to go to work at once. I had a hundred dollars to pay back. Already I had used five of it. If I stayed here a few weeks without working, it would rapidly disappear. Then, even when I did get a position, suppose they gave me only a beginner's salary, how could I do more than pay my board from that? The possibility of getting that hundred dollars together again would then be remote, remote. And if I could not get it, how, then, was I to see *him* again?

I would stick to my first resolve. I would not write to him until I could send him back that money—that dirty money. I felt that it stood between us like a ghost.

I wonder if many girls suffer from this passionate sensitiveness about money. Or was I exceptional? *He* has said so, and yet I wonder.

ONOTO WATANNA

I was determined to get work at once. I would learn and practise type-writing at night, but I would not wait till I had learned it, but look for work just the same through the day. Secretly I thought to myself that if Estelle took three weeks in which to learn the type-writer, as she said she did, I could learn it in two days. That may sound conceited, but you do not know Estelle. I take that back. I misjudged Estelle. Ignorant and slangy she may have been, but she was sharp-witted, quick about everything, and so cheerful and good-humored that I do not wonder she was able to keep her position for four or five years. In fact, for the kind of house she was in—a clothing firm—she was even an asset, for she "jollied" the customers and at times even took the place of a model. She said she was "a perfect thirty-six, a Veenis de Mylo."

Conceit carries youth far, and if I had not had that confidence in myself, I should not have been able to do what I did.

All next day I tramped the streets of Chicago, answering advertisements for "experienced" (mark that!) stenographers and type-writers. I was determined never to be a "beginner." I would make a bluff at taking a position, and just as I had made good with Mr. Campbell, so I felt I should make good in any position I might take. I could not afford to waste my time in small positions, and I argued that I would probably lose them as easily as the better positions. So I might as well start at the top.

XIII

I hate to think of those nightmare days that followed. It seemed to me that a hundred thousand girls answered every advertisement. I stood in line with hundreds of them outside offices and shops and factories and all sorts of places. I stood or sat (when I could get a seat) in crowded outer offices with scores of other girls, all hungrily hoping for the "job" which only one of us could have.

Then I began to go from office to office, selecting a building, and going through it from the top to the bottom floor. Sometimes I got beyond the appraising office boys and clerks of outer offices, and sometimes I was turned away at the door.

I have known what it is to be pitied, chaffed, insulted, "jollied"; I have had coarse or delicate compliments paid me; I have been cursed at and ordered to "clear out—" oh, all the crucifying experiences that only a girl who looks hard for work knows!

I've had a fat broker tell me that a girl like me didn't need to work; I've had a pious-looking hypocrite chuck me under the chin, out of sight of his clerks in the outer offices. I've had a man make me a cold business proposition of ten dollars a week for my services as stenographer and type-writer, and ten dollars a week for my services as something else. I've had men brutally touch me, and when I have resented it, I have seen them spit across the room in my direction, and some have cursed me.

And I have had men slip into my hand the price of a meal, and then apologize when they saw they had merely hurt me.

When the day was done, I've wearily climbed aboard crowded cars and taken my stand, packed between a score of men and women, or clung to straps or doors, and I have envied those other people on the car, because I felt that most of them were returning from work, while I was looking for it.

And then I've gone back to my room in the Y. W. C. A., hurrying to get there before the chattering, questioning Estelle, and counted over my ever-diminishing hundred dollars, and lain down upon my bed, feverishly to think ever and only of *him*! Oh, how far, far away now he always seemed from me!

Sometimes, if I came in early enough, and if I were not too desperately tired, I would write things. Odds and ends—what did I not write? Wisps of thoughts, passionate little poems that could not bear analysis; and then one day I wrote a little story of my mother's land. I had never been there, and yet I wrote easily of that quaint, far country, and of that wandering troupe of jugglers and tight-rope dancers of which my own mother had been one.

A week passed away, and still I had found no work. What was worse, I had no way of learning type-writing, even with the machine before me; for Estelle, despite her promises, went out every night with Albert. She had merely shown me one morning how to put the paper on and move the carriage back and forth. I used to sit before that type-writer and peck at the type, but my words ran into one another, and sometimes the letters were jumbled together.

I now knew a few of the girls in the house to speak to slightly, but I hesitated to ask any of them to show me something that perhaps I ought to pay to learn; for I did not want to spend the money for that. So I waited for Estelle to keep her promise.

Sometimes I would approach a group of girls, with the intention of asking one of them to come with me up to my room, and then when she was there, ask her about the type-writer; but the girls at the Y. W. C. A. were always occupied in one way or another in the evening, and a great many of them, like myself, were looking for work.

They used to cluster together in the lower halls and reading-room and talk over their experiences. Snorts of indignation, peals of laughter, strenuous words of advice—all these came in a stream from the girls. You'd hear one girl tell an experience, and another would say, "I tell you what *I'd* have done: I'd have slapped him in the face!" Or again, a girl would say, "I just gave him one look that petrified him." From all of which I gathered that my own experiences while looking for work were common ones. Alas! most of us had passed the stage where we "smacked" or "slapped" a man in the face or "petrified" him with a stare when he insulted us. What was the use? I had got so that I would take a nasty proposition from a man with a shrug and a smile, and walk out gamely.

I dare say there are people who cannot believe men are so base. Well, we girls who work see them at their worst, remember, and sometimes we see them at their best. There are men so fine and great in the business world that they compensate for all the contemptible wolves who prey upon creatures weaker and poorer than they are.

I did not have time in those days to notice much that happened in the house, and yet small riots and strikes were on all sides of us. Girls were protesting about this or that. I remember one of the chief grievances was having to attend certain amateur theatrical performances given by patronesses of the association. We poor girls were obliged to sit through these abortive efforts at amusing us. Most of us, as Estelle said, could have "put it all over" these alleged actors. Then, not all of the girls cared to attend the religious services and prayer meetings. It was a real hardship to be obliged to sit through these when one would have much preferred to remain in one's room. The ten-o'clock rule was the hardest of all. At that hour all lights went out. We were supposed to be in bed unless we had permission to remain out later. Vehement protests against this rule were daily hurled at the powers that were, but in vain. The girls asserted that as there were no private parlors in which to see their company, they were obliged to go out, and it was cruel to make it obligatory to be in so early.

So, you see, pleasant as in many ways the association was, it had its drawbacks. Even I, who was charmed with the place, and grateful for the immediate shelter it gave me, revolted after I had been working some time.

One day a statue of General Logan was to be unveiled opposite our place, and a great parade was to mark the occasion. Naturally the windows of our house that faced the avenue were desirable and admirable places from which not only to see the parade, but to watch the unveiling exercises. Promptly the patrons and patronesses descended upon us, and our windows were demanded. We girls were told we would have to give up our rooms for that afternoon and go to the roof.

I'll tell you what one girl did. When the fine party that was to occupy her room knocked upon her door, she called, "Come in!" and when they entered, they found the young person in bed. She declined to get up.

Threats, coaxings, the titterings and explosive laughter of the association's "honored guests" (they were of both sexes) fell upon deaf ears. She declined to get up, and dared any one of them to force her up. She said she had paid for that room, and she, and no one else, was going to occupy it that day. That girl was I. I suppose I would have been put out of the place for that piece of unheard-of defiance but for the fact that one of the patronesses undertook to champion me. She said I was perfectly right, and as she was a most important patroness, I was not disturbed, though I received a severe lecture from Miss Secretary.

Taken on the whole, however, it was a good place. We had a fine gymnasium and even a room for dancing. There were always lectures of one kind or another, and if a girl desired, she could acquire a fair education.

At the end of my second week, and while I was still looking for a place, I made my first real girl friend and chum. I had noticed her in the dining-room, and she, so she said, had specially selected me for consideration. She called upon me one evening in my room. Of course she was pretty, else I am afraid I should not have been attracted to her. Pretty things hypnotize me. She was several years older than I, and was what men call a "stunning-looking" girl. She was tall, with a beautiful figure, which she always showed to advantage in handsome tailor-made suits. Her complexion was fair, and she had laughing blue eyes. She was the wittiest and prettiest and most distinguished-looking girl in the house. I forgot to describe her hair. It was lovely, shining, rippling hair, the color of "Kansas corn," as one of her admirers once phrased it.

Estelle was out that evening, and while I was forlornly picking at my type-writer, some one tapped at my door, and then Lolly—her name was Laura, but I always called her Lolly—put her head in.

She said:

"Anybody but yourself at home?" and when I said no, she came in, and locked the door behind her. She was in a pink dressing-gown so pretty that I could not take my eyes from it. I had never had a dressing-gown.

Lolly stretched herself out on my bed, brought forth a package of cigarettes, a thing absolutely forbidden in the place, offered me one, and lit and began to smoke one herself. To be polite, I took her cigarette and tried to smoke it; but she burst into merry laughter at my effort, because I blew out instead of drawing in. However, I did my best.

Of course, like girls, we chatted away about ourselves, and after I had told her all about myself, Lolly in turn told me her history.

It seems she was the daughter of a prominent Texas politician whose marriage to a stepmother of whom Lolly heartily disapproved had induced her to leave home. She was trying to make a "sort of a livelihood," she called it, as a reporter for the newspapers.

When she said this carelessly, I was so surprised and delighted that I jumped on the bed beside her, and in a breath I told her that that was the work I had done, and now wanted to do. She said that there "wasn't much to it," and that if she were I, she'd try to get something more practical and dependable. She said she had a job one day and none the next. At the present time she was on the *Inter Ocean*, and she had been assigned to "cover" the Y. W. C. A. (she called it "The Young Women's Cussed Association") and dig up some stories about the "inmates" and certain abuses of the officials. She said she'd have a fine "story" when she got through.

How I envied her for her work! Hoping she might help me secure a similar position, I read to her my latest story. She said it was "not bad," but still advised me to get a stenographer's place in preference. She said there were five thousand and ninety-nine positions for stenographers to one for women reporters, and that if I got a good place, I would find time to write a bit, anyway. In that way I'd get ahead even better than if I had some precarious post on a newspaper, as the space rates were excessively low. She said that she herself did not make enough to keep body and soul together, but that she had a small income from home. She said her present place was not worth that, and she blew out a puff of smoke from her pretty lips. Any day she expected that her "head would roll off," as she had been "falling down" badly on stories lately.

In her way Lolly was as slangy as Estelle, but there was a subtle difference between their slangs. Lolly was a lady. I do not care for the word, but gentlewoman somehow sounds affected here. Estelle was not. Yet Lolly was a cigarette fiend, and, according to her own wild tales, had had a most extraordinary career.

Lolly had the most charming smile. It was as sunny as a child's, and showed a row of the prettiest of teeth. She was impulsive, and yet at times exceedingly moody.

I told her I thought she was quite the prettiest girl in the place, whereupon she gave me a squeeze and said:

"What about yourself?"

Then she wanted to know what I did with myself all the time. I said:

"Why, I look for work all day."

"But at night?"

Oh, I just stayed in my room and tried to write or to practise on the type-writer.

"Pooh!" said Lolly, "you'll die of loneliness that way. Why don't you get a sweetheart?"

I suppose my face betrayed me, for she said:

"Got one already, have you?"

"No, indeed," I protested.

"Then why don't you get one?"

"You talk," I said, "as if sweethearts were to be picked up any day on the street."

"So they are, as far as that goes," said Lolly. "You just go down the avenue some night and see for yourself."

That really shocked me.

"If you mean make up to a strange man, I wouldn't do a thing like that, would you?"

"Oh, yes," said Lolly, "if I felt like it. As it is now, however, I have too many friends. I've got to cut some of them out. But when I first came here, I was so d—— lonely"—she used swear-words just like a man—"that I went out one night determined to speak to the first man who got on the car I took."

"Well?"

Lolly threw back her head and laughed, blowing her smoke upward as she did so.

"He was a winner from the word go, my dear. Most of the girls get acquainted with men that way. Try it yourself."

No, I said I wouldn't do that. It was too "common."

"Pooh!" said Lolly, "Lord knows I was brought up by book rule. I was the bell of D——, but now I'm just a working-girl. I've come down to brass tacks. What a fool I'd be to follow all the conventional laws that used to bind me. Then, too, I'm a Bohemian. Ever hear of that word?" she interrupted herself to ask.

I nodded.

Mama used to call papa that when she was angry with him.

"Well," said Lolly, "I'm the bona-fide Bohemian article. My family think I'm the limit. What do you think?"

"I think you are trying to shock me," I said.

"Well, have I?"

"No, not a bit."

"Then you're the only girl in the house I haven't," she said with relish. "You know, I'm in pretty bad here, a sore spot in the body politic. Out I'd go this blessed minute if it wasn't for the fact that they're all afraid of me—afraid I'll show 'em up scorchingly."

"Would you do that?" I asked.

"Watch me!" said Lolly, laughing.

The lights went out, and then she swore. She had to scramble about on the bed to find her cigarettes. When she was going out, she said:

"Oh, by the way, if you like, I'll give you a card to a fellow out in the stock-yards. You go out there to-morrow and see him. He may have something for you."

Have I, I wonder, in this first rough picture of Lolly done her an injustice? If so, I hasten to change the effect. Lolly was a true adventurer; I dare not say adventuress, for that has a nasty sound. I wonder why, when adventurer sounds all right. Though at heart she was pure gold, though her natural instincts were refined and sweet, she took a certain reckless pleasure in, as it were, dancing along through life with a mocking mask held ever before her. For instance, she took an almost diabolic delight in painting herself in black colors. She would drawl off one startling story after another about herself as with half-closed eyes, through the smoke, she watched my face to judge of the effect of her recital. Sometimes she would laugh heartily at the end of her confidences, and then again she would solemnly assert that every word was true.

The morning after her first visit she woke me up early and, although Estelle grumbled, came airily into our room and got into bed with me.

A queer sort of antagonism existed between Lolly and Estelle, which I never quite understood at the time, though perhaps I do now. Lolly, with her reckless, handsome stylishness and dash represented the finished product of what poor Estelle tried to be. To make a crude sort of comparison, since Estelle herself worked in a clothing house and used clothing-house figures of speech, it was as if Lolly were a fine imported model and Estelle the pathetic, home-made attempt at a copy. She had copied the outlines, but not the subtle little finishing touches. Lolly, moreover, was acutely, amusedly aware of this, and she took a wicked and heartless delight in teasing and gibing at Estelle with words fully as slangy as Estelle's own, but which fairly stung with their keenness and caustic wit.

I could understand why Estelle hated Lolly, but I never could understand Lolly's contempt for Estelle. She always dismissed her as "Trash, Nora, trash!"

So now Estelle turned over in bed and snorted loud and long as Lolly got into mine.

Lolly said:

"George! how the *hoi-polloi* do snore!"

Estelle lifted her head from the pillow, to show she was not sleeping, and, as she would have put it, "petrified" Lolly with one long, sneering, contemptuous look.

ONOTO WATANNA

Lolly had come in, in fact, on an errand of mercy toward me, to whom she had taken a sudden fancy very much reciprocated by me. She said she wanted me to go out to the stock-yards as early as possible, as she understood this man she knew there wanted a stenographer right away. His name, she said, was Fred O'Brien, and she gave me a card which read, "Miss Laura Hope, the *Inter Ocean*." On the back she had written:

"Introducing Miss Nora Ascough."

I was delighted. It was like having another reference. I asked her about this Mr. O'Brien. She said, with a smile and significantly, that she had met him on a recent expedition to the yards in an inquiring mood for the *Inter Ocean* in regard to the pigs'-hair department, of which he was then manager.

"Pigs' hair!"

I had never heard of such a thing, and Lolly burst into one of her wildest peals of laughter, which made Estelle sit up savagely in bed.

"You'll be the death of me yet," said Lolly.

That was all the explanation she gave me, but all the way to the stock-yards, and as I was going through them, I kept wondering what on earth pigs' hair could be. I must say I did not look forward with any degree of delight to working in the pigs'-hair department.

XIV

Have you ever ridden through the Chicago stock-yards on a sunny day in the month of June? If you have, you are not likely to forget the experience.

As I rode with about twenty or thirty other girls in the bus, all apparently perfectly contented and happy, I thought of some of my father's vivid stories of old Shanghai, the city of smells.

I shall not describe the odors of the Chicago stock-yards. Suffice it to say that they are many, varied, and strong, hard to bear at first, but in time, like everything else, one becomes acclimated to them, as it were. I have heard patriotic yards people, born and reared in that rarefied atmosphere, declare that they "like it." And yet the institution is one of the several wonders of the world. It is a miraculous, an astounding, a mighty organization.

Again, as on that first day in Chicago, at the railway station, I was one of many atoms pouring into buildings so colossal that they seemed cities in themselves. I followed several of the stenographers— only the stenographers rode in the busses; the factory girls of the yards walked through, as did the men—up a few flights of stairs, and came to a vast office where, I believe, something like three thousand clerks are employed on one floor. Men, women, girls, and boys were passing along, like puppet machines, each to his own desk and chair.

The departments were partitioned off with oak railings. There was a manager and a little staff of clerks for every department, and, oh! the amazing number of departments! During all the months I worked there I never knew the names of more than half the departments, and when I come to think of what was on the other floors, in other buildings, the great factories, where thousands were employed, I feel bewildered and stupendously impressed.

To think of the stock-yards as only a mighty butcher shop is a great mistake. It is better to think of them as a sort of beneficent feeder and provider of humanity, not merely because of the food they pour out into the world, but for the thousands to whom they give work.

I heard much of the abuses there, of the hateful actions of many of the employers; but one loses sight of these things in contemplating the great general benefit of this astounding place. Of course I, in the offices, saw perhaps only the better and cleaner side of the yards, and therefore I cannot tell what went on elsewhere.

I asked a boy for Mr. O'Brien, and he said:

"Soap department."

I went along the main railing, inquiring for the soap department, and a sharp-eyed youth (in the pickled snouts department) with a pencil on his ear, undertook to take me to O'Brien.

As I passed along with him, I found myself the attacked of many eyes. A new girl is always an object of interest and speculation in the yards. I tried to look unconcerned and unaware, an impossibility, especially as some of the clerks coughed as I went by, some grinned at me, one winked, and one softly whistled. I felt ashamed and silly, and a fierce sort of pity for myself that I should have to go through this.

"Lady for you, Fred," at last sang out my escort as we approached an inclosure, and then smiling, he opened a little gate, and half pushed, half led, me in.

I found myself at the elbow of a long, lanky young man who was doubled over in such a position that his spine looked humped up in the middle. He had a large box before him, in which were a lot of pieces of soap, and he kept picking up pieces and examining them, sometimes smelling them. There was one other person in the inclosure, or department, and he was a very red-haired, freckle-faced boy of about twelve.

For some time the long, lanky young man did not even look up, but continued to examine the soap. I was beginning to think he was ignorant of my presence at his elbow when he said, without taking his nose out of the box, and shifting his unlighted cigar from one side of his mouth to the other, in a snarling sort of voice, like the inquiring bark of a surly dog:

"Wa-al, what d' yer want?"

"A position as stenographer," I answered promptly.

He straightened up in his seat at that, and took a look at me. His cheek-bones were high and lumpy; he had a rather pasty-colored skin, sharp-glancing eyes, and a humorous mouth. It was a homely face, yet, curiously enough, not unattractive, and there was something straightforward about it. He wore his hat on the back of his head, and he did not remove it in honor of me. After scrutinizing me in one quick glance, in which I felt he had taken in all my weaknesses and defects, he said in a less-snarling tone:

"Sit down."

I sat.

Lolly's card I timidly proffered. He took it, stared at it with an astonished expression, and then snorted so loudly it made me think of Estelle, and I felt a quaking fear that Lolly's card was a poor recommendation. He spat after that snort, looked at me again, and said:

"Well, I like her nerve!"

Of course, as I was not aware of just what he meant by that (I subsequently learned that Lolly had gone to work for O'Brien supposedly as a stenographer, and then had written up and exposed certain conditions in the yards), I stared at him questioningly, and he repeated with even more eloquent emphasis:

"Well, I like her *nerve*! It beats the *Dutch*!"

Then he chuckled, and again scrutinized me.

"That all the reference you got?" he asked.

I produced Mr. Campbell's, and as I watched him read it with a rather puzzled expression, I hastily produced Canon Evans's reference as to my character, which my father had sent me for the Y. W. C. A. O'Brien handed the letters back to me without comment, but he kept Lolly's card, putting it carefully away in his card-case, and chuckling as he did so.

"What do you know?" at last he said to me. "Good stenographer, are you?"

"Yes, very good," I eagerly assured him.

"Humph! How much salary do you expect to get?"

"I got ten a week in the West Indies," I said. I never even thought that that "free board" at the hotel amounted to something, too. Ten dollars was my salary, and so I said ten.

He hugged his chin reflectively, studying me, and after a moment he said:

"I wasn't expecting to take any one on for a day or two, but so long as you're here, and come so highly recommended,"—and he grinned,— "you may stay. Salary fifteen per."

"Oh, thank you!" I said so fervently that he got angrily red, and turned away.

The red-haired office boy, who had been acutely listening to the conversation, now came up to me and pertly asked me if I was engaged. Which insolent question I at first declined to answer. When I realized that he did not mean engaged to be married, but engaged for the position, then I said, with scarlet face, that I was.

"Red Top," as they called him, then showed me my desk, next to Mr. O'Brien's, filled my ink-wells, brought me pens, pencils, and note-books. I was inwardly congratulating myself that there was no sign of a type-writer when the boy pulled up the lid of my desk, and, lo! there was a fine, glistening machine.

I suppose some girls really take a sort of pride in their machine, just as a trainer does in his horse. I confess that I felt no fond yearnings toward mine, and while I was debating how in the world I was ever going to copy the letters, Mr. O'Brien pulled out a slat on my desk, leaned over, and began to dictate. All the time he was dictating he was chewing tobacco, stopping once in a while to spit in a cuspidor at his feet, and watching my face out of the corner of his eye. This was a sample of the letters I took, and you can judge of my feelings as I wrote:

Messrs. So and So.
Gentlemen:
   I send you F.O.B. five hundred broken babies, three hundred cracked babies, one thousand perfect ones, etc.

Broken babies, cracked babies, perfect ones! What sort of place was this, anyway? The pigs' hair department was mystifying and horrifying enough, and I *had* heard that sausages were made from dogs and horses; but a trade in *babies*—cracked and broken!

I suppose my face must have betrayed my wonder and perhaps horror, for O'Brien suddenly choked, though I don't know whether he was laughing or coughing, but he made a great noise. Then he said, clearing his throat:

"Got all that?"

I nodded.

"That's all," he said, and turned back to his soapbox. There was nothing for me to do now but to type-write those letters. I stared at that machine blindly, and to put off the evil moment, I tried to engage my "boss" in conversation while pretending to dust the machine.

"Mr. O'Brien, have—have you many babies here?" I asked.

"Thousands," he returned.

"It must be like a hospital," said I.

He grunted. I've often thought that O'Brien delighted to put stenographers through that "baby" joke, but I don't suppose any other girl was ever quite so gullible as I.

"I'd like to see some of them," I said.

"You're looking at them now," said he.

I looked about me, but I saw no babies. O'Brien was digging down in the box. Suddenly he tossed up a handful of odd-shaped pieces on his desk. Then I understood. They were all in the shape of babies— Wool-Soap babies! O'Brien, with his tobacco in his cheek, thought it a good joke on me.

I stuck the paper into the type-writer, and then I began slowly to write, pecking out each letter with my index-finger. I felt rather than saw O'Brien slowly turning round in his seat, and though I dared not look up, I felt both his and Red Top's amazed eyes on my slowly moving fingers. Suddenly O'Brien stood up.

"Well, upon my word," said he, "you sure are a twin of that friend of yours! I like your nerve!"

I sat still in my seat, just staring at the type, and a fearful lump came up in my throat and almost choked me. I could not see a thing for the tears that came welling up despite myself, but I held them back fiercely.

Suddenly O'Brien snapped out in his most angry and snarling tone:

"Say, who are you staring at, anyway?"

I thought he meant me, and I started to protest that I was merely looking at the type, when I heard the feet of Red Top shuffle, and he said, oh, so meekly and respectfully:

"Yes, sir; I ain't staring at *her*, sir."

I was relieved, anyway, of a part of the pressure, for the office boy was now busy at some files. I found enough courage at last to look at O'Brien. He was studying me as if I were some strange curiosity that both amused and amazed him.

"You're a nice one, aren't you," said he, "to take a job at fifteen per as an experienced and expert stenographer and—"

I said quickly:

"I am an expert stenographer. It's just the type-writing I can't do, and, oh! if you'll only give me a chance, I'll learn it in a few days, honestly I will. I'm cleverer than most girls, really I am. I taught myself shorthand, and I can type-writing, too. I'll practise every night, and if you'll just try me for a few days, I'll work so hard—and you won't be sorry; I'm sure you won't."

I got this all off quickly and warmly.

To this day I do not know what impulse moved Fred O'Brien to decide that he wanted me as his stenographer. His was an important department, and he could have had as good a stenographer as fifteen dollars a week will get, and that's a fair salary for work of that kind. Here was I, palpably a green girl, who could not type a line! No man's voice ever sounded nicer than that gruff young Irishman's when he said that I could stay, that for the first week I could do the letters by hand; but I was to practise every opportunity I got, and I could help him a lot if I would write the letters without making it necessary for him to dictate them.

In justification of my boast to O'Brien that I would "make good," let me say that I stayed in his department all the time I was at the yards, and this is the reference he gave me when he himself left to take charge of the New York office:

To Whom it may Concern:
　　This is to certify that Miss Nora Ascough, who has been in my employ for the past few months as stenographer and typewriter, is an A No. 1 Crack-a-Jack.
　　　　　　　　　　　Smith & Co. Per, Fred O'Brien, Mgr.

Some one once said of me that I owed my success as a writer mainly to the fact that I used my sex as a means to help me climb. That is partly true not only in the case of my writing, but of my work as a stenographer. I have been pushed and helped by men who liked me, but in both cases I *made good* after I was started.

I think it would have broken my heart not to have "made good" to Fred O'Brien after he had trusted me in this way. This man, the first I worked for in America, was probably the best friend I ever had or will have. I do not mean so much while I worked for him, but later in my life.

I have spoken of the mild sensation I made as I walked down that main aisle. All through the day, in whatever direction I looked, I encountered interested eyes bent upon me. Some were those of girls like myself, some office boys, a number of department managers, and nearly all the clerks in my vicinity. Some craned their necks to get a glimpse of me, some came officiously to talk to O'Brien. Thus it was an embarrassing day for me, especially at luncheon-hour, when I did not know quite what to do. Then a girl from another department came over and asked me to go to luncheon with her. She said that her "boss," whose name was Hermann, and who was a chum of O'Brien, had bade her look out for me.

She pointed Hermann out to me as we passed along, and he seized his hat, and came after us; but as he was passing our department, O'Brien seized him, and, looking back, I saw them both laughing, and I felt sure O'Brien was telling him about me.

Hermann was about twenty-five. He had a stiff thatch of yellow hair which he brushed up straight, and which stood up just like bristles on his head. He had wide-awake eyes, and looked like a human interrogation-point, dressed very dudishly, and flirted right and left with all the girls. Though born in America, and wiry and active, nevertheless there was the stamp of "Made in Germany" everywhere upon him. Later in the afternoon he stuck so insistently about our department that O'Brien finally introduced us, and then said with a grin:

"Now clear out. You got what you wanted."

Two or three departments to the left of me I had noticed a very blond, plumpish, rather good-looking young man, who watched me unceasingly throughout the day, but, whenever I looked at him, would blush, like a girl, and look down and fuss with papers on his desk. Well, about the middle of the afternoon, and while O'Brien was away from the department, a boy came over and laid a note on my desk. It was folded ingeniously, twisted into a sort of bowknot, and it was addressed, "Stenographer, Soap Dept."

I thought it was some instruction from O'Brien, especially as the boy said:

"Any answer?"

I unfolded the note, and this is what I read:

I'm stuck on you. Will you keep company with me?

I had to laugh, though I knew my furiously red swain was watching me anxiously.

"Any answer?" again asked the boy. I wrote on a piece of paper the one word, "Maybe."

People who have called me clever, talented, etc.,—oh, all women writers get accused of such things!—have not really reckoned with a certain weak and silly side of my character. If as I proceed with this chronicle I shock you with the ease and facility with which I encouraged and accepted and became constantly engaged to men, please set it down to the fact that I always felt an inability to *hurt* by refusing any one who liked me enough to propose to me. I got into lots of trouble for this,—call it moral lack in me,—but I could not help it at the time. Why, it's just the same way that I once felt in a private Catholic hospital, and little Sister Mary Eulalia tried to convert me. Out of politeness and because I loved *her*, I was within an ace of acknowledging her faith, or any other faith she might choose.

If you could have seen the broad smile of satisfaction that wreathed the face of my first stock-yards "mash," you, in my place, would not have regretted that little crumb of hope that I had tossed him. Yet I had no more intention of "keeping company" with him that I had of flying.

It pleases me much to record that on this my first day in the yards I received three "mash" notes, which one of the girls later told me "was going it some for fair."

My second note was a pressed flower, accompanied by these touching lines:

> *The rose is red; the violet's blue,*
> *Honey's sweet, and so are you!*
> *And so is he, who sends you this,*
> *And when we meet we'll have a kiss.*

I don't know who sent me this, but I suspected an office boy in a neighboring department.

My third note came just about an hour before leaving. It was from Hermann, and in a sealed envelop. It was as follows:

> *How about "Buffalo Bill" to-night?*

O'Brien leaned over me as I opened the note, deliberately took it from me, and read it. As he did so, Hermann stealthily pelted him with tightly chewed wads of paper, though, from his hunched-over position at his desk, no one would have suspected who was throwing those pellets. I saw him, however, and he winked at me as if I were in a conspiracy with him, and as much as to say:

"We'll fix him."

O'Brien, his cigar moving from one side of his mouth to the other, answered the note for me.

"Nothing doing," was his laconic response to Hermann's invitation, and he despatched it by Red Top. He let me out with the five-thirty girls instead of the six, and he said:

"Now step lively, and if you let Hermann catch up with you, I'll fire you in the morning."

I went flying down the aisle with my heart as light as a feather. Next to being in love, there is nothing finer in the world, for a working-girl, than to have a good "job" and to know that some one is "stuck" on you.

XV

My type-writing was practised under difficulties, for girls kept coming in and out of my room, and Lolly, who was there nearly every evening, taught me. By this time I was getting acquainted with a great many of the girls in the house, and for some reason or other I was popular. The "good" girls wanted me to join this or that Christian Society or Endeavor Club, and the "bad" girls—alleged by the good ones to be bad—were always urging me to "come on out and have a good time."

In those days Lolly was my chum. We were always together, much to Estelle's disgust. Every evening Lolly would come into my room unless she had an engagement, and, heavens! men came after Lolly like flies to the honey-pot. With a box of cigarettes and a magazine, or one of my own stories, all of which she was revising for me, she would curl up on my bed while I worked. Sometimes I practised till ten o'clock, when the lights would go out.

After a long, if not hard, day in the yards—and even if one did not work at all, the incessant movement and buzz of the great work factory was exhausting—and two or three hours of type-writing practice at night, you may be sure I was pretty tired when finally I crept into bed.

Then for some time thereafter I would lie wide awake. Like a kaleidoscopic panorama, the scenes of my day's work would slide in and out of my mind, then slowly pass away, as the figures in a strange dance. Visions would then come to me—the wavering, quaint persons and plots of the stories I would write. Dreams, too, came of the days when I would be famous and rich, and all my dear people would be lifted up from want. My poems would be on every one's tongue, my books in every home. And I saw myself facing a great audience, and bowing in acknowledgment of their praise of my successful play.

A few years later, when the name of a play of mine flashed in electric letters on Broadway, and the city was papered with great posters of the play, I went up and down before that electric sign, just to see if I could call up even one of the fine thrills I had felt in anticipation. Alas! I was aware only of a sad excitement, a sense of disappointment and despair. I realized that what as an ignorant little girl I had thought was fame was something very different. What then I ardently believed to be the divine sparks of genius, I now perceived to be nothing but a mediocre talent that could never carry me far. My success was founded upon a cheap and popular device, and that jumble of sentimental moonshine that they called my play seemed to me the pathetic stamp of my inefficiency. Oh, I had sold my birthright for a mess of potage!

We arrive at a stage of philosophic despair when we calmly recognize our limitations; but long before we know them, what wild dreams are those that thrill, enthrall, and torment us! Well, the dreams at least were well worth while.

I was now part of a vast, moving world of work, and, strangely enough, I was, in a way, contented. It takes very little to make the average normal girl contented. Take the girls who worked as I did. Given fair salaries and tolerable conditions under which to work, they were for the most part light-hearted and happy. You had only to look at groups of them about the Y. W. C. A. to realize that. Not that most of us did not have some little burden to carry; a few of us cherished wistful ambitions beyond our sphere, and all of us, I think, had our romances.

In the yards there was probably one girl to every three or four hundred men. They were obliged to pay good salaries, moreover, as many girls hesitated to go away out there to work, and the aristocrats of our profession balked at the sights and smells of the yards. Anyhow, the firm for which I worked treated us well. Special busses brought us to and from the yards. Excellent dressing-rooms and luncheon-rooms were assigned to us, and we were always treated with courtesy.

We girls were all appraised when we entered, and soon afterwards were assigned certain places in the estimation of the men of the yards. That is to say, a girl was "good," "bad," a "worker," a "frost," or a "peach."

The "good" girls were treated with respect; the "bad" girls made "dates" for dinners with the various "bosses," had fine clothes, jewels, were loud, and had privileges; the "frosts" were given a wide berth. They were the girls who were always on the defensive with the men, expecting and looking for insults and taking umbrage on the slightest provocation. The "workers" were of course the backbone of our profession. They received high salaries and rose to positions almost as good as the men's. Boys and men stepped lively for them, and took their orders unblinkingly. Finally, the title of "peach" was bestowed upon the girls whom the men decided were pretty and approved of in other ways. If one was in the "peach" class, she was persistently courted by all well-meaning or bad-meaning men who could get near her. She was a belle of the yards.

Under which head I came, I never knew. I think I was the strange gosling that had sprung up somehow in this nest, and no one knew quite where I should be assigned. There was a wavering disposition at first to put me in the "peach" class, but I rather think I degenerated within a few weeks to the "worker" class, for Fred O'Brien early acquired the habit of leaving most of the details of our department entirely to me.

Twenty-four men asked me to "go out" with them the first week I was there. I kept a note of this, just to amuse myself and O'Brien, who was vastly interested in the sensation he fatuously believed I was creating. He took a comical pride in my "success"! Ah, dear Fred! No one, not even I, was ever prouder of my later "success" than he. Every day he would ask me, "Well, who's asking you out to-night?" and I would show him my "mash" notes, most of which he confiscated, later, I suspect, to torment their authors.

The men out here did not ask if they could call upon a girl. Their way of becoming better acquainted, or "going after" a girl, as they called it, was to invite her to "go out" with them, meaning for a ride, to the theaters, the parks, restaurants, or other places of amusement. I never "went out" with any of the men of the yards except O'Brien and Hermann, who had been acting like a clown for my special benefit by coming over to our department every day, and talking a lot of nonsense, telling jokes, and sending me countless foolish notes, until at last O'Brien took pity on him, and said they would call upon me one night.

That was an illuminating occasion. "Fellows" were few and far between who called at the Y. W. C. A., and every girl who possessed a "steady" was marked. Whenever a new "fellow" appeared there, he was the object of the united curiosity of a score of girls, who hung about the halls and the parlors to get a look at him.

Now, Hermann called upon me in great state. Much to my surprise and Lolly's hilarious joy, he came in silk hat and frock coat, with a gold-topped cane. I hardly knew him, when I descended in my own best, a white polka-dotted Swiss dress, with a pink sash, and found him sitting erect and with evident discomfort on the edge of a sofa in the parlor, the admired target of a score of eyes, all feminine. He was making a manful effort to appear at his ease, and unaware of the sensation he had made. Men with silk hats, you must know, do not call every day upon girls at the Y. W. C. A. It was plain to be seen that the poor fellow was suffering a species of delicious torture. In the hall, within direct sight of the sofa, Lolly was leaning against the wall, and looking her wickedest and prettiest. She had already tormented and teased me unmercifully about my "first beau."

Hermann rose gallantly as I entered, and he bowed, as I did not know he could bow, over my hand, shaking it in the then approved and fashionable high manner; but I could not resist a little giggle as I heard Lolly chokingly cough in the hall, and I knew she was taking it all in.

"O'Brien's waiting for us outside," said Hermann. "Wouldn't come in. Acted just like a man with a sore tooth. Ever seen a man with a sore tooth, Miss Ascough?"

No, I had never had that pleasure, I told him.

"Well," said Hermann, "the man with a sore tooth groans all day and night, and makes every one about him suffer. Then first thing in the A.M. he hikes off to the nearest dentist. He gives one look at the sign on the dentist's door, and that's enough for him: he's cured. Christian Science, you see. Now, that's how it is with O'Brien to-night. He was dead stuck on coming along, but got stage-fright when he saw the girls."

"*You* weren't afraid of us, were you, Mr. Hermann?" said I, admiringly and flatteringly.

"Me? What, me afraid of girls? Sa-ay, I like that!" and Hermann laughed at the idea as if it amused him vastly. "Tell you what you do. Get another girl; there's a peach looking in at us now—don't look up. She's the blonde, with the teeth. What do you say to our all going over to the S—— Gardens for a lobster supper, huh?"

Now, the peach, of course, was Lolly, who, with her dimples all abroad and her fine white teeth showing, was plainly on view at the door, and had already worked havoc in the breast of the sentimental Hermann.

O'Brien didn't like the idea of the S—— Gardens. He said it was "too swift" for *me*, though he brutally averred it might do for Hermann and Lolly. Lolly and he sparred all the time, just as did Lolly and Estelle. He said, moreover, that it would not do at all for us to be seen together, and we would be sure to run across some yards people at the S—— Gardens. If he were seen out with his stenographer, every tongue in the office would be wagging about it next day.

So he suggested that we take a long car ride, and get off at L—— Park, where there was a good restaurant, and we could get something to eat and drink there. Fred and I paired off together, and Hermann, who had been utterly won away from me by Lolly, who was flirting with him and teasing him outrageously, brought up behind us as we started for the cars. After he had explained to me why we should not be seen together, O'Brien said, with an air of great carelessness:

"Now, look a-here, girl, I don't want you to get it into your head that I'm stuck on you, for I'm not; but I like you, and if you don't pull my leg too hard, I'll take you out with me all you want."

"Pull your leg!" I repeated, shocked. I had never heard that expression before. American slang was still a source of mystification, delight, and wonder to me. Lolly heard my horrified exclamation, and moved up, laughing her merriest.

"Limb's the polite term," she corrected Fred.

"Eh?" said he. Then as he saw I did not really understand, he explained to me what he meant.

"Oh," said I, "you needn't worry about me. If you don't believe that I care nothing about money, look at this."

There were a few coins in my pocketbook. I poured them into my hand, and deliberately and impulsively I tossed them out into the road. I am sure I don't know why I did such a senseless thing as that. It was just the impulse of a silly moment.

The subjects we two girls and boys discussed were varied and many, but always by persistent degrees they seemed to swing back to the yards, wherein of course the interests of our escorts naturally centered. The boys entertained us with tales of the men and even cattle of this "city," as they called it. There was a black sheep called "Judas Iscariot" who led the other sheep to slaughter, and was always rewarded with a special piece of meat. There was a big black pig that wandered about the offices of a neighboring firm, and was the mascot of that office.

There was a man who had been born in the yards, married in the yards, and whose heir had recently been born there. And so forth.

I got into trouble at the Y. W. C. A. for the first time that night. We had forgotten to ask permission to be out after ten, and it was after eleven by the time we got back. The door girl let us in, but took our names, and we were reported next day. I was let off with a reprimand from the secretary, but Lolly had a stormy time of it with this unpleasant personage, upon whom, I am happy to say, she never failed to inflict deserved punishment. It seems Lolly was an old offender, and she was accused of "leading Miss Ascough astray." I, by the way, was now in high favor with the secretary, though I never liked her, and I never forgave her for that first day. Also I had seen many girls turned away, sometimes because they did not have the money to pay in advance, and sometimes because they had no references. My heart used to go out to them, as with drooping shoulders these forlorn little waifs who had applied for shelter were turned from the very doors that should have opened for them.

That night as we felt our way in the dark through the unlighted halls to our rooms, Lolly, swearing audibly and picturesquely, said she was "darned tired" of this "old pious prison," and as she now had all the "dope" she wanted upon the place, she was going to get out, and she asked me to go with her. I said that I would.

XVI

I worked for five weeks in the stock-yards before I could make up the deficit in my hundred dollars caused by those first three weeks of idleness and the consequent expenses of my board. I am very bad at figures. I still calculate with my fingers. Every night, however, I counted my little hoard, and I had it all reckoned up on paper how soon I would have that hundred intact again.

Out of my fifteen a week I had to allow five dollars for my board, and so much for luncheon, car-fare, and the little articles I added to my wardrobe. I used about eight dollars a week on myself and I sent home two. That left me only five a week, and as I had used twenty-five of the hundred before I got my position, it took me over five weeks to make it up. As each week my little pile grew larger, the more excited I became in anticipation of that moment when I could write!

I would lie awake composing the wonderful letter that would accompany that hundred dollars, but when the sixth Saturday (pay-day) actually came, and I had at last the money, I found myself unable to pen the glowing letter of my dreams. This was the letter I finally sent, and unless he read between the lines, goodness knows it was a model of businesslike brevity, showing the undoubted influence of the Smith & Co. approved type of correspondence:

> Y. W. C. A.
> Chicago, Ill., Aug. 8-19
> Roger Avery Hamilton, Esq.

Dear Sir

I send you herewith inclosed the sum of one hundred dollars, being in full the amount recently lent by you to,
> Very faithfully yours,
> NORA ASCOUGH

It was with a bursting heart that I folded that cold and brief epistle. Then I laid it on top of that eloquent pile of bills—"dirty money." Just before I did up the package, the ache within me grew so intense that I wrote on the envelop:

"Please come to see me now."

I made a tight little package of the money and letter, and I sent it off by registered mail. I knew nothing about post-office orders or checks. So the money went to him just like that.

Now my life really changed. On the surface things went on as ever. I progressed with my type-writing. I "made good" at the office. The routine of the daily work in the yards was brightened by various little humorous incidents that occurred there. For instance, one of the firm, a darling old man of seventy, took a great fancy to me, and every day he would come down the main aisle of the office with a fresh flower in his hand, and lay it on my desk as he passed. Not bad for an old "pork-packer," was it? Every one teased me about him, and so did he himself. He called me "black-eyes," and said I was his "girl." Other men gave me flowers, too, but I prized that one of Mr. Smith's more than the others. Also I had enough candy given to me, upon my word, to feed me, and I could have "gone out" every night in the week, had I wanted to; but, as I have said, this was only part of my life now—my outer life. The life that I conjured up within me was about to come to reality, and no one knew anything about it, not even Lolly.

She had been very much engaged in "educating" Hermann, who was madly in love with her. Lolly accepted his adoration with amused delight. She considered him a "character," but she never took him seriously.

As the days passed away, the fever within me never waned. Though I went about my work as ever, my mind was away, and I was like one whose ear is to the ground, waiting, waiting.

But he did not come, and the weeks rolled away, and two months passed.

One night a man from Lolly's home came to call upon her. His name was Marshall Chambers. He was one of those big-shouldered, smooth-faced, athletic-looking men who make a powerful impression upon girls. According to Lolly, he was a wealthy banker whom she had known during her father's administration as mayor of her home town. I knew as soon as I saw them together that my poor Lolly was deeply in love with him, and I felt at once a sense of overwhelming antagonism and dislike toward him. I cannot explain this, for he was specially attentive to me, and although Lolly and he had not seen each other for some time, he insisted that I should accompany them to dinner at R——'s.

When we went to our rooms to dress, Lolly asked me what I thought of this man, and I said:

"I like Hermann better. *He's* honest."

That remark in ordinary circumstances would have sent Lolly into one of her merry peals of laughter,—she always laughed about Hermann,—but she gave me a queer look now, her cigarette suspended in her hand. Her face was flushed, and her eyes were so brilliant they looked like turquoises.

"You're dead right," she said solemnly.

But a moment later she was her old self again. I was putting on a little white dress when Lolly swung me round and examined me.

"Here, you can't go to R——'s in duds like these," she said. "Wait a minute."

She disappeared into her own room, and came back with her arms full of dresses; Lolly had beautiful clothes. I suppose her tailored suits would have looked ludicrous, as she was larger than I, but a little cream-colored chiffon frock, trimmed with pearl beads, was very becoming to me. She also lent me an evening cap, and a red rose (artificial) for my waist.

"Now look at yourself," said she, "and after this don't let me catch you mooning in your room at night. Get out and show yourself. You'll only be young once."

Lolly was in blue, the color of her eyes, and she looked, as always, "stunning." Beside her, I'm afraid, I appeared very insignificant, for Lolly was a real beauty. I never went anywhere with her but people—men and women, too—would stare at her, and turn around for a second look. People stared at me, too, but in a different sort of way, as if I interested them or they were puzzled to know my nationality. I would have given anything to look less foreign. My darkness marked and crushed me, I who loved blondness like the sun.

Mr. Chambers did everything very splendidly. He had a carriage to take us to dinner, and he was extremely gallant in his manner to both Lolly and me, just as attentive, I thought wistfully, as if we were society girls, and not poor girls of the Y. W. C. A. Lolly and he talked a good deal in an undertone, and although they did not ignore me, I was left out of most of their conversation. I did not mind this. I was happy to lean back in that carriage, and indulge in my own fine dreams.

I should have enjoyed the dinner more if our host had been some one other than this man Chambers. He made me uncomfortable and secretly angry by looking at me in a meaning sort of way when Lolly did not see him. I felt as if he were trying to establish some sort of intimacy with me behind Lolly's back. He sat beside Lolly, and I opposite them, and he would lean back in his seat, inclined toward Lolly, and over her shoulder he would make his bold eyes at me. No, I did not like that man, and I avoided his glances as much as I could. But Lolly, my poor Lolly, seemed infatuated with him, and all her pretty banter and chaff had departed. She scarcely ate anything, but played nervously with her food, and she would look at him in such a way that I wanted both to shake her and to cry for her.

But this is my story, not Lolly's, though hers perhaps would make a better tale than mine.

Chambers said he could tell one's fortune from one's palm, and that he would like to see mine. Lolly said:

"Nora carries her fortune in her head."

"And you," I said, "in your face."

He reached over the table for my hands, and Lolly said:

"Let him, Nora. Sometimes he makes pretty good guesses."

Chambers began to reel off a fine fairy-story, which he said was to be my fortune. We were all laughing, Lolly leaning over, and making merry and mocking interpolations, and I eagerly drinking in every word, and, though I laughed, believing most of it, when suddenly I had a queer, nervous feeling that some one other than ourselves was listening to us and was watching my face. There is something in telepathy. I was afraid to look up, and my heart began to beat in a frightened way, for I knew, even before I had turned my head, that *he* was somewhere there in the room with us. And then I saw him directly behind Marshall Chambers. Their chairs, back to back, were almost touching, but he had turned about in his seat, so that he was looking directly at me, and I shall never forget the expression of his face. It was as though he had made some discovery that aroused both his amusement and contempt.

What had I done that he should look at me like that? I wanted to go to him, to beg him to speak to me; but some one with him—a woman, I think, for curiously enough, I was capable of seeing only him, and noted not at all his companions—said something to him, and he moved his chair till his back was turned toward me. I felt like some dumb thing unjustly punished.

Lolly said:

"What's the matter, Nora? You look as if you had seen a ghost."

I suppose my face had blanched, for I was shivering, and I wanted to cover my face with my hands and to cry and cry.

"Oh, Lolly," I said, "I want to go home!"

Chambers took me by the arm, and we passed, like people in a dream, between the tables—ah! past where he was sitting, and out into the street and then home!

THE FOLLOWING MORNING I WAS passing languidly by the secretary's desk, in the main office, when she called to me:

"Miss Ascough, you will have to ask your men visitors to call earlier in the evening if they wish to see you. You know our rules."

"My men visitors?" I repeated stupidly.

"Yes," she returned sharply; "a gentleman called here last night at nearly nine-thirty. Of course we refused to permit him to see you."

"Oh," I said faintly, for before I had looked at that little card I knew who had at last come to see me. I went out with his card held blindly in my hand, and all that day, whenever my work paused or slackened, I found myself vaguely wondering why he had called so late, and I felt a dumb sense of helpless rage toward that hateful secretary who had turned him away.

XVII

Lolly came flying into my room just a little while before eight that evening, with her cheeks red and her eyes sparkling. She had dined down town with Marshall Chambers, and they had come back to get me to go to the theater with them.

"Hurry up, Nora!" she cried. "Get dressed! Marshall has seats for Sothern and Harned in 'The Sunken Bell.'"

Up to this time I had never been inside a theater. I had come to America in late May. It was now the beginning of September, and the theaters were just opening. Of course I had never been to a play of any sort at home, except some little church affairs. So, unhappy as I was, I dressed in Lolly's pretty chiffon dress, and we went down to join Mr. Chambers, who was waiting for us in the parlor. On the way down in the elevator, Lolly had handed me a number of advertisements of rooms and flats that she had cut from the papers, and while she was drawing on her gloves in the lower hall and I was glancing through these, a page called my name, and said a gentleman was waiting for me inside.

As I went into the parlor, Marshall Chambers stood up, held out his hand, and said something to me; but I scarcely saw him, and I know I did not answer him. I saw, in fact, nothing in the world save Roger Hamilton, who had come across the room to me, and, with an odd air almost of proprietorship, had taken me quietly from Chambers.

Without saying a word to each other, we sat for some time in the Y. W. C. A., with girls coming and going. I glanced only once at his face, and then I looked away, for I could not bear his expression. It was like that of the previous night. It was as if he examined me critically, cruelly, not only my face, but even my clothes and my gloved hands. Presently he said in a low voice:

"There are too many people here. We shall have to go out somewhere."

I found myself walking with him down Michigan Avenue. We said nothing as we walked, but presently we came to a little park, and found a bench facing the lake, and there we sat, I staring out at the water, and he looking at me. After a while he said:

"Who was your friend of last night?"

I said:

"Her name is Lolly Hope."

"I mean the *man*."

"He is her friend," I said. "I never met him till last night."

It was pretty dark, and I could not see his face, but insensibly I felt him lean toward me to look at mine; and then he said in a low voice:

"Are you sure of that?"

"Why, yes," I said. "I don't know the man at all. Did you think that I did?" He did not answer me, and I added, "Was it because of *him* you did not speak to me last night?"

"I did bow to you," he said, and then added reluctantly, "though I can't say I admired the looks of your party."

I said:

"I didn't even see the people with *you*, and it wouldn't have made any difference to me who they were."

He put his arm along the back of the bench behind me, but not touching me.

"Where did you get the clothes you had on—the dress you're wearing now?" he asked in a strained voice.

"Lolly lent them to me," I said. "She said mine were not fine enough."

After a pause he moved nearer to me, and I thought he was going to put his arm about me, but he did not. He said in a low voice:

"You can have all the fine clothes you want."

"I wish I could," I returned, sighing; "but one can't dress very beautifully on the salary I get."

"What do you get?" he asked, and I told him. Then he wanted me to tell him all about myself—just what I had been doing, whom I had met, what men, and to leave out nothing. I don't know why, but he seemed to think something extraordinary had happened to me, for he repeated several times:

"Tell me *everything*, every detail. I want to know."

So I did.

I told him of the Y. W. C. A. woman who had met me; of my failure with the newspaper offices; of my long hunt for work; of the insults and propositions men had made to me; of my work at the yards; and of O'Brien, my "boss," who had taken me on trust and had been so good to me.

He never interrupted me once, nor asked me a single question, but let me tell him everything in my own way. Then when I was through, he took his arm down, put his hands together, and leaned over, with his elbows on his knees, staring out before him. After a while he said:

"Do you mean to tell me you *like* living at this—er—Y. W. C. A.?"

I nodded.

"And you are contented to work at the Union Stock Yards?"

"No, I don't say that; but it's a stepping-stone to better things, don't you see? It's a living for me for the present, and perhaps by and by I'll sell some of my poems and stories, and then I'll be able to leave the yards."

He turned sharply in his seat, and I felt him staring at me.

"When on earth do you get *time* to write, if you work all day from nine till five-thirty?"

"Sometimes I get up very early," I said, "at five or six, and then I write a bit; and unless the girls bother me at night, I have a chance then, too, though I wish the lights didn't go out at ten."

"But you will kill yourself working in that way."

"No, I won't," I declared eagerly. "I'm awfully strong, and, then, writing isn't work, don't you see? It's a real pleasure, after what I've had to do all day, really it is, a sort of balm almost."

"But you can't keep that up. I don't want you to. I want you to go to school, to begin all over again. If you can, you must forget these days. I want you to blot them out from your mind altogether."

I thought of that question he had asked me on the train when I had read to him my poem: "Wouldn't you like to go to school?" Now, indeed, neither my pride nor my vanity was piqued. I could even smile at his tone of authority. He was so sure I would obey him; but I was not going to let him do anything in the world for me unless he could say to me what I was able to say to him.

"Well?" after a moment he prompted me.

"No, Mr. Hamilton," I said, "I am not going to school. I cannot afford to."

"I will send you," he said.

"You cannot do that if I refuse to go."

"Why should you refuse?" he said.

"Because it would cost you money—dirty money," I said.

"Nonsense!" He said that angrily now. "I *want* you to go."

"Thank you; but, nevertheless, I am not going."

He sat up stiffly, and I could feel his frown upon me. He shot out his words at me as if he wished each one to hit me hard:

"You are an ignorant, untrained, undisciplined girl. If you wish to accomplish the big things you plan, you will have to be educated. Here is your chance."

"I'm sorry, but I'll have to get along the best way I can."

"You are stubborn, pig-headed, foolish. Don't you *want* to be educated? Are you satisfied with your present illiterate condition?"

"I can't afford to be," I said.

"But if I am willing—"

I broke in:

"I took nearly six weeks to earn the money to pay you back. I told you I'd never take another cent from you, and I never will."

"Why not?"

"Because I want you to know that I care nothing, nothing at all— nothing, nothing, about your money, that you said every one else wanted. *I* only care for *you*. I do."

I had run along headlong with my speech, and now I was afraid of what I had said.

He did not say a word after that, and presently I added shakily:

"Don't you see that I can't let you help me again unless you care for me as I do for you? Don't you see that?"

He poked at the gravel with his cane, and after a moment he said very gently:

"I see that you are a very foolish little girl."

"You mean because I—care for you?" I asked.

"Because you've made yourself believe you do," he said.

"I *do*," I said earnestly. "I haven't thought of anything else except you."

"Nonsense! You mustn't get sentimental about me. Let's talk of something else. Have you been writing anything lately?"

I told him of the stories I was writing about my mother's land, and he said:

"But you've never been there, child."

"I know," I said; "but, then, I have an instinctive feeling about that country. A blind man can find his way over paths that he intuitively feels. And so with me. I feel as if I knew everything about that land, and when I sit down to write—why, things just come pouring to me, and I can write *anything* then."

I could feel his slow smile, and then he said:

"I believe you can. I don't doubt that you will accomplish all that you hope to. You are a *wonderful* girl."

He stood up, and held out his hand to help me, saying we had better be returning now, as he expected to take a train at eleven. My heart sank to think that his visit was to be so short, and I felt a passionate regret that there was nothing I could do or say that would keep him longer.

As we were walking down the avenue, he put the hand nearest me behind his back, and with the other swung his cane slightly. He seemed to be thinking all the time.

I asked him whether he was going to come and see me again, and he said quickly:

"If you do what I tell you."

"You mean about the school?" I asked.

"No-o. We'll let that go for the present; but you've got to get out of both that er—institution—"

"The Y. W. C. A.?" I queried, surprised.

"Yes, your precious Y. W. C. A."

He was talking in a low and rather guarded voice, as if anxious that no one passing should hear us.

"I want you to get bright, pretty rooms. You'll feel better and work better in attractive surroundings."

"I did intend to move, anyway," I said. "Lolly and I were planning to look for rooms to-morrow."

He said quickly:

"I wouldn't go with her. Get a place of your own."

"Well, but, you see, together we can get a better room for less money," I explained.

He made an impatient sound, as if the discussion of expense provoked him.

"Get as nice a place as you can, child," he said, and added growlingly, "If you don't, I'll not come to see you at all."

"All right," I said; "I'll get a nice place."

"And now about your position—"

"It's not bad," I asseverated. "Fred's awfully good to me."

"Fred?"

"Yes; he's my boss—Fred O'Brien."

"You call him Fred?"

"Yes; every one does at the yards."

"Humph! I think it would be an excellent plan for you to leave those yards just about as expeditiously as you can."

"But I can't. Why, I might not be able to get another position. Just look how I tramped about for weeks before I got that."

He stopped abruptly in the street.

"Don't you know, if you stay in a place like that, every bit of poetry and—er—charm—and fineness in you, and every other worth-while quality that you possess, will be literally beaten out of you? Why, that is no place for a girl like you. Now you get a pretty room—several, if you wish—and then go to work and write—write your poetry and stories and anything you want."

"But, Mr. Hamilton, I can't afford to do that."

He switched his cane with a sort of savage impatience.

"Nonsense!" he said. "You can afford to have anything you want. I'll give you anything—anything you want."

He repeated this sweepingly, almost angrily, and after a moment I said:

"Well, why should you do this for me?"

I was saying to myself that I would let him do anything for me if he did it because he cared for me. If not, I could take nothing from him. I waited in a sort of agony for his answer. It came slowly, as if he were carefully choosing his words:

"I want to do it," he said, "because I am interested in you; because it pleases me to help a girl like you; because I believe you are, as I have said, a wonderful girl, an exceptionally gifted girl, and I want to give you a chance to prove it."

"Oh!" I tried to speak lightly, but I wanted to sob. His belief in my talent gave me no pride. I vastly preferred him to care for me personally. "Thank you," I said, "but I can't let you give me a room and support me any more than I can let you send me to school."

We had now reached the Y. W. C. A. I could see the door girl watching us through the glass. It was after ten, and I had to go in. I held out my hand, and he took it reluctantly and immediately let it go. His manner plainly showed that I had offended him.

"Don't think," I said, "because I can't let you help me that I'm not grateful to you, for I am."

"Gratitude be damned!" he said.

Estelle and I had a little stock of candles, and when the lights went out before we were in bed, we used to light one. I had trouble finding one in the dark that night, and I tripped over the rocking-chair and hurt my ankle. Estelle sat up in petulant wrath.

"Say, what's biting you lately, anyhow?" she demanded. "Getting gay in your old age, are you?" she inquired.

"You shut up!" I said crossly, nursing my ankle. "I believe you hide those candles, anyway."

"I sure do," retorted Estelle. "If you think I'm going to let your swell friend burn my little glimmers, you've got one more guess coming."

By my "swell friend" she meant Lolly.

She got out of bed, however, felt under the bureau, and produced and lighted a candle. Then she examined and rubbed my ankle, and, grumbling and muttering things about Lolly, helped me undress and into bed. When I supposed she had dropped off asleep, she sat up suddenly in bed.

"Say, I'd like to ask you something. Have you got a steady?" she said.

"No, Estelle; I wish I had," I replied mournfully.

"Well," said Estelle, "you sure are going the way about *nit* to get one. You let them swell guys alone that come nosing around you. Say, do you know *I* thought you were in for a nice, steady fellow when I seen Pop-eyes"—Pop-eyes was her term for Hermann—"hanging round here. Then I seen *Miss* Hope"—with a sneer—"had cut you out. Say, I'd 'a' like' to have handed her one for that. Who was the swell took you out last night?"

"His name's Chambers. He's Lolly's friend."

"And who was the man to see you to-night? Looked to me as if *he* were stuck on you."

I sat up in bed excitedly.

"Oh, Estelle, did it?"

"Humph! I was right there next to you, on the next sofa with Albert, but, gee! you didn't see nothing but him, and he was looking at you like he'd eat you up if you give him half a chance."

I sighed.

"I gave him a chance all right," I said mournfully.

"And nothing doing?" asked Estelle, sympathetically.

"No—nothing doing, Estelle," I said.

"Well, what do you care?" said my room-mate, determined to comfort me. "Say, what does any girl want with an old grand-pop like him, anyway?"

I laughed, I don't know why. Somehow, I was *glad* that Mr. Hamilton was old. Oh, yes, forty seems old to seventeen.

XVIII

I don't know whether it was the effect of Mr. Hamilton's visit or not, but I was not so contented after that. Things about the Y. W. C. A. that I had not noticed before now irritated me.

A great many unjust requirements were made of the girls. It was not fair to make us attend certain sermons. Goodness knows, we were tired enough when we got home, and most of us just wanted to go to our rooms; and if we did desire entertainment or relaxation, we wanted to choose it for ourselves. I believe some of these old rules are not enforced to-day.

Then that ten o'clock rule! Really it *was* a shame! Just fancy writing feverishly upon some beautiful (to me it was beautiful) story or poem, and all of a sudden the lights going out! That was maddening, and sometimes I swore as Lolly did, and I cried once when I had reached a place in my story that I simply *had* to finish, and I tried to do it in the dark.

So I was determined to move, and Lolly went about looking for rooms for us. I told her I'd like anything she got.

Meanwhile life in the yards began to "get upon my nerves." I never before knew that I *had* nerves; but I knew it now. No one, not even a girl of the abounding health and spirits I then enjoyed, could work eight hours a day at a type-writer and two or three hours writing at night, and be in love besides, and not feel some sort of strain.

And I *was* in love. I don't suppose any girl was ever more utterly and hopelessly in love than I was then. No matter what I was doing or where I was,—even when I wrote my stories,—he was always back there in my mind. It was almost as though he had hypnotized me.

Loving is, I suppose, a sort of bliss. One can get a certain amount of real joy and excitement out of loving; but it's pretty woeful when one must love alone, and that was my case. You see, though I knew I had made a kind of impression upon Mr. Hamilton, or, as he himself put it, he was "interested" in me, still he certainly was not in love with me, and I had little or no hope now of making him care for me.

I realized that he belonged to a different social sphere. He was a rich, powerful man, of one of the greatest families in America, and I—I was a working-girl, a stenographer of the stock-yards. Only in novels or a few sensational newspaper stories did millionaires fall in love with and marry poor, ignorant working-girls, and then the working-girl was sure to be a beauty. I was not a beauty. Some people said I was pretty, but I don't think I was even that. I had simply the fresh prettiness that goes hand in hand with youth, and youth gallops away from us like a race-horse, eager to reach the final goal. No, I was not pretty. I looked odd, and when I began to wear fine clothes, I must have appeared very well, for I had all sorts of compliments paid to me. I was told that I looked picturesque, interesting, fascinating, distinguished, lovely, and even more flattering things that were not true. It showed what clothes will do.

I was not, however, wearing fine clothes at this time. My clothes were of the simplest—sailor shirtwaist, navy-blue cloth skirt, and a blue sailor hat with a rolled-up brim. That was how I dressed until the night Lolly lent me some of her finery.

My only hope lay in pulling myself up by my talent. If I achieved fame, that, perhaps, I felt, would put me on a level with this man. But fame seemed as elusive and as far away as the stars above me.

Then, his insistence that I should be educated and his statement that I was illiterate made me pause in my thought to take reckoning of myself. If, indeed, my ignorance was so patent that it was revealed in my mere speech, how, then, could I hope to achieve anything? I felt very badly about that, and when I read over some of my beloved poems, instead of their giving me the former pride and delight, I felt, instead, a deep-seated grief and dissatisfaction, so that I tore them up, and then wept just as if I had destroyed some living thing.

Yes, I was very unhappy. I kept at my work, doing it efficiently; but the place now appeared hideous and abhorrent to me, and every day I asked myself:

"How much longer can I bear it?"

I remember leaving my desk one day, going to the girls' dressing-room, and just sitting down alone and crying, without knowing just what I was crying about—I who cried so little!

I suppose things would have gone from bad to worse for me but for two things that happened to distract me.

We moved, Lolly and I. I can't say that our rooms were as attractive and clean-looking as the ones we had at the Y. W. C. A., and of course they cost more. Still, they were not bad. We had two small rooms. Originally one large room, a partition had made it into two. By putting a couch in the outer room, we made a sitting-room, and were allowed to have our company there. Whichever one was up the last with company was to sleep on the couch.

Lolly made the rooms very attractive by putting pretty covers over the couch and table, and college flags that some men gave her on the wall, with a lot of pictures and photographs. The place looked very cozy, especially at night, but somehow I missed the cleanly order of my room of the Y. W. C. A.

I wrote a letter to Mr. Hamilton and gave him our new address. I could not resist telling him that I had been very unhappy; that I realized he was right, and that I could never go very far when my equipment in life was so pitifully small. However, I added hopefully that I intended to read a lot that winter, and that Lolly and I were going to join the library. I could take a book with me to work. There were many intervals during the day when I could read if I wished to; in the luncheon hour, for instance, and on the cars going to and from work. One could always snatch a moment. Didn't he think I would improve myself much by reading?

He did not answer me, but a few days later three large boxes of books came to the house for me.

Lolly and I were overjoyed. We had a great time getting shelves for the books and setting them up. We had Balzac, Dumas, Flaubert, Gautier, Maupassant, Carlyle's "French Revolution," and the standard works of the English authors. Also we had the Encyclopædia Britannica. I was so happy about those books that my depression dropped from me in a moment. I felt that if my little arms could have embraced the world, I should have encircled it. It was not merely the delight of possessing books for the first time in my life, but because *he* had chosen and sent them to me.

The second thing that came up to divert me from a tendency to melancholia at this time happened at the yards immediately after that.

One day O'Brien did not come to work till about five in the afternoon. As soon as he came in I noticed that there was something wrong with him. His hat was tipped over one eye, and his mouth had a crooked slant as he moved his cigar from side to side. Without noticing me, he took his seat, and slightly turned his back toward me. I chanced just then to catch Hermann's eye. He made a sign to me. I could not understand at first what he meant till he lifted an empty glass from his desk, held it to his lips, and then pretended to drain it. Then I knew: Fred had been drinking.

I suppose I ought not to have spoken to a man in his condition, but I think for the first time in my life there swept over me a great wave of maternal feeling toward this big uncouth boy who had been so good to me. I said:

"Fred!"

He turned around slightly, and looked at me through bleary eyes. His lips were dirty and stained with tobacco, and the odor that came from him made me feel ill. His voice, however, was steady, and he had it under control.

"Nora," he said, "I'm soused."

"You'd better go home," I whispered, for I was afraid he would get into trouble if one of the firm were to see him. "I'll finish your work for you. I know just how."

"I'm not going home till *you* do," said Fred. "I'm going with you. You'll take care of me, won't you, Nora?"

"O Fred," I said, "please do go home!"

"I tell you I'm going with you. I want to tell you all about myself. I never told you before. Got to tell you to-night."

"I'd rather hear it to-morrow night."

"Don't care what you'd rather. I'm going to tell you to-night," persisted Fred, with the irritable querulousness of a child.

"But I go out on the bus with the girls," I said. "And that leaves at 5:30."

"Tha' 's true," said Fred. "Tell you what I'll do. I'll start off now, and I'll meet you at the end of the yards when the bus comes out. See?"

I nodded. Fred settled his hat more crookedly on his head, and, with an unlighted cigar twisting loosely in his mouth, went staggering down the aisle.

Hermann came over to my desk, and when I told him what Fred had said, he advised me to slip off the bus quickly and make a run for the nearest car. He said if Fred "got a grip" on me, he'd never let go "till he had sobered up."

I asked Hermann how long that would take, and he said:

"Well, sometimes he goes on a long drunk, for weeks at a time. It depends on who is with him. If he can get any one to drink with him, he'll keep on and on, once he's started. Once a prize-fighter just got a hold of him and punched him into sensibility, and he didn't touch a drop for a year afterward. He can, if he tries, sober up in a few hours. He goes months without touching a thing, and then all of a sudden he reverts."

ONOTO WATANNA

Hermann then told me that Fred had once been jilted by a girl in Milwaukee, and that had started him to drinking.

As the bus took us through the yards, I thought how terrible and sad it was for a man who was in such a condition to be left to his own devices. It was just as if one left a helpless baby to mind himself, or threw a poor sick person out upon the street, expecting him to be cured without treatment. What was drink but a disease, anyhow? And I said to myself that I wished I were a prize-fighter. Fred had been good to me. I come of a race, on my mother's side, which does not easily forget kindnesses, and somehow I could think of nothing save how Fred had treated me that first day, and had given me a chance when no one else would.

So when I stepped from the bus, and Fred came lurching toward me, I simply had not the heart to break away from him. All the girls were watching us, and some of the men tried to draw Fred aside by the arm.

He became wildly excited, and said he could "lick any son of a gun in the Union Stock-Yards."

One of the men told me to "beat it" while they took care of Fred; but Fred did look so helpless and so inexpressibly childish as he cried out his defiance, and as I was mortally afraid that they might get fighting among themselves, and, anyhow, though drunk, he was not offensive, I said:

"I'll take him home. I'm not afraid of him."

Some of them laughed, and some protested; but I didn't care anything about any of them except Fred, and I helped him on an open car that went near our house.

I took him to our rooms, and there Lolly tried to sober him by making him black coffee, and Hermann, who came, too,—he had kept right up with Fred and me,—said he'd take care of Fred while Lolly and I got our dinner. We took our meals out.

When we got back,—it was about eight then,—there was Fred sitting on the door-step. Hermann was trying to drag him to his feet, but he wouldn't move, and he kept saying: "Nora's going to take care of me. S-she's m' stenographer, you know."

Hermann explained that our landlady had ordered them out, as Fred had begun to sing after we went. Hermann wanted Lolly and me to go into the house, and he said he'd take care of Fred, even if he had to "land him in a cell" to do it. He said that in such a nasty way that poor Fred began to cry that he hadn't a friend in the world, and that made me feel so badly that I told him that I was his friend, and that I'd take good care that Hermann didn't put him in a cell. Then I had an inspiration.

I suggested that we all take a long street-car ride and that the open air might clear his head, and if it didn't, we could get off at some park and walk around. Fred exclaimed that walking was the one thing that always "woke" him up.

Lolly said:

"Not for me!" and went into the house.

So Hermann and I, with Fred between us, made for the nearest car. I got in first, then Fred, and then as Hermann was getting on, Fred seized his hat and threw it out into the road. A wind caught it, and Hermann had to chase after it. While he was doing this, Fred pulled the bell-rope, and the car started.

We rode to the end of the line, Fred behaving very well. Here we got off, and we went into the park. I asked Fred how he was feeling, and he said "tip-top," and that he would be all right after walking about a bit.

We *walked*!

At first Fred was garrulous in a wandering sort of way, and he tried to tell me about the girl who had jilted him. He said he had never liked a girl since except me, and then he pulled himself up abruptly and said:

"But don't think I'm stuck on you, because I ain't. I got stuck on one girl in my life, and that was enough for me."

"Of course you're not," I said soothingly, "and I'm not stuck on you, either. We're just good pals, aren't we?"

"Best ever," said Fred, drowsily.

Then for a long time—my! it seemed hours and hours—we just tramped about the park. Curiously enough, I didn't feel a bit tired; but by and by I could tell by the way he walked that Fred was just about ready to drop from exhaustion. He had been up drinking all the previous night and all the day. So presently I found a bench under a big tree, and I tried to make him sit down; but nothing would do but that he must lie down at full length on the bench, with his head on my lap. He dropped off almost immediately into a sound sleep or stupor, breathing heavily and noisily.

I don't know how long we were there. I grew numb with the weight of his heavy head upon my knee. A policeman came along and asked me what we were doing. I told him truthfully that Fred had been drinking, and was now asleep, and I asked him, please not to wake him. He called Fred my "man," and said we could stay there. We did stay there. Nothing

ONOTO WATANNA

I believe could have awakened Fred. As for me, well, I made up my mind that I was "in for it." I thought of trying to go to sleep with my head against the back of the seat, but it was too low. So I had to sit up straight.

It was a still, warm night in September, with scarcely a breeze stirring. I could see the giant branches of the trees on all sides of us. They shot up like ghostly sentinels. Even the whispering leaves seemed scarcely to stir.

I saw the stars in a wide silver sky, staring and winking down upon us all through that long night. I looked up at them, and thought of my father, and I thought of that great ancestor of mine who had been an astronomer, and had given to the world some of its chief knowledge of the heavens above us. It would be strange, I whimsically thought, if somewhere up there among the stars, he was peering down at me now on this microscopic earth; for it was microscopic in the great scheme of the universe, my father had once said.

To sit up all night long in a quiet, beautiful park, under a star-spotted sky, with a drunken man asleep on your lap, after all, that is not the worst of fates. *I* know, because I have done it, and I tell you there have been less happy nights than that in my life.

As we rush along in the whirligig of life, we girls who must work so hard for our daily bread, we get so little time in which to *think*. For one cannot think save disjointedly, while working. Now I had a long chance for all my thoughts, and they came crowding upon me. I thought of my little brothers and sisters, and I wistfully longed that I might see them again while they were still little. I thought of my sister Marion, whom I had left in Boston. Had she fared as well as I? She had written me two or three times, and her letters were cheerful enough, but just as I told her in my letters nothing of my struggles, so she told me nothing of hers. Yet I read between the lines, and I *knew*—it made my heart ache, that knowledge—that Marion was having an even more grim combat with Fate than I; I was better equipped than she to earn a living. For one's mere physical beauty is, after all, a poor and dangerous asset. And Marion was earning her living by her beauty. She was a professional model, getting fifty cents an hour.

I thought of other sisters, one of whom had passed through a tragic experience, and another—the eldest, a girl with more real talent than I—who had been a pitiful invalid all her days. She is dead now, that dear big sister of mine, and a monument marks her grave in commemoration of work she did for my mother's country.

It seemed as if our heritage had been all struggle. None of us had yet attained what the world calls success. We were all straining and leaping up frantically at the stars of our ancestor; but they still stared aloofly at us, like the impenetrable Sphinx.

It seemed a great pity that I was not, after all, to be the savior of the family, and that my dreams of the fame and fortune that not alone should lift me up, but all my people, were built upon a substance as shifting as sand and as shadowy as mist. For, if what Mr. Hamilton had said was true, there was, alas! no hope in me. Perhaps I was doomed to be the wife of a man like the fat, blond clerk at the yards, or even of Fred. To think now of Mr. Hamilton as a possible husband was to do so with a cynical jeer at my own past ingenuousness. Since that visit of his, I had been awakened, as it were, to the clear knowledge that this man could never be to me what I had so fondly dreamed. Well!

I don't know when the stars began to fade. They just seemed to wink out one by one in the sky, and it grew gray and haggard, as it does just before the dawn. Even in the dark the birds began to call to one another, and when the first pale streak from the slowly rising sun crept stealthily out of the east, these winged little creatures dropped to earth in search of food, and a small, soft, inquiring-eyed squirrel jumped right in the path before me, and stood with uplifted tail and pricked-up head, as if to question my presence there.

Perhaps it was the whistling chatter of the birds that awoke Fred. He said I called to him, but he was mistaken.

He was lying on his back, his head upturned on my lap, and suddenly he opened his eyes and stared up at me. Then slowly he sat up, and he leaned forward on the bench and covered his face with his hands. I thought he was crying, but presently he said to me in a low, husky voice:

"How long have we been here?" and I said:

"All night, Fred."

"Nora Ascough, you're a dead-game sport!" he answered.

XIX

It may sound strange, but I really felt very little the worse for that long night's vigil. I went home, took a cold bath, had breakfast in a near-by restaurant (one of those, ten, twenty, twenty-five-cent places), and went to work just the same as ever. What is more, I had a specially hard day at the yards, for of course Fred was not there, and I had to do a good part of his work.

Frank Hermann wanted to know just how I got away from Fred, and I told him just what had happened. He said admiringly:

"Gee! you're one corker, Nora!"

"Fred gave me my job," I said, but I may as well add that I felt rather proud. Not every girl can be called a "dead-game sport" and a "corker."

Hermann said he had told the men about the place who had seen me go home with Fred that he had joined us, and later had himself taken Fred home. I felt grateful to Hermann for that. Personally I cared very little what these stock-yard people thought of me. Still it was good of Frank to undertake to protect me. He was a "good sort," I must say.

One of the girls in the bus said as we were going home that evening that I looked "fagged out," so I suppose I had begun to show the effects of the night; but I was not aware of any great fatigue until I got on the street car. All the seats were taken, and I had to stand in a crush all the way home, holding to a strap. I was glad enough to get home, I can tell you.

I thought Lolly was in when I saw the light in my room, and that surprised me, because her hours were very irregular. She seldom came home for dinner, and often worked at night.

I suppose it was the surprise and shock of finding him there, and, of course, my real state of weakness, but I nearly fainted when I saw Mr. Hamilton in my room. His back was turned to the door when I went in, as he was looking at the books he had sent me. Then he turned around and said:

"Well, how's the wonderful girl?"

I couldn't answer him, and I must have looked very badly, for he came over to me quickly, took both my hands, and drew me down to the couch beside him. Then he said roughly:

"You see, you can't stand work like this. You're all trembling and pale."

I said hysterically:

"I'm trembling because you are here, and I'm pale because I'm tired, and I'm tired because I've been up all night long."

"What!" he exclaimed.

I nodded.

"Oh, yes. Fred was drunk, and he wanted me with him; so I walked with him in L—— Park, and then he fell asleep on a bench with his head on my lap."

He jumped to his feet, and looking up, I saw his face. It was so black with astounded fury that I thought he was going to strike me; but I was not afraid of him. I felt only a sudden sense of wonder and pain. His voice, though low, had a curious sound of suppressed rage.

"Do you mean to tell me that you have been out all night with that man?"

I looked into his face, and then I nodded, without speaking. He gave me a hard look, and then he laughed shortly, brutally.

"So you are *that* sort, are you?" he said.

"Yes," I returned defiantly, "I am that sort. Fred was good to me. He took me on trust. If I had left him last night, he might have gone on drinking, or a policeman would have arrested him. You can't imagine the state he was in—just like a helpless child."

While I was speaking he kept staring at me. I was so nervous that I wrenched my hands together. And then I saw his face change, just as if it were broken, and in place of that hard, sneering expression there came that beautiful look that I had seen on his face that day on the train when he had asked me if I would like to go to school.

He came over and sat down again beside me on the couch. He took my hands in his, and held them as if he were warming them. Then I put my face against his arm and began to cry. He didn't say a word to me for the longest time. Then he asked me very gently to tell him all over again just what happened. So I did. He wanted to know if Fred had said anything offensive to me, or if he had been familiar or tried to kiss me. I said, "No; Fred is not that kind." If he had been, he asked me, what would I have done? I didn't know, I told him.

"You'd have permitted him to?" he demanded sharply, and I said I didn't think I would; but then, of course, one couldn't tell what a drunken man might do. He said that that was the whole point of the matter, and that I could see for myself that I had done a very foolish and dangerous thing.

By this time he was walking up and down. After a while, when he had gotten over his excitement and wrath about Fred, he shook up all

ONOTO WATANNA

the sofa pillows on the couch, and made me lie down. When I sat up, he lifted up my feet, and put them on the couch, too. So I had to lie down, and I was so tired and happy that he was there, and *cared*, that I would have done anything he ordered me to. Then he drew up a chair beside me, and began to talk again on the subject of my going to school. Goodness! I had thought that matter was settled. But, no; he had the persistency of a bull-dog in matters about which he cared.

He said it was nonsense for me to be expending my strength like this, when I ought to be studying and developing myself. He said association at my age meant everything; that I had the impressionable temperament of the artist, and was bound either to be benefited or hurt by the people with whom I associated.

I let him go on, because I loved to hear him talk, anyway, even though he was so cross about it. He kept frowning at me, as if he were administering a scolding, and driving the fist of his right hand into the palm of his left in a way he had when talking. When he was through, I said:

"If I go to school, will you come to see me, like this?"

"Of course I'll come to see you," he said. "Not—like this exactly; but I shall make it a point of coming to see you."

"Well, would I be alone with you ever?" I asked.

He said, yes, sometimes, but that I ought to know what boarding-schools were like. I smiled up at him at that, and he frowned down at me, and I said:

"I'd rather live like this, with all my besotted ignorance, and have you come to see me, and be with me all alone, just like this, than go to the finest boarding-school in the world."

He said, "Nonsense!" but he was touched, for he didn't say anything more about my going to school then. Instead, he began to urge me to leave my position at the yards. When I said I couldn't do that, he grew really angry with me. I think he would have gone then, for he picked up his hat; but I told him I hadn't had any dinner. Neither, of course, had he, as I had come in about six-thirty. So then I made him wait while I dressed, and he took me out to dinner.

There were a number of restaurants near where I lived, but he knew of a better place down-town; so we went there, by carriage, instead. On the way he asked me where I got the suit I had on, and I told him. Then he wanted to know what I paid for it, and I told him $12. It was a good little blue serge suit, and I had a smart hat to go with it. In fact, I was beginning to dress better, and more like American girls. I asked him if he liked my suit. He said roughly:

"No," and then he added, "it's too thin." After a moment he said:

"I'm going to buy you decent clothes first of all."

I had a queer feeling that so long as I took nothing from this man, I should retain his respect. It was a stubborn, persistent idea. I could not efface from my mind his bitter words of that day on the train, and I wanted above all things to prove to him that I cared for him only for himself and not for the things I knew he could give me and wanted to give me. I never knew a man so anxious to give a woman things as was Mr. Hamilton to do things for me from the very first. So now I told him that I couldn't let him get clothes for me. That made him angrier than ever, and he wouldn't speak to me all the rest of the way. While we were having dinner (he had ordered the meal without reference to me at all, but just as if he knew what I should like), he said in that rough way he often assumed to me when he was bent upon having his way about something:

"You want me to take you with me when I come to Chicago, don't you—to dinner, theaters, and other places?"

I nodded. I did want to go with him, and I was tremendously proud to think that he wanted to take me.

"Very well, then," he said; "you'll have to dress properly."

I couldn't find any answer to that, but I inwardly vowed that I would spend every cent I made above my board on clothes.

I think he was sorry for having spoken unkindly to me, because he ceased to urge me about the school, my position, my lodgings, which he did not like at all, and now my clothes. He made me tell him all over again for the third or fourth time about last night. He kept asking me about Fred, almost as if he were trying to trap me with questions, till finally I grew so hurt by some of his questions that I wouldn't answer him. Then again he changed the subject, and wanted to know what I had been writing. That was a subject on which he knew I would chatter fluently, and I told him how I had actually dared to submit my latest to a mighty publication in New York. He said he wished he were the editor. I said:

"Would you take my stories?"

"You better believe I would," he said.

"Why?"

"Well, why do you suppose?"

"Because you think my stories are good or because you like me—which?"

He laughed, and told me to finish my coffee.

I said:

"You must like me *some*, else you wouldn't have cared about Fred."

He tried to frown at me for that, but instead laughed outright, and said if it gave me any satisfaction to believe that, to go on believing it.

My happiness was dashed when he said he had to return to Richmond on the eleven o'clock train. I had been secretly hoping he would remain in Chicago a few days. When I faltered out this hope, he said rather shortly:

"I can only run down here occasionally for a day or a few hours at a time. My affairs keep me in Richmond."

Little things exhilarate me and make me happy, and little things depress me and make me sad. So while I was light-hearted a moment before, I felt blue at the thought of his going. I said to myself that this was how it would always be. He would always come, and he would always go, and I wondered if a day would ever come when he would ask me to go with him.

He saw that I was depressed, and began to talk teasingly:

"Do you know," he said—we were now at the steps of my boarding-house—"that you are a very fickle little person?"

"I? Why I'm foolishly faithful," I declared.

"I say you are fickle," he asserted with mock seriousness. "Now I know one chap that you used to think the world and all about, but whom you have completely forgotten. The poor little fellow came to me, and told me all about it himself."

I couldn't think whom in the world he could mean, and thought he was just joking, when he said:

"So you've forgotten all about your little dog, have you?"

"Verley!"

"Yes, Verley."

"Oh, you've seen him?"

I think it gave him all kinds of satisfaction to answer me as he did.

"I've got him. He's mine now—ours, shall we say?"

"Oh, did Dr. Manning give him to you?"

He laughed.

"Not much. He *sold* him to me."

"He had no right to do that. Verley was my dog."

"But you owed Dr. Manning for your fare from Boston."

"That's true. Did he tell you that?"

"No, but I knew it, and I didn't like the idea of your owing anything to any one except—me," and he gave me one of his warmest smiles when he said that. "I did not see the doctor myself, but a friend arranged the matter for me. By the way, he owes you a considerable little sum over the amount he paid for your fare from Boston, though we are not going to bother collecting it. We'll let it go."

"What do you mean?"

"It seems he considered the dog a very expensive article. I paid him three hundred dollars for Verley, whose high-bred ancestry I very much doubt."

"Three hundred dollars! Oh, what a shame! He wasn't worth anything like that," I cried.

He said after a moment, during which he looked at me very steadily:

"Yes, he was worth that to me: he was—*yours*."

I caught my breath, I was so happy when he said that.

"Now I know you do like me," I said, "else you wouldn't say things like that."

"Nonsense!" he said.

"Why do you bother about me at all, then?" I asked.

He had put the key in the lock now. He didn't look up when he answered that, but kept twisting the key.

"I told you why. I'm interested in you—that's all," he said.

"Is that—*really*—all?" I asked tremulously.

"Yes," he said in a rough whisper; "that is really all, little girl."

"Well, anyway," I said, "even if you don't love me, I love you. You don't mind my doing that, do you?"

I could *feel* his smile in the darkness of that little porch as he said:

"No, don't stop doing *that*, whatever happens. That would be a calamity hard to bear—now."

It's not much to have permission to love a person, who doesn't love you, but it was a happy girl who slept on the couch that night. Lolly came in after I did, but I made her sleep inside. She wanted to know why on earth I had all the pillows on the couch. I didn't answer. How could I tell her that I wanted them about me because *he* had put them there?

In the morning, on the table, I found half a cigar that he had smoked. I rolled it up in tissue-paper and put it in the drawer where I kept only my most cherished treasures.

XX

Now that the lights no longer went out at ten, I did considerable writing at night. I had to work, however, under difficulties, for Lolly had no end of men callers. She had discouraged men calling on her at the Y. W. C. A., but now that we had a place of our own, she liked them to come. As she gaily put it to me one day: "Beaux make great meal tickets, Nora."

And then, too, she liked men. She told me once I was the only girl chum she had ever had, though she had had scores of men chums, who were not necessarily her admirers as well.

Lolly was a born flirt. Hermann was her slave and her shadow now, and so were several newspaper men and editors who seemed devoted to her. There was only one man, however, for whom she cared a "button," so she told me, and that was Marshall Chambers; and yet, she quarreled with him constantly, and never trusted him.

Lolly's men friends were kind to me, too. They tried many devices to entrap me to go with them. It was all I could do to work at night, for even when I shut myself into the inner room, Lolly was always coming in with this or that message and joke, and to urge me to "come on out, like a good fellow, just for to-night." Though, to do Lolly justice, many a time, when she thought the story I was working on was worth while, she would try to protect me from being disturbed, and sometimes she'd say:

"Clear out, the whole bunch of you! Nora's in the throes of creation again."

However, I really don't know how I managed to write at all there. Hermann came nearly every night in those days, and even when Lolly was out, he used to sit in that outer room and wait, poor fellow, for her to return. He never reproached Lolly, though he certainly knew she did not return his love. Hermann just waited, with a sort of untiring German patience and determination to win in the end. He was no longer the gay and flippant "lady-killer." In a way I was glad to have Hermann there at nights, for I was afraid of Chambers. Whenever he found me alone, he would try to make love to me, and tell me he was mad about me and other foolish things.

I asked him once what he would do if I told Lolly. He replied, with an ugly smile, that he guessed Lolly would take his word before mine.

That marked him as unprincipled, and I hated him more than ever. Of course I never told him I disliked him. On the contrary, I was always very civil and joking with him. It's queer, but I have a good streak of the "Dr. Fell" feeling in me. Hermann and I once talked over Marshall Chambers, and his efforts to make love to me. Hermann said that that was one of the reasons he was going to be there when he could. He said that some day Lolly was going to find out, and he (Hermann) wanted to be there to take care of her when that day came. Such was his dog-like affection for Lolly, that, although he knew she loved this man, he was prepared to take her when she was done with the other.

Occasionally Fred, too, came to see me in the evening, but if I was writing, he would go away at once. My writing to Fred loomed as something very important. He believed in me. Hamilton had called me a wonderful girl, but Fred believed I was an inspired genius. He let me copy all my stories on the type-writer at the office, and would literally steal time for me in which to do it, making Red Top do work I should have done.

Fred was "in bad" at the yards. It seems that his last "drunk" had completely exasperated certain heads of the firm, and there was a general opinion, so Hermann told me, that Fred's head might "come off" any day now.

I was so worried about this that I tried to warn him. He stuck his tongue in one cheek and winked at me. Then he said:

"Nora, I have an A No. 1 pull with old man Smith, and there ain't nobody going to get my job here; but I'm working them for the New York job. I want to go east."

That made me feel just as badly, for, if Fred was transferred to the New York branch, what would become of me? I could not go, too, and I disliked the thought of working under another.

I felt so badly about it that I wrote to Mr. Hamilton, who had not been to see me for three weeks. I suppose if I had not been working so hard, I should have felt worse about that, because I had thought he would be sure to come and see me again soon. But he did not; nor did he even write to me, though I wrote him four letters. My first letter was a very foolish one. It was this:

I know you do not love me, but I do you.

NORA

I felt ashamed of that letter after I mailed it. So then I sent another to say I didn't mean it, and then I sent another immediately to say that I did.

Then, for a time, as I received no answers, I didn't write to him, but tried to forget him in my writing. It's a fact that I was fairly successful. Once I started upon a story, my mind centered upon nothing else; but as soon as I was through with it, I would begin to think about him again, and I suppose he really was in my mind all the time.

But to get back to Fred. I wrote Mr. Hamilton that Fred was likely to be transferred to the New York office, and in that event he would take me with him. Of course it would be a fine opportunity for me, as all the best publishing houses and magazines were in New York, and I would have a chance to submit my work directly to the editors. Then, too, if Fred was placed in charge of the New York offices, it would be much pleasanter than in the stock-yards, since there would be merely a handful of clerks. He never answered that letter, either. I wondered why he never wrote to me. His silence made me blue and then reckless.

Lolly, who by this time knew all about Mr. Hamilton, offered me her usual consolation and advice. The consolation was a cigarette, but I didn't care for it at all. Cigarettes choked me every time I tried to smoke them, and I couldn't for the life of me understand why she liked them. She must have smoked a dozen packages a day, for she smoked constantly. Her pretty fingers were nicotine-stained, and I've known her even in the night to get up and smoke. So I could not accept Lolly's consolatory cigarette. I did, however, follow her advice in a way. She said:

"Nora, the only way to forget one man is to interest yourself in another—or many others."

So toward the end of the month I began to go about with some of Lolly's friends.

They took me to dinners, theaters, and some social and Bohemian clubs and dances. At one of these clubs I met Margaret Kingston, a woman lawyer, who became my lifelong friend. I don't know how old she was, but to me then she seemed very "grown-up." I dare say she was no more than forty or forty-five, though her hair was gray. She was a big woman physically, mentally, and of heart. Good-humored, full of sentiment, and with a fine, clear brain, I could not but be attracted to her at once. She was talented, too. She wrote, she painted, she was a fine musician, and a good orator. She was a socialist, and when very much excited, declared she was also an anarchist. With all her talents, possibly because of a certain impractical and sort of vagabond streak in her, she was always poor, hard up, and scraping about to make both ends meet.

She came over to the table where I was sitting with Lolly and Hermann and a newspaper man, and she said she wanted to know the "little girl with the black eyes." That was I. We liked each other at once, just as Lolly and I had liked each other. I form attachments that way, quickly and instinctively, and I told her much about myself, my writing, etc., so that she became at once interested in me and invited me to her house. She said she "kept house" with another "old girl."

I went to see them that very next night. They had a pretty house on G—— Avenue. Mrs. Kingston took me through the place. I suppose I looked so longingly at those lovely rooms that she asked me if I wouldn't like to come and live with them. She said she needed a couple of "roomers" to help with the expenses, and offered me a dear little room—so dainty and cozy!—for only seven dollars a week, with board. There were to be no other boarders, so she said; but there was a suite of two rooms and a bath in front, and these she intended to rent without board. She laughingly said that as these rooms were so specially fine, she'd "soak the affluent person who took them" enough to carry our expenses. I wanted badly to move in at once, but I was afraid Lolly would be offended, so I said I'd see about it.

On that very first visit to Mrs. Kingston, who asked me, by the way, to call her "Margaret"—she said she felt younger when people called her that; and if it didn't sound so ugly, she would even like to be called "Mag"—I met Dick Lawrence, a *Tribune* reporter.

One never knows why one person falls in love with another. See how I loved Hamilton despite his frankly telling me he was only "interested" in me. Dick Lawrence fell in love with me, and just as Hermann was Lolly's shadow, so Dick became mine. He was as ambitious as I, and quite as impractical and visionary. He wrote astonishingly clever things, but never stuck at anything long enough to succeed finally. He was a born wanderer, just like my father, and although still in his early twenties, had been well over the world. At this time the woes of Cuba occupied the attention of the American press, and Lawrence was trying to get out there to investigate conditions. This was just prior to the war.

I never really thought he would go, and was much astonished when only two weeks after I met him he turned up one night for "two purposes," as he said. The first was to tell me that he loved me, and the second to bid me good-by. Some newspaper syndicate was sending him to Cuba. Dick asked me if I would marry him. I liked him very much. He carried me away with his eloquent stories of what he was going to do. Moreover I was sorry to think of his going out to hot and fever-wracked Cuba, among those supposedly fiendish Spaniards; also he reminded me of Verley Marchmont, so that I could not help accepting him. You see, I had given up all hope of hearing from Mr. Hamilton again. He had not answered my letters. I was terribly lonesome and hungry for some one to care for me. Dick was a big, wholesome, splendid-looking boy, and his tastes were similar to mine. Then he said he'd "move mountains," if only I'd become engaged to him. He appeared to me a romantic figure as I pictured him starting upon that perilous journey.

The long and short of it is, that I said, "All right." Whereupon Dick gave me a ring—not a costly one, for he was not rich—and then, yes, he kissed me several times. I won't deny that I liked those kisses. I would have given anything in the world to have Mr. Hamilton kiss me; but, as I said, I had reached a reckless stage, where I believed I should not see him again, and next to being kissed by the man you love, it's pleasant to be kissed by a man who loves you. However, that may be with his strong young arms about me and his fervent declaration that he loved me, I felt comforted and important.

Meantime Lolly came in soon after we were engaged, and she had a party of men with her. Dick made me promise to tell no one. He sailed the next morning for Cuba. I never saw him again.

When I told Lolly about my engagement she laughed, and told me to "forget it." She said Dick had been on her paper a while, and she knew him well. She said he never took girls seriously, and although he did seem "hard hit" by me, he'd soon get over it once he got among the pretty Cuban and Spanish *señoritas*. That was a dubious outlook for me, I must say. Just the same, I liked to wear his ring, and I felt a new dignity.

It's queer, but in thinking of Mr. Hamilton at this time I felt a vindictive sort of satisfaction that I was now engaged. It was good to know that even if he didn't love me enough to answer my letters, some one did.

One day Fred came in very late from luncheon. I thought at first from something strange in his attitude that he had been drinking again, but he suddenly swung around in his seat and said:

"Do you know Mott?"

"No. Who is he?"

"Manager of the—Department."

"I don't know him by name," I said. "Point him out to me."

Fred said ominously:

"That's him; but he's not looking quite his usual handsome self."

I saw a man several departments off who even from that distance looked as if his face and nose were swollen and cut.

"Then you never went out with him?" demanded Fred.

"Why, of course not," I declared. "I've never been out with any yards men except you and Hermann. You know that."

"I thought so. Now look a-here," and he showed me his fists. The skin was off the knuckles, and they had an otherwise battered look.

"That son of a blank," said Fred, "boasted that you had been out with him. I knew that he lied, for no decent girl would be seen with the likes of him; so I soaked him such a swig in the nose that he'll not blow it again for a month."

I tell this incident because it seems to be a characteristic example of what certain contemptible men say about girls whom they do not even know. I have heard of men who deliberately boasted of favors from girls who despised them and who assailed the character of girls who had snubbed them. This was my first experience, and my only one of this kind. That a man I had not known existed would talk lightly about me in a bar-room full of men seemed to me a shameful and cruel thing. That a man who did know me had defended me with his fists thrilled and moved me. At that moment I almost loved Fred.

This incident, however, thoroughly disgusted me with everything connected with the yards. I made up my mind that I would go with Fred to New York. We talked it over, and he said that even if the firm would not send me, he himself would engage me after he was settled there. So I began to plan to leave Chicago, though when I paused to think of Mr. Hamilton I grew miserable. Still, the thought of the change excited me. Lolly said I'd soon forget him—I knew I wouldn't—and that there was nothing like a change of scene to cure one of an infatuation of that kind. She always called my love for Hamilton "infatuation," and pretended never to regard it as anything serious. She said I was a hero-worshipper, and made idols of unworthy clay and endowed them with impossible attributes and virtues. She said girls like me never really loved a man at all. We loved an image that we ourselves created.

I knew better. In my love I was simply a woman and nothing else, and as a woman, not an idealist, I loved Hamilton. I never pretended he was perfect. Indeed, I saw his faults from the first, but despite his faults, not because of them, I loved him.

XXI

Fred was to leave for New York on the first of November, and that was only a week off. The firm had decided to retain me, after all, in the Chicago offices, but I was determined I would not remain there, and planned to go to New York as soon as possible, when Fred would immediately engage me. He said he'd "fire" any girl he had then for me.

I had been saving from week to week for my fare and a set of furs. My suit, though only two months old, had already begun to show wear, and it was thin, as Mr. Hamilton had said. The girls at the yards were already wearing furs, but furs were beyond my purse for months to come. Lolly had beautiful furs, black, silky lynx, that some one had given her the previous Christmas.

It was now five weeks since I had seen Mr. Hamilton, and two since Dick had gone. I had had a few letters from Dick. They were not exactly love-letters. Dick's letters were more, as it were—well, written for publication. I don't know why they seemed like that to me. I suppose he could not help writing for effect, for although he said tender things, and very brilliantly, too, somehow they did not ring true to me.

I did not think very seriously of our engagement, though I liked my ring, and showed it to all the girls at the yards.

My stories came back with unflattering regularity from the magazines to which I sent them. Lolly, however, gave two of my stories to her paper, and I was to be paid space rates (four dollars a column, I think it was) on publication. I was a long time waiting for publication.

Dissatisfied, unhappy, and restless, as I now really was, I did not even feel like writing at night. I now no longer ran up-stairs to my room, with an eager, wishful heart, hoping that *he* might be there. Alas! I felt sure he had abandoned me forever. He had even ceased, I told myself, to be interested in me.

Then one night he came. I had had a hard day at the yards. Not hard in the sense of work; but Fred was to leave the following day, and a Mr. Hopkins was to take his place. We had spent the day going over all the matters of our department, and it's impossible for me to say how utterly wretched I felt at the thought of working under another "boss" than Fred.

So I came home doleful enough, went out and ate my solitary dinner in a nearby restaurant, and then returned to the house.

He called, "Hello, little girl!" while I was opening the door.

I stood speechlessly staring at him for a moment, so glad was I to see him. It seemed an incredible and a joyous thing to me that he was really there, and that he appeared exactly the same—tall, with his odd, tired face and musing eyes.

"Well, aren't you glad to see me?" he asked, smiling, and holding out his hand.

I seized it and clung to it with both of mine, and I wouldn't let it go. That made him laugh again, and then he said:

"Well, what has my wonderful girl been doing?"

That was nearly always his first question to me.

"I wrote to you four times," I said, "and you never answered me once."

"I'm not much of a hand at letter-writing," he said.

"I thought that you'd forgotten me," I told him, "and that you were never going to come and see me again."

He put his hand under my chin, raised my face, and looked at it searchingly.

"Would it have mattered so much, then?" he asked gently.

"You know very well I'm in love with you," I told him desperately, and he said, as always:

"Nonsense!" though I know he liked to hear me say that.

Then he wanted to inspect me, and he held me off at arm's-length, and turned me around, too. I think it was my suit he was looking at, though he had seen it before. Then he made me sit down, and said we were going to have a "long talk." Of course I had to tell him everything that had happened to me since I had seen him. I omitted all mention of Dick!

I told him about Fred's wanting me to join him in New York, and he remarked:

"Fred can jump up. You're not going."

I did not argue that with him. I no longer wanted to go. I was quite happy and contented now that he was here. I didn't care whether he returned my love or not. I was satisfied as long as he was with me. That was much.

He always made me tell him every little detail of my life, and when I said I found it difficult to write, because of so many men coming to see Lolly,—I didn't mention that they were coming to see me, too!—he said:

"You're going to move out of this place right away. We'll look about for rooms to-morrow."

So then I knew he was not going back that night, and I was so glad that I knelt down beside him and cuddled up against his knee. I wished that he would put his arm about me, but all he did was to push back the loose hair that slipped over my cheek, and after that he kept his hand on my head.

He was much pleased with my description of the rooms at Mrs. Kingston's. He said we'd go there the next day and have a look at them. He said I was to stay home from work the next day, but I protested that I couldn't do that—Fred's last day! Unless I did just what he told me, it exasperated him always, and he now said:

"Then go away from me. I don't want anything to do with a girl who won't do even a trifling thing to please me."

I said that it wasn't trifling, and that I might lose my position; for the new man was to take charge to-morrow, and I ought to be there.

"Damn the new man!" he said.

He was a singularly unreasonable man, and he could sulk and scowl for all the world like a great boy. I told him so, and he unwillingly laughed, and said I was beyond him. To win him back to good humor, I got out some of my new stories, and, sitting on the floor at his feet, read them to him. I read two stories. When I was through, he got up and walked up and down, pulling at his lower lip in that way he had.

"Well," I challenged, "can I write?"

He said:

"I'm afraid you can." Then he took my manuscripts from me, and put them in his pocket.

It was late now, for it had taken me some time to read my stories, but he did not show any signs of going. He was sitting in our one big chair, smoking, with his legs stretched out in front of him, and although his eyes were half closed, he was watching me constantly. I began to yawn, because I was becoming sleepy. He said he supposed I wanted him to get out. I said no, I didn't; but my landlady probably did. She didn't mind our having men callers as long as they went before midnight. It was nearly that now. He said:

"Damn the landlady!" just as he had said, "Damn the new man!" Then he added, "You're not going to be run by every one, you know."

I said mischievously:

"Just by you?"

"Just by me," he replied.

"But when you stay away so long—"

It irritated him for me to refer to that. He said that there were certain matters I wouldn't understand that had kept him in Richmond, and that he had come as soon as he could. He added that he was involved in some lawsuit, and that he was being watched, and had to be "careful." I couldn't see why he should be watched because of a lawsuit, and I asked:

"Would you be arrested?"

He threw back his head and laughed, and said I was a "queer little thing," and then, after a while, he said very seriously:

"It's just as well, anyway. We mustn't get the habit of *needing* each other too much."

I asked:

"Do you think it possible *you* could ever need *me*?" To which he replied very soberly:

"I need you more than you would believe."

Mr. Hamilton never made a remark like that, which revealed any sentiment for me, without seeming to regret it a moment later. Now he got up abruptly and asked me which room I slept in. I said generally in the inner one, because Lolly came in late from her night work and engagements.

"I want to see your room," he said, "and I want to see what clothes you need."

He knew much about women's clothes. I felt ashamed to have him poking about among my poor things like that, and I grew very red; but he took no notice of me, and jotted down some things in his notebook. He said I would need this, that, and other things.

I said weakly:

"You needn't think I'm going to let you get me clothes. Honestly, I won't wear them if you do."

He tilted up my chin, and spoke down into my face:

"Now, Nora, listen to me. Either you are going to live and dress as I want you to, or I am positively not coming to see you again. Do you understand?"

"Well, I can get my own clothes," I said stubbornly.

"Not the kind I want you to have, not the kind *I* am going to get you."

He still had his hand under my chin, and I looked straight into his eyes.

"If you tell me just once," I said, "that you care for me, I'll—I'll— take the clothes then."

"I'll say anything you want me to," he said, "if you'll do what I tell you."

I took him up at that.

"All right, then. Say, 'I love you,' and you can buy pearls for me, if you want to."

He gave me a deep look that made me thrill, and I drew back from his hand. He said in a low voice:

"You can have the pearls, anyway."

"But I'd rather have the words," I stammered, now ashamed of myself, and confused under his look.

"Consider them said, then," he said, and he laughed. I couldn't bear him to laugh at me, and I said:

"You don't mean it. I made you say it, and therefore it has no meaning. I wish it were true."

"Perhaps it is," he said.

"Is it?" I demanded eagerly.

"Who knows?" said he.

Lolly came in then. She did not seem at all pleased to see Mr. Hamilton there, and he left soon after. When he was gone, she told me I was a very silly girl to have taken him into my room. I told her I hadn't; that he had just walked in. Lolly asked me, virtuously, whether I had ever seen *her* let a man go in there, and I confessed I had not. She wanted to know whether I had told Mr. Hamilton about Dick. Indeed, I had not! The thought of telling him frightened me, and I besought Lolly not to betray me. Also I took off Dick's ring. I intended to send it back to him. It was impossible for me to be engaged to him now.

Lolly said if she were I, she wouldn't let Mr. Hamilton buy clothes for her. She said once he started to do that, he would expect to pay for everything for me, and then, said Lolly, the first thing I knew, people would be saying that he was "keeping" me. She said that I could take dinners, flowers, even jewels from a man,—though in "high society" girls couldn't even do that; but working-girls were more free,—and I could go to the theater and to other places with him; but it was a fatal step when a man began to pay for a girl's room and clothes. Lolly added that once she had let a man do that for her, and—She blew out a long whiff of smoke from her lips, saying, "Never more!" with her hand held solemnly up.

So then I decided I couldn't let him do it, and I felt very sorry that I had even weakened a little bit in my original resolve not to let him spend money on me. I went to sleep troubled about the matter.

ONOTO WATANNA

XXII

As soon as I got up next day I called him on the telephone. It was so early that I probably woke him up, but I had to tell him what was on my mind.

"It's Nora," I said.

He replied:

"Last time you telephoned to me you were in trouble; do you remember? Are you in trouble now, little girl?"

I said I wasn't, but I just wanted to say I *couldn't* and wouldn't let him buy clothes for me.

I knew just as well as if I could see him how he was looking when I said that. He was used to having his own way, and that I dared to set my will against his always made him angry. After a moment he said:

"Will you do something else to please me, then?"

"What?"

"Don't go to work to-day."

"I've *got* to; truly I have."

"You only think that. Call up O'Brien and ask to be excused. If you don't, I will. Now I'll be up at your place about ten. I've something special to give you, anyway."

"What?"

"I can't tell you on the 'phone."

"We-ell," I weakened; "all right, then."

I was rewarded beautifully for that.

"That's *my* little girl!" he said.

Then he rang off. I never would have.

So I stayed home from work, the first time since I had been at the yards—and Fred's last day! Mr. Hamilton came over about ten. Lolly was still sleeping, so I had to see him down-stairs in the parlor. As soon as I saw him, I held out my hands and said:

"Where's the special thing?"

He laughed. I could make him laugh easily now, though I don't believe any one else could. He pinched my chin and said:

"Get your hat on. We're going shopping."

"Now, Mr. Hamilton, I am not going to let you buy things for me."

"Did I say I was going to do that?" he demanded.

"Well, then, how can we shop?"

"You have some money of your own, haven't you?"

"Yes, but I was saving it for furs and to go to New York."

"Well, you can get the furs later, and you're not going to New York. The main thing is you need a decent suit and a—er—heavy coat to wear to work, since you *will* work; and you need gloves and—let me see your shoes—" (I showed them) "and shoes, a hat and—"

"I haven't the money for all those things."

"Yes, you have. I know a place where you can get all kinds of bargains. Ever hear of bargain-shops?"

No, I had never heard of bargain-shops, though I had of bargain-sales, I told him. Well, it was the same thing, he said, except that this particular shop made a specialty of selling nothing but bargains.

That, of course, tempted me, and I went up to my room and put on my coat and hat. I had thirty dollars, and I borrowed ten from Lolly. So I was not so badly off. He was right; I really needed new things, and I might as well let him choose them for me.

That was a happy morning for me! All girls love to "shop," and there was a joy in trying on lovely things, even if I couldn't afford them. It was a small shop to which he took me, but the things there were really beautiful and astonishingly cheap. He made them try many things on me, not only suits, but negligées and evening gowns.

Then he chose a soft dark-blue velvet suit, trimmed with the loveliest gray fur at the neck and sleeves. I thought it must be very expensive, but the saleswoman said it was only fifteen dollars. I had never *heard* of such a bargain, especially as a hat, trimmed with the fur, and a muff also went with the suit. I made up my mind I'd bring Lolly here. I told the lady who owned the store that I would bring a friend. That made her laugh, but she stopped, because Mr. Hamilton frowned and looked very angry. He liked to laugh at me himself, but he didn't want others to do so, and I liked him for that.

Still, I felt uncomfortable. The woman's laugh had been peculiar, and the saleswomen were watching me. I bought, too, a heavy navy-blue coat, with a little cape, and belted, just the thing for every day, and gloves and two pairs of shoes. She said that, as I'd bought so much, she'd give me silk stockings to go with the shoes.

Of course I know now that I was a blind fool; but then I was only seventeen, and nine months before I had never been outside my home city, Quebec. For that matter, I hardly knew Quebec, so limited and confined is the life of the poor. I thought my forty dollars paid for all; I *did* think that!

Mr. Hamilton was in a fine humor now, and he made me wear the velvet suit and the hat to go to luncheon with him, and where do you suppose he took me? Right to his own hotel. There he introduced me to a man named Townsend who was waiting for him. I didn't at all like the way Mr. Townsend looked at me; but Mr. Hamilton did not seem to mind it, though he was quick to notice such things. When I had dined with him before, if any man stared at me, he used to lean over and say, without the slightest suggestion of a smile:

"Well, what shall I do to him? Turn the seltzer on him or push his face in?"

Mr. Townsend, however, was not trying to flirt with me, as, for instance, Mr. Chambers always was. He studied me curiously and, I thought, suspiciously. He talked in an undertone to Mr. Hamilton, and I am sure they were talking about me. I did hope that Mr. Townsend had not noticed any mistakes I made about the knives and forks.

I was glad when luncheon was over. We entered a cab again, and Mr. Hamilton directed the driver to take us to Mrs. Kingston's. I asked him who Mr. Townsend was. He said he was his lawyer, and began to talk about something else. He wanted to know if I wasn't curious to know what that special thing was he had to give me. I had forgotten about it. Now, of course, I wanted to know.

"Well," he said, "'open your mouth and shut your eyes, and in your mouth you'll find a prize.'"

I thought he was going to give me a candy, so I shut my eyes and opened my mouth, just like a foolish child; and then he kissed me. It wasn't like a kiss at all, because my mouth was open; but he seemed to think it very funny, and when I opened my eyes, he was sitting back in the carriage, with his arms folded, laughing hard. I think he thought that a good joke on me, because I dare say he knew I wanted him to kiss me. I didn't think it a good joke at all, and I wouldn't speak to or look at him, and my face grew hot and red, and at last he said teasingly:

"I'll have to keep you angry all the time, Nora. You look your prettiest then."

I said with dignity:

"You know very well I'm not even a little bit pretty, and I wish you wouldn't make fun of me, Mr. Hamilton."

He was still laughing, and he said:

"You know very well you are pretty, you little fraud, and my name is Roger."

I never called him Mr. Hamilton after that.

XXIII

When I introduced Mr. Hamilton to Mrs. Kingston, she put on her glasses and examined him curiously, and he said, with a rather formal smile, not at all as he smiled at me:

"I've heard quite a lot about you from Miss Ascough, and am very glad to meet you."

"I've known all about you for some time," she said, chuckling. And then she added, "I don't know what I expected to see, but you don't quite measure up to Nora's extravagant ideal."

"No, I suppose not," he said, his eyes twinkling. "I doubt if any man could do that."

We were all laughing, and I said:

"Oh, well, I know he's not much to look at; but I'm crazy about him, anyhow, and he wants to see the rooms."

He didn't think the little room nearly good enough for me, but he said that big suite of rooms in front was just the thing. That made me laugh. Did he suppose any stenographer could afford a luxurious suite of rooms like that? There was a long room that ran across the front of the house, with big bay-windows and a great fireplace, and opening out from this room was a large bedroom, with a bath-room adjoining it. As one may see, they weren't exactly the rooms a girl getting fifteen dollars a week could afford.

I said:

"Tell him just how much you intend to 'soak' your prospective roomer for these palatial chambers."

She started to say, "Twenty-five dollars a week," which was what she had told me she expected to charge, when I saw him make a sign to her, and she hesitated. Then I knew he intended to get her to name a cheap price just for me, and pay the difference himself. But now I was too quick for him. He had actually deceived me about those clothes. I had not the remotest idea till months afterward that he had paid for them and for many other things I subsequently bought, or thought I bought; but Mrs. Kingston had already told me the price of that room. So I said:

"It's no use. I know the price."

"Yes, but for a friend," he replied, "I'm sure Mrs. Kingston would make—er—a considerable reduction."

She said nothing. I don't know how she felt. Of course she knew that I was in love with him, but, as she told me afterward, she couldn't quite make out just what our relations were.

"That's all very well," I said, "but Mrs. Kingston has to get her rent."

Then he said:

"Well, but—er—I'm sure her practice is going to soar from now on. A great lawyer like Mrs. Kingston need not rent rooms at all."

Still she said nothing; but I saw her watching us both. He went on to urge me to have these rooms, but of course the idea was absurd. It was really provoking for him to keep pressing me to have things I simply could not afford and did not greatly want. I said all this. Besides, I added, it would be foolish for me to make any change at this time. Things were uncertain with me at the yards, now that Fred was leaving, and I should have to speak to Lolly, anyhow.

He argued that if I expected to write, I should have to move. No one could write in such disturbing circumstances. Of course that was true enough, and I said I'd talk it over that night with Lolly.

He took out some money then, and wanted to pay Mrs. Kingston so much down on the rooms, when I exclaimed that even if I did leave Lolly, I didn't mean to take these rooms, but the little one, if Mrs. Kingston was still willing to let me have it. She said she certainly was; that she badly wanted me to come. Both she and Mrs. Owens (the woman with her) needed a young person about the place to make them forget what old fogies they were, and that it would be like a real home to have me there, and we'd all be very happy.

It ended like this: *he* took that suite of rooms. He said they'd be there for me to have at any time I wanted them. I told him it was just a waste of money, for I simply would not let him pay for my room any more than I would let him pay for my clothes, and that was all there was to it.

He smiled curiously at that, and asked Mrs. Kingston what she thought of my clothes. She said:

"I haven't been able to take my eyes off them. Nora is *wonderful*! Does it seem possible that clothes can make such a difference?"

She wanted to know where I got them. I told her, and how cheap they were. She was amazed at the price, and Mr. Hamilton went over to the window and looked out. How clearly this all comes back to me now!

All the way back to my rooms he argued with me about the matter. He said if I had a pleasant place like that to live in, I'd soon be writing masterpieces (ah, he knew which way my desires ran!), and soon I'd not have to work in offices at all. To take rooms like those, he said, was really an investment. Business men all did things that way. It was part of the game. He wanted me to try it, for a while, and at last I said in desperation:

"What's the use of talking about it? I tell you, I haven't got the money."

Then he said (I never knew a man who could so persist about a thing on which he had set his heart):

"Now, look here, Nora, I've got more money than is decent for any one person to have, and I *want* to spend it on *you*. I want to give you things—comforts and luxuries and all the pretty things a girl like you ought to have. If you could see yourself now, you'd realize what a difference even clothes make. And so with other things. I want to take hold of you and make you over. I never wanted to do anything so much in my life before. Now you're going to be a good girl, aren't you, and not deny me the pleasure—the real *joy* it gives me to do things for you, dear little girl?"

By this time I was nearly crying, but I set my teeth together, and determined not to be won over to something I knew was not right.

"You told me once," I said, "that all any one had ever wanted of you was your money—your 'dirty money,' you called it; and now, just because I won't take it from you, you get angry with me."

"Well, but, confound it! I didn't mean you then."

"Oh, yes, you did, too; because you said I'd be sending for more money in a week, and you said that I was made to have it, and men would give—"

He put a stop to my too vivid recollections.

"But, *child*, I had no *idea* then of the kind of girl you were,"—he lowered his voice, and added tenderly, he was trying so hard to have his way!—"of the exceptional, wonderful little girl you are."

"But I wouldn't be exceptional or wonderful," I protested, "if I took your money. I'd be common. No; I'm not going to let people say you *keep* me!"

"Where did you hear that word?" he demanded roughly.

"From Lolly—and the girls at the Y. W. C. A. Oh, don't you suppose I know what that means?" I was looking straight at him now, and I saw his face turn red, but whether with anger or embarrassment, I do not know. He said in a sort of suppressed way:

"Don't you know that men who keep women are their lovers?"

I nodded.

He sat up stiffly now, and he gave me a cold, almost sneering, look that made me shiver. Then he said:

"Have I ever given you the slightest reason to suppose I wanted to be *your* lover?"

I shriveled up not only at his words, but at his look, and I turned my face away, and looked out of the window of the cab without seeing anything. It was true he had never pretended to care for me. I was the one who had done all the caring, and now it almost seemed as if he were throwing this up to me as something of which to be ashamed. But though my face was burning, I felt no shame, only a sort of misery.

"Well?" he prompted me, for I had not answered that last brutal query. Without looking at him, I said, in a shaking little voice, for I was heartbroken to think that he could use such a tone to me or look at me in that way:

"No, you haven't. In fact, if you had, perhaps I might have done what you wanted."

He came closer to me in the carriage when I said that, but I shrank away from him. I was nearer to disliking him then than at any time in my acquaintance with him.

"You mean," he said, "that if I *were* your lover, you *would* be willing to—live with me—like that? Is that what you mean, Nora?"

"Oh, I don't know what I mean," I said. "I don't pretend to be respectable and good in the way the women of your class are. I suppose I have no morals. I'm only a girl in love with a man; and if—if—he cared for me as I did for him, I'd be willing to do anything in the world he wished me to. I'd be willing to die for him. But if he didn't—if he didn't care for me, don't you see, I couldn't take *anything* from him. I should feel degraded."

It was a tangled, passionate sort of reasoning. For a long time after that we rode along in silence, I looking out of the window, and he looking constantly at me. I could *feel* his eyes on me, and I did not dare to turn around. Then presently he said:

"I'm all kinds of a rotter, Nora, but I'm straight about you. You're my wonderful girl, the oasis in my life. I wouldn't harm a hair of your precious little head. If I were to tell you I loved you, I would precipitate a tragedy upon you that you do not deserve. So I am not going to say any such thing to you." He cleared his throat, and as I said nothing, he went on strongly, it seemed to me:

"Your friend, Lolly, is right about men, and I'm not different from other men as far as women are concerned; but in your case I am. My desire to do things for you is based on no selfish design. I assure you of that. I simply have an overwhelming desire to take care of you, Nora, to help you."

I said with as much composure as I could command:

"Thank you, I don't need help. I'm not so badly off as you think. I make pretty good money, and, anyway, I'm independent, and that's a big thing."

"But you have to work like a slave. I can't bear to think of that, and as for being independent, you won't be any the less so if you let me do things for you. You may go on with your life in your own way. I'll never interfere or try to dictate to you about anything."

Almost hysterically I cried out:

"Oh, please stop talking about this! Every time you come here you scold me about something."

"Why, Nora," he said aggrievedly, "I have never asked you to do anything but this. That's the only thing I ever scolded you about."

"Look how you acted that first night, when you saw me with Lolly and Mr. Chambers, and then the night I was up with Fred. You wanted to *beat* me! I saw it in your face. You could no more help dictating to and scolding me than you can help coming to see me now."

The last sentence slipped out before I knew it, and he sat up sharply at that, and then laughed, uncomfortably.

"I am a dog in the manger as far as you are concerned," he said; "but I'll turn over a new leaf if you'll let me do these things for you."

I smiled ruefully, for I was beginning to know him so well now, and I sighed. He asked me why I sighed, and then I asked him in turn just why he wanted to do these things for me. He paused a moment, and then said slowly, and not without considerable emotion:

"I've told you why before, Nora. I'm interested in you. You're my find, my discovery. I take a special pride in everything connected with you. You're the one thing in life I take a real interest in, and I want to watch you, and see you develop. I haven't the slightest doubt of your eventual success."

"Hum! You look upon me as a sort of curiosity, don't you?"

"Nonsense! Don't talk so foolishly!"

But I knew that that was just how he did regard me, and it made me sick at heart. My beautiful day had clouded over. I supposed that nothing in the world would ever induce this man to admit any feeling for me but interest. Well, I wanted to love and to be loved, and it was a cold sort of substitute he was offering me—pretty clothes and fine rooms. I could earn all those things myself in time.

"Now, then," he said, "you *are* going to be my darling, reasonable little girl, aren't you? After all, it isn't so much I am asking of you. All I want you to do is to leave your position and go to live with this Mrs. Kingston. She struck me as being all right, and the rooms are exceedingly attractive, though we'll furnish them over ourselves. And then you are going to let me get you the proper kind of clothes to wear. I'll choose them myself for you, Nora. Then, since you won't go to school,—and, you see, I'm willing to let that go,—why, we can arrange for you to take special lessons in languages and things like that, and there are certain English courses you can take up at Northwestern. And I want you to study music, too, piano and vocal—the violin, too, if you like. I'm specially fond of music, and I think it would be a good thing for you to take it up. Then in the spring you shall go abroad. I have to go myself about that time, and I want to see your face when you see Europe, honey." That was the only Southern endearing term he ever applied to me, and I had never heard it used before. "It will be a revelation to you. And now the whole thing is settled, isn't it?"

I hated, after all this, to have to refuse again, so I didn't answer him, and he said, taking my hand, and leaning, oh, so coaxingly toward me:

"It's all settled, isn't it, dear?"

I turned around, and shouted at him almost hysterically:

"No, it *isn't*. And I wish you'd shut up about those things. You only make me miserable."

If I had stung him, he could not have drawn back from me more sharply.

"Oh, *very* well," he said, and threw himself back in his seat, his face looking like a thunder-cloud.

He didn't speak another word to me, and when the carriage stopped at my door, he got out, assisted me from the carriage, and then immediately got in again himself. I stood at the curb, my hand on the door of the carriage, and I said:

"Please don't go like this."

"I'm sorry, but I am taking the 6:09 train."

"Take a later train."

"No, thank you."

"Please!"

"Sorry. Good-by."

"Please don't be angry with me!"

He didn't answer. It was terrible to have him go like that, and I asked him when he was coming back.

"I can't say," was his curt response. Then his angry glance fixed me, and he said slowly:

"You can let me know when you take those rooms I chose for you. I'll come then—at once."

And that is the cruel way he left me. I was heartbroken in a way, but I was angry, too. I went up to my room, and sat on the couch, and as I slowly pulled off my new gloves, I was not thinking kindly of Mr. R. A. Hamilton. No man had a right to impose his will in this way on a girl and to demand of her something that she could not do without losing her self-respect. I asked myself whether, because I loved this man, I was willing to make of myself a pusillanimous little door-mat, or if I had enough pride to stand by my own convictions?

I had humbled myself enough to him; indeed, I had virtually offered myself to him. But he did not want me. He had made that clear enough. If, in the circumstances, I took from him the gifts he offered me, I would roll up a debt I could never wipe out. Now, although poor and working, I was a free woman. What I had, I honestly earned. I was no doll or parasite who needed to be carried by others. No! To retain my belief in my own powers, I must prove that they actually existed. Only women without resources in themselves, without gifts or brains, were "kept" by men, either as mistresses or wives or from charity, as Hamilton wished to "keep" me. I had the youthful conviction that *I* was one of the exceptional souls of the world, and could carry myself. Was I, then, to be bought by the usual foolish things that attract the ordinary woman? No! Not even my love could alter my character.

Now, there really was a fine streak in me, for I did want pretty things (what young girl does not?), I hated my work, and I loved this man, and wanted above all things on earth to please him.

Lolly said, to jerk one's mind from too much brooding over one man, one should think of another, I discovered another method of distraction. Pretty clothes are a balm even to a broken heart, and although I was clever, I was also eternally feminine. My things had arrived from the shop, and they were so lovely,—so much lovelier than I had thought,— that I was enchanted. Lolly came in while I was lifting the things from the boxes. I hadn't taken off my suit, and she turned me around to look at me.

"Isn't it stunning, Lolly?" I asked. "And, just think, it was only fifteen dollars, suit, hat, muff, and all."

Lolly's unbelieving glance swept me, then she threw her cigarette down, and said spitefully:

"For the love of Mike, Nora, cut it out! You're a poor little liar!"

"Liar! What do you mean, Lolly Hope?"

I was furious at the insult, capping all I had gone through.

"That suit you have on never cost one penny less than $150. The fur alone is easily worth half of that. It's silver fox, an inch of which is worth several dollars, and that muff—" She laughed disgustedly. "What do you take me for, anyhow, to try to spring that fifteen-dollar gag on me?"

"It was marked down, I tell you, at a bargain sale."

"Oh, come off, Nora! Don't try that on me. I know where you got those clothes. That man Hamilton gave them to you. You didn't follow my advice, I see." She shrugged her shoulders. "Of course it's your own affair, and I'm the last to blame you or any other girl for a thing like that, but, for heaven's sake, don't think it necessary to make up fairy-tales to me!"

"Lolly, I swear to you that I paid for these myself."

"Tell it to the marines!" said Lolly.

"Then see for yourself. Here are the price-tags, and here's the bill," I cried excitedly, and I thrust them upon her. Everything came to exactly forty dollars. Lolly looked the bill over carefully; then she put her cigarette in her mouth, and looked at me. All of a sudden she began to laugh. She threw her head back upon the sofa pillows and just laughed and laughed, while I became angrier and angrier with her. I waited till she was through, and then I said, very much injured:

"Now you can apologize to me, Lolly Hope."

"You blessed infant," she cried, "I'm in the dust at your feet. One thing's sure, and I guess friend Hamilton is wise to that: there's no one like *you* in this dull old world of ours!"

XXIV

My new "boss" at the yards was a sharp-nosed, sharp-eyed old-young man who seemed to think that his chief mission in life was to crack a sort of mental whip, like an overseer, over the heads of those under him, and keep us all hustling and rushing like frightened geese.

I had been accustomed to answer the correspondence of the soap department myself, Fred merely noting a few words in pencil on each letter, giving the gist of what he wanted said; but Mr. Hopkins dictated everything, and as soon as I was through one batch of correspondence, he would find something else for me to do. It seemed to give him a pain for my typewriter to be idle a moment. I think I was on his mind all the time except when he was thinking up work for Red Top.

My position, therefore, had become a very hard one. I worked incessantly from nine till six. Fred had let me off at five-thirty and often at five; but Mr. Hopkins kept me till six. I think he'd have made it seven, but the bell rang at six, and the office was supposed to close after that.

Many a time I've seen him glance regretfully at the clock or make an impatient movement with his shoulders at the clanging of the bell, at which moment I always banged my type-writer desk, and swiftly departed.

How I missed Fred! He had made life at the yards tolerable and even amusing for me with his jokes and confidences. And, then, there's a pleasure in working for some one you know approves of you and likes you. Fred *did* like me. In a way, I don't think any one ever liked me better than poor Fred did.

It makes me sad to think that the best girl friend I ever had, Lolly, and the best man friend, Fred, are now both gone out of this world, where I may have still such a long road to travel.

I hated my position now. I was nothing but an overworked machine. Moreover, the routine of the work was deadening. When I answered the letters myself, it gave a slight diversion; but now I simply took dictation and transcribed it, and when I was through with that, I copied pages of itemized stuff. My mind became just like a ticker that tapped off this or that curt and dry formula of business letter in which soap, soap, soap stood out big and slimy.

I now neither wrote at night nor went out. I was too tired from the incessant labor at the type-writer, and when I got to sleep,—after two or three hours, in which I lay awake thinking of Mr. Hamilton and wondering whether I would ever see him again; I always wondered about that when he was away,—I declare, I would hear the *tap-tapping* of that typewriter all night long! Other type-writists have had the same experience. One ought to escape from one's treadmill at least in sleep.

But this is a world of miracles; doubt it who can.

There came a glorious day late in the month of November—to be exact, it was November 24. No, Mr. Hamilton did not come again. He was still waiting for my capitulation anent the rooms at Mrs. Kingston's.

This is what happened: I was type-writing, when Red Top came in with the mail. He threw down on my desk some personal letters that had come for me. Although Mr. Hopkins was at his desk, and I knew it was a criminal offense to stop any office work to attend to a personal matter, I reached over and picked up my letters. I heard my "boss" cough significantly as I glanced through them. Two were from home, and I put them down, intending to read them at noon. One was from Fred. I put that down, too. And the other! Oh, that other! It was from—listen! It was from the editor of that great magazine in New York! I opened it with trembling fingers. The words jumped up at me and embraced me! My story was accepted, and a check for fifty dollars accompanied that brief, but blessed, note.

Mr. Hopkins was clearing his throat so pronouncedly now that I turned deliberately about in my chair and grinned hard at him. He glared at me indignantly. Little idiot! He thought I was trying to flirt with him!

"Are you through, Miss Ascough?" he asked.

"No, Mr. Hopkins," I responded blandly, "and I never will be now. I've just come into some money, and I'm not going to work for you any more."

"What! What!" he said in his sharp little voice, just like a duck quacking.

I repeated what I had said, and I stood up now, and began gathering my things together—my pocketbook, handkerchief, odds and ends in my desk, and the rose that Mr. Smith had given me that day.

Mr. Hopkins had a nasal, excitable, squeaking sort of voice, like the querulous bark of a dog—a little dog.

"But, Miss Ascough, you don't mean to say you are leaving now?"

"Yes, I do mean to say it," I replied, smiling gloriously.

"But surely you'll finish the letter on the machine."

"I surely will not," said I. "I don't *have* to work any more. Good-by." And out I marched, or, rather, flew, without waiting to collect three days' pay due me, and resigning a perfectly good fifteen-dollar-a-week job on the first money I ever received for a story!

I did not walk on solid ground, I assure you. I flew on wings that carried me soaring above that Land of Odors, where I had worked for four and a half hard months, right up into the clouds, and every one knows the clouds are near to heaven.

Mr. Hamilton? Oh, yes, I did remember some such person. Let me see. He was the man who thought I was incapable of taking care of myself, and who grandiloquently wanted to "make me over"; who once said I was "ignorant, uncivilized, undisciplined," and would never get anywhere unless I followed his lordly advice. How I laughed inwardly at the thought of the effect upon him of those astounding conquests that I was to make in the charming golden world that was smiling and beckoning to me now.

As soon as I got to my room, I sat down and wrote a letter to him. I wanted *him* to know right away. In fact, I had a feeling that if *he* didn't know, then all the pleasure of my triumph might go. This is what I said to him:

> Dear Roger
>   (Yes, I called him Roger now.)
>   Read, mark, learn, and inwardly digest the inclosed thrilling, extraordinary, and absorbing indorsement of
> > Your abused and forsaken
> > NORA

How had he the heart not to answer that letter of mine, I wondered.

Girls love candies, pretty clothes, jewelry, geegaws, and, as the old song has it, "apples and spices and everything nicest," they like boys and men and all such trifling things. Those are the things that make them giggle and thrill and weep and sometimes kill themselves; but I tell you there isn't a thrill comparable with that electric and ecstatic shock that comes to a young girl writer when, after many rebuffs, her first story is accepted. Of course, alas! that thrill is brief, and soon one finds, with wonder, that the world is actually going on just the same, and, more wonder of wonders! there are still trouble and pain and tragedy and other ugly things crawling about upon the face of the earth. Ah me!

They say the weird, seeking sound of a new soul is the most beautiful music on earth to the ears of a mother. I think a poet feels that way toward his first poem or story that comes to life. The ecstasy, the pain, and thrill of creating and bearing—are they not all here, too? I know that often one's "child" is unworthy, uncouth, sometimes deformed, or, worse, a misshapen and appalling monster, a criminal product, as it were; but none the less he is one's own, and one's love will accompany him, even as a mother's, to the gallows.

"It never rains but it pours," says a homely old adage. I thought this was the case with me now. Within a few days after I got that letter and check, lo and behold! I had three stories accepted by a certain Western magazine. I was sure now that I was not only going to be famous immediately, but fabulously wealthy.

Three stories, say, at fifty dollars each, made a hundred and fifty; add the fifty I had from the New York magazine, and you perceive I would possess two hundred dollars. Then do not forget that I had as well a little black suitcase full of other stories and poems, and an abortive effort at a novel, to say nothing of a score of articles about Jamaica. Besides, my head was teeming with extraordinary and unusual plots and ideas,—at least they seemed extraordinary and original to me,—and I felt that all I had to do was to shut myself up somewhere alone, and out they would pour.

I now sat down on the floor, with my suitcase before me, and I made a list of all my stories, put prices opposite them, added up the list, and, bedad! as O'Brien would say, I was a rich girl!

In fact I felt so confident and recklessly happy that nothing would do but I must treat Lolly and Hermann to a fine dinner and the theater. My fifty dollars dropped to forty. But of course I was to get one hundred and fifty for those other three stories. It's true, the letter accepting them did not mention the price, but I supposed that all magazines paid about the same, and even though in the case of the Western magazine I was to be "paid upon publication," I was sure my stories would be published soon. In fact, I thought it a good thing that I was not paid all at once, because then I might be tempted to spend the money. As it was, it would come in just about the time I was through with the fifty.

If my ignorance in this matter seems infantile, I think I may confidently refer my readers to certain other authors who in the beginning of their careers have been almost as credulous and visionary as I. It's a matter of wonder how any person who is capable of writing a story can in other matters be so utterly impractical and positively devoid of common sense.

I never saw fifty dollars fly away as quickly as that fifty dollars of mine. I really don't know *what* it went for, though I did swagger about a bit among my friends. I took Mrs. Kingston and Mrs. Owens, the woman who lived with her, to the theater, and I went over to the Y. W. C. A. several times and treated Estelle and a lot of my old acquaintances to ice-cream sodas and things like that.

I avidly watched the news-stands for the December number of that Western magazine to appear, and when it did come out, I was so sure at least one of my stories was in it, that I was confounded and stunned when I found that it was not. I thought some mistake must have been made, and bought two other copies to make sure.

I was now down to my last six dollars. I awoke to the seriousness of my position. I would have to go to work again and immediately. The thought of this hurt me acutely, not so much because I hated the work, but because I realized that my dream of instant fame and fortune was in fact only a dream.

The December number of the New York magazine also was out, but my story was not in it. I wrote to the editors of both the Eastern and Western magazines, and asked when my stories would appear. I got answers within a few days. The New York magazine said that they were made up for several months ahead, but hoped to use my story by next summer,—it was the first week in December now,—and the Western magazine wrote vaguely that they planned to use my stories in "the near future."

I wrote such a desperate letter to the editor of that Western magazine, imploring him to use my stories very soon, that I must have aroused his curiosity, for he wrote me that he expected to be in Chicago "some time next month," and would be much pleased to call upon me and discuss the matter of the early publication of my stories and others he would like to have me write for them.

I said my fifty dollars flew away from me. I except the last six dollars. I performed miracles with that. I paid my share of our room-rent for a week—three dollars—and lived eleven days on the other three. At the end of those eleven days I had exactly ten cents.

For two reasons I did not tell Lolly. In the first place, while I had not lied to her, I had in my egotistical and fanciful excitement led her to believe that not only had I sold the four stories, but that they had been paid for. And in the second place, Lolly at this time was having bitter troubles of her own. They concerned Marshall Chambers. She was suffering untold tortures over that man—the tortures that only a suspicious and passionately jealous woman who loves can feel. She had no tangible proof of his infidelities, but a thousand little things had occurred that made her suspect him. They quarreled constantly, and then passionately "made up." So I could not turn to Lolly.

I had not heard a word from Mr. Hamilton, and after that glowing, boastful letter I had written, how *could* I now appeal to him? The mere thought tormented and terrified me.

Toward the end, when my money had faded down to that last six dollars, I had been desperately seeking work. I think I answered five hundred advertisements at least, but although now I was well dressed, an asset to a stenographer, and had city references (Fred's), I could get nothing. My strait, it will be perceived, was really bad, and another week's rent had fallen due.

I didn't have any dinner that evening when I went over to Mrs. Kingston's, but I had on my beautiful blue velvet suit. My luncheon had been a single ham sandwich. Mrs. Kingston had called me up on the telephone early in the day, and invited me over for the evening, saying she had some friends who wished to meet me.

Her friends proved to be two young men from Cincinnati who were living and working in Chicago. One, George Butler, already well known as a Socialist, was head of a Charities Association Bureau (I hysterically thought it an apropos occasion for me to meet a man in such work), and the other, Robert Bennet, was exchange editor of the *News*. Butler was exceedingly good-looking, but he had a thick, baggy-looking mouth, and he dressed like a poet,—at least I supposed a poet would dress something like that,—wearing his hair carelessly tossed back, a turn-over soft collar, flowing tie, and loose-fitting clothes that looked as if they needed to be pressed.

Bennet had an interesting face, the prominent attribute of which was an almost shining quality of *honesty*. It illuminated his otherwise rugged and homely countenance, and gave it a curious attraction and strength. I can find no other word to describe that expression. He wore glasses, and looked like a student, and he stooped a little, which added to this impression. Both boys were in their early twenties, I should say, and they roomed together somewhere near Jane Addams's Hull House, where both worked

ONOTO WATANNA

at night, giving their services gratuitously as instructors in English. They were graduates of Cornell.

Butler talked a great deal about Socialism, and he would run his hand through his hair, as Belasco does on first nights. Bennet, on the other hand, was a good listener, but talked very little. He seemed diffident and even shy, and he stammered slightly.

On this night I was in such a depressed mood that, despite Mr. Butler's eloquence, I was unable to rouse myself from the morbid fancies that were now flooding my mind. For the imagination that had carried me up on dizzying dreams of fame now showed me pictures of myself starving and homeless; and just as the first pictures had exhilarated, now the latter terrified and distracted me.

Mrs. Kingston noticed my silence, and asked me if I were not feeling well. She said I did not seem quite myself. I said I was all right. When I was going, she asked me in a whisper whether I had heard from Mr. Hamilton, and I shook my head; and then she wanted to know whether he knew of my "success." Something screamed and cried within me at that question. My success! Was she mocking me then?

Bennet had asked to see me home, and as it was still early,—only about nine,—he suggested that we take a little walk along the lake.

It was a beautiful night, and though only a few weeks from Christmas, not at all cold. Mrs. Kingston had apparently told Mr. Bennet of my writing, for he tried to make me talk about it. I was not, however, in a very communicative mood. I talked disjointedly. I started to tell him about my stories, and then all of a sudden I remembered how I was fixed, and then I couldn't talk at all. In fact, I pitied myself so that I began to cry. It was dark in the street, and I cried silently; so I didn't suppose he noticed me until he stopped short and said:

"You're in trouble. Can't you tell me what is the matter?"

"I've got only ten cents in the world," I blurted out.

"What!"

"Just ten cents," I said, "and I *can't* get work."

"Good heavens!" he exclaimed. "You poor girl!"

He was so sorry for me and excited that he stammered worse than ever, and I stopped crying, because, having told some one my secret, I felt better and knew I'd get help somehow.

So then I told him all about how I had come down to such straits; how I had worked all those months, and my implicit belief that that fifty dollars would last till I was paid for the other three stories.

When I was through, Bennet said:

"N-now, l-look here. I get thirty dollars a week. I don't need but half of that, and I'm going to give you fifteen a week of it till you get another place."

I protested that I wouldn't think of taking his money, but I was joyfully hailing him in my heart as a veritable savior. Before we had reached my lodging-place, I had not only allowed him to give me ten dollars, but I agreed to accept ten dollars a week from him till I got work.

It is curious how, without the slightest compunction or any feeling even of hurt pride or shame, I was willing to accept money like this from a person whom I had never seen before; yet the thought of asking Hamilton filled me with a real terror. I believe I would have starved first. It is hard to explain this. I had liked to think of myself as doing something very unusual and fine in refusing help from Hamilton, and yet where was my logic, since without a qualm I took money from Bennet? Our natures are full of contradictions, it seems to me. Perhaps I can explain it in this way, however. There was something so tremendously *good* about Bennet, so overpoweringly human and great, that I felt the same as I would have felt if a woman had offered to help me. On the other hand, I was desperately in love with Hamilton. I wanted to impress him. I wanted his good opinion. I unconsciously assumed a pose—perhaps that is it—and I had to live up to it. Then I have often thought that almost any woman would have confidently accepted help from Bennet, but might have hesitated to take anything from Mr. Hamilton.

Some men inspire us with instant confidence; we are "on guard" with others. I can write this analysis now; I could not explain it to myself then.

ONOTO WATANNA

XXV

Now my life assumed a new phase. No man like Bennet can come into a woman's life and not make a deep impression. I have said that Dick was my "shadow." Bennet was something better than that. He was my protector, my guide, and my teacher. He did not, as Dick had done, begin immediately to make love to me, but he came persistently to see me. Always he brought some book with him, and now for the first time in my life the real world of poetry began to open its doors for me. I a poet! Oh, me!

Hamilton had filled my bookshelves with novels, chiefly by French authors. They were of absorbing interest to me, and they taught me things just as if I had traveled; but Bennet read to me poetry—Keats, Shelley, Byron, Browning, Tennyson, Heine, Milton, and others. For hours I sat listening to the jeweled words. No, I could not write poetry,—I never shall,—but I had the hungry heart of the poet within me. I know it; else I could not so vividly, so ardently have loved the poetry of others.

I cannot think of my acquaintance with Bennet without there running immediately to my mind, like the refrain of an old song, some of those exquisite poems he read to me—read so slowly, so clearly, so subtly, that every word pierced my consciousness and understanding. Else how could a girl like me have gasped with sheer delight over the "Ode to a Grecian Urn"? What was there in a poem like that to appeal to a girl of my history?

When we did not stay in and read, Bennet would take me to some good theater or concert, and I went several times with him to Hull House. There twice a week he taught a class in English poetry. The girls in his class were chiefly foreigners,—Russian Jewesses, Polish and German girls,—and for the most part they worked in factories and stores; but they were all intelligent and eager to learn. They made me ashamed of my own indolence. I used to fancy that most of his pupils were secretly in love with Bennet. They would look at his inspired young face as if they greatly admired him, and I felt a sense of flattering pride in the thought that *he* liked only me. Oh, I couldn't help seeing that, though he had not then told me so.

Sometimes he took me over to his rooms. They were two very curious, low-roofed rooms down in the tenement-house district, completely lined with books. Here Butler, with his pipe in his loose mouth, used to entertain me with long talks on Socialism, and once he read me some of Kipling's poems. That was my first acquaintance with Kipling. It was an unforgettable experience. In these rooms, too, Bennet read me "Undine," some of Barrie's stories, and Omar Khayyam.

Those were clean, inspiring days. They almost compensated for everything else that was sad and ugly in my life. For sad and ugly things were happening to me every day, and I had had no word, no single sign, from Mr. Hamilton. I tried to shut him from my mind. I tried hard to do that, especially as I knew that Robert Bennet was beginning to care for me too well. Through the day, it was easy enough. I could do it, too, when Bennet read to me from the poets; but, ah, at night, that was when he slipped back insidiously upon me! Sometimes I felt that if I did not see him soon, I should go mad just from longing and desire to see his dear face and hear the sound of his cruel voice.

I got a position about two weeks after I met Bennet. It was in a steel firm; I stayed there only two days. There were two other stenographers, and the second day I was there, the president of the firm decided to move me from the outer to his private office, to do his work. Both of the girls looked at each other so significantly when my desk was carried in that I asked them if anything was the matter. One of them shrugged her shoulders, and the other said:

"You'll find out for yourself."

Within ten minutes after I entered that inner office I did. I was taking dictation at a little slat on the desk of the president when he laid a photograph upon my book, and then, while I sat dumfounded, trying to look anywhere save at what was before me, he laid more photographs, one after the other, on top of that first one, which was the vilest thing I have ever seen in my life.

The girls at the Y. W. C. A. and the girls at the stock-yards used to talk about their experiences in offices, and we used to laugh at the angry girls who declared they did this or that to men who insulted them. As I have written before, I had become hardened to such things, and when I could, I simply ignored them. They were one of the dirty things in life that working-girls had to endure. But now, as I sat at that desk, I felt rushing over me such a surge of primitive and outraged feeling that I could find no relief save in some fierce physical action. I seized those photographs, and slammed them into the face of that leering old satyr.

After that I went from one position to another. I took anything I could get. Sometimes I left because the conditions were intolerable; sometimes because they did not pay me; usually I was allowed to go after a brief trial in which I failed to prove my competence. I was very bad at figures, and most offices require a certain amount of that kind of work from their stenographers. These were the places where I failed.

Of course, changing my position and being out of work so much, I made little progress, and although I had had only twenty dollars from Bennet, I was unable to pay him back. I had hoped to by Christmas, now only a week off.

And now something happened that caused a big change in my life; that is, it forced me at last to separate from Lolly. For some time she had been most unhappy, and one evening she confided to me her suspicions of Chambers. She said she had "turned down" Hermann, who wanted to marry her, for Chambers, though friends had warned her not to trust him; but that though he had at times been brutal to her, she adored him. Pacing up and down the room, she told me that she wished she knew some way to prove him. It was then that I made my fatal offer. I said:

"Lolly, I could have told you long ago about Chambers. I *know* he is no good. If I were you, I'd have nothing more to do with him."

Lolly stopped in her pacing, and stared at me.

"*How* do you know?" she demanded.

"Because," I said, "he's tried several times to make love to me."

"You lie, Nora Ascough!" she cried out in such a savage way that I was afraid of her. If I had been wiser, perhaps, I might have reassured her and let her think I did lie. Then the matter would have ended there; but I had to plunge in deeper.

"Lolly, I'll prove it to you, if you wish."

"You can't," retorted Lolly, her nostrils dilating.

"Yes, I can, I say. He's coming to-night, isn't he? Well, you stay in that inner room, by the door. Let me see him alone here. Then you'll see for yourself."

She considered the suggestion, with her eyes half closed, blowing the smoke slowly from her lips, and looking at the tip of her cigarette. Then she shrugged her shoulders and laughed sneeringly.

"The trouble with you, Nora, is that because a lot of muckers at the Union Stock-Yards got 'stuck' on you, a few poor devils of newspaper men are a little smitten, and a fast rich man tried to keep you, you imagine every other man is after you."

I couldn't answer that. It was untrue. None the less, it hurt. I had never in my life boasted to Lolly about men. I supposed she knew that, like every other girl who is thrown closely into contact with men, I naturally got my share of attention. I had long ago realized the exact value of this. The girls at the yards, for instance, used to say that the men would even go after a hunchback or a girl that squinted if she gave them any encouragement. And as for Robert Bennet and Dick, it was mean of Lolly to refer to them in that contemptuous way. Lolly, I think, regretted a moment later what she had said. She was as generous and impulsive as she was hasty in temper. Now she said:

"Forget I said that, Nora. Just for fun I'll try your plan. Of course, it's ridiculous. Marshall has never looked upon you as anything but a joke. I mean he thinks you're a funny little thing; but as for anything else—" Lolly blew forth her cigarette smoke in derision at the notion.

Chambers came about eight-thirty. They never announced him, but we knew his double knock, and Lolly slipped into the inner room, but did not close the door tight.

I had taken up Lolly's mandolin, and now I painfully tried to pick out a tune on the strings. Chambers stood watching me, smiling, and when I finally did manage "The Last Rose of Summer," he said:

"Bully for you!"

Then he looked about quickly and said:

"Lolly out?"

I nodded. Whereupon he sat down beside me.

"Want to learn the mandolin?" he asked.

I nodded, smiling.

"This is the way," he said. He was on my left side, and putting his arm about my waist, and with his right hand over my right hand, he tried to teach me to use the little bone picker; but while he was doing this he got as close to me as he could, and as I bent over the mandolin, so did he, till his face came right against mine, and he kissed me.

Then something terrible happened. Lolly screamed. She screamed like a person gone mad. Chambers and I jumped apart, and I felt so weak I was afraid to go inside that room. Just then Hermann came rushing in with the landlady. She had heard Lolly's screams, and she wanted to know what was the trouble. I said Lolly was ill; but as soon as she went out, I told Hermann the truth. When Chambers realized that he was the victim of a trap, and while Lolly was still crying,—a moaning sort of cry now,—he picked up his hat and made for the door. There he encountered Hermann, all of whose teeth were showing. Hermann's hand shot up to Chambers's collar, and he threw him bodily from the room. How he did this, I am sure I don't know, for Chambers was a larger and seemingly much stronger man than Hermann. Then Hermann went in to Lolly, and I, feeling like a criminal, followed.

I had never seen a woman in hysterics before. Lolly was lying on her back on the bed, with her arms cast out on each side. Her face was convulsed, and she was gasping and crying and moaning and laughing all at the same time. Hermann put his arms about her, and tried to soothe and comfort her, and I, crying myself now, begged her to forgive me. She screamed at me, "Get out of my sight!" and kept on upbraiding and accusing me. She seemed to think that I must have been flirting with Chambers for some time, and she said I was a snake. She said she hated me, and that if I did not go "at once! at once! at once!" she'd kill me.

I didn't know what to do, and Hermann said:

"For God's sake! Nora, go!"

I packed my things as quickly as I could. I had no trunk, but two suitcases, and I made bundles of the things that would not go into them. I told Hermann I'd send for the things in the morning. Then I put on my coat and hat, and took the suitcase with my manuscripts and my night things. Before going, I went over to the bed and again begged Lolly to forgive me, assuring her that I never had had anything to do with Chambers till that night. I told her that I loved her better than any other girl I knew, better than my sisters even, and it was breaking my heart to leave her in this way. I was sobbing while I talked, but though she no longer viciously denounced me, she turned her face to the wall and put her hands over her ears. Then I kissed her hand,—women of my race do things like that under stress of emotion,—and, crying, left my Lolly.

XXVI

I went direct to Mrs. Kingston's. As soon as I walked in with my bag in my hand, she knew I had come to stay, and she was so delighted that she seized me in her arms and hugged me, saying I was her "dearest and only Nora." She took me right up to what she thought were to be my rooms, but I said I preferred the little one, and after we had talked it over a bit, she said she agreed with me. It was much better for me to have only what I myself could afford.

I didn't tell her a word about Lolly. That was my poor friend's secret; but I told her of my straitened affairs, my poor position and that I owed money to Bennet. When I ended, she said:

"That boy's an angel. I can't wish you any better luck than that you get him."

"Get him?"

"He is simply crazy about you, Nora. Can't talk about anything else, and you couldn't do better if you searched from one end of the United States to the other. He's of a splendid family, and he's going to make a big name for himself some day, you mark my words."

I agreed with all her praise of Bennet, but I told her I thought of him only as a friend, as I did of Fred O'Brien for instance.

She shook her head at me, sighed, and said that she supposed I still cared for "that man Hamilton," and I didn't answer her. I just sat on the side of the bed staring out in front of me. After a moment she said:

"Of course, if that's the way you feel, for heaven's sake! let poor Bennet alone; though if I were you, it wouldn't take me long to know which of those two men to choose between."

"You'd take Bennet, wouldn't you?" I asked heavily, and she replied:

"You better believe I would!"

"Don't you like Mr. Hamilton?" I asked wistfully.

"I don't entirely trust him," said she. "Candidly, Nora, that was a nasty trick he tried to play us here. I was 'on to him,' but I didn't know just where you stood with him, and I'm not in the preaching business. I let people do as they like, and I myself do what I please; and then, of course, Lord knows I need all the money I can get." She sighed. Poor woman, she was always so hard up! "So if he wanted to take those rooms and pay the price, I wasn't going to be the one to stand in the way. Still, I was not going to let him pull the wool over your eyes, poor kiddy."

"I suppose not," I assented languidly. I was unutterably tired and heartsick, with the long strain of those weeks, and now with this quarrel with Lolly, and I said, "Yet I'd give my immortal soul to be with him again just for a few minutes even."

"You would?" she said. "You want to see him as much as all that?"

I nodded, and she said pityingly:

"Don't love any man like that, dear. None of them is worth it."

I didn't answer. What was the use? She said I looked tired out, and had better go to bed, and that next day she would send the man who looked after the furnace for my belongings.

Mrs. Kingston was really delighted to have me with her. She said she could have had any number of girls in her house before this, but that she had set her heart on having just me, because I was uncommon. She had a funny habit of dismissing people and things as "ordinary and commonplace." I was not that, it seems.

Here was I now in a really dear little home, not a boarder, but treated like a daughter not only by Mrs. Kingston, but by Mrs. Owens, who quickly made me call her "Mama Owens." She was a pretty woman of about sixty, with lovely dark eyes, and white wavy hair that I often did up. She had periodical spells of illness, I don't know just what. Both Mrs. Kingston and Mrs. Owens were widows.

I brightened up a bit after I got there, for they wouldn't give me a chance to be blue. We had a merry time decorating the house with greens and holly, and we even had a big Christmas-tree. Mama Owens said she couldn't imagine a Christmas without one. Just think, though I was one of fourteen children (two of the original sixteen had died), I can never remember a Christmas when we had a tree!

Bennet came over and helped us with the decorations, and he and Butler were both invited to the Christmas dinner. Butler could not come, as he was due at some Hull House entertainment, but Bennet expected to have dinner with us before going to work. He was working nights now, and would not have Christmas off.

I was getting only twelve dollars a week at this time, so I had little enough money to spend on Christmas presents. I did, however, buy books for Bennet and Mrs. Kingston and Mrs. Owens. Also for Lolly, to whom I had written twice, begging her to forgive me. She never answered me, but Hermann wrote me a note, advising me to "leave her alone till she gets over it."

I had to walk to work for two days after that, as I didn't have a cent left, and I did without luncheon, too. I rather enjoyed the walk, but it was hard getting up so early, as I had to be at the office at eight. I was working for a clothing firm not unlike the one Estelle was with, and I had obtained the position, by the way, through Estelle.

On Christmas eve Margaret had to go to the house of a client in regard to some case, so mama and I were left alone. We were decorating the tree with strings of white and colored popcorn and bright tinsel stuff, and I was standing on top of a ladder, putting a crowning pinnacle on the tree,—a funny, fat, little Santa Claus,—when our bell rang. Our front door opened into the reception hall, where our tree was, so when mama opened the door and I saw who it was, I almost fell off the ladder. He called out:

"Careful!" dropped his bag, came over to the ladder, and lifted me down. You can't lift a girl down from a ladder without putting your arms about her, and I clung to him, you may be sure. He kept smoothing my hair and cheek, and saying,—I think he thought I was crying against his coat,—"Come, now, Nora, it's all right! Everything's all right!" and then he undid my hands, which were clinging to his shoulders, and shook himself free.

Mama Owens had never met him, so I had to introduce them. She scolded me dreadfully afterward about the way I had acted, though I tried to explain to her that it was the surprise and excitement that had made me give way like that.

It was queer, but from the very first both Margaret and Mama Owens were prejudiced against him. Both of them loved me and were devoted to Bennet. They were planning to make a match between us. Hamilton was the stumbling-block; and although in time he partly won Margaret over, he never moved mama, who always regarded him as an intruder in our "little family."

I now hinted and hinted for her to leave us alone, but she wouldn't budge from the room for the longest time. So I just talked right before her, though she kept interrupting me, requiring me to do this or that. She didn't ask him to do a thing, though if Bennet had been there, she would have seated herself comfortably and let him do all the work.

However, I was so happy now that it didn't matter if all the rest of the world was disgruntled. I hugged Mama Owens, and told her if she didn't stop being so cross, Mr. Hamilton and I would go out somewhere and leave her "all by her lonesome." I could do almost anything with her and Margaret, and I soon had her in a good humor; she even went off to get some Christmas wine for Mr. Hamilton.

I had in a general way told Roger something of what I had been doing since I had seen him; but I did not tell him of the straits to which I had come, or of the money I had borrowed from Bennet. He suspected that I had passed through hard times, however. He had a way of picking up my face by the chin and examining it closely. The moment we were alone, he led me under the gas-light, and looked at me closely. His face was as grave as if he were at a funeral, and I tried to make fun of it; but he said:

"Nora, you don't look as well as you should."

I said lightly:

"That's because you didn't come to see me."

"I came," he returned, "as soon as you did what I told you. As soon as Mrs. Kingston sent me word that you were here, I came, though it was Christmas eve, and I ought to be in Richmond."

I saw what was in his mind: he thought I had taken those rooms! I put my arm through his, just to hold to him in case he went right away, while I told him I had only the little room.

He said, with an expressive motion:

"Well, I give you up, Nora."

I said:

"No, please, don't give me up. I'll die if you do."

Margaret came in then, and she greeted him very cordially. She chuckled when I called her a "sly thing" for writing to him, and she said she had to let him know, since he had paid for the big room.

"Yes, but you didn't tell him I had the little room," I said.

"What does it matter?" laughed Margaret. "You two are always making mountains out of molehills. Life's too short to waste a single moment of it in argument."

Roger said:

"You are perfectly right. After this, Nora and I are not going to quarrel about anything. She's going to be a reasonable child."

I had to laugh. I knew what he meant by my being reasonable. Nothing mattered this night, however, except that he had come. I told him that, and put my cheek against his hand. I was always doing things like that, for although he was undemonstrative, and the nearest he came to caressing me was to smooth my cheek and hair, I always got as close to him as I could. I'd slip my hand through his arm, or put my hand in his, and my head against him; and when we were out anywhere, I always had my hand in his pocket, and he'd put his hand in over mine. He liked them, too, these ways of mine, for he used to look at me with a queer sort of grim smile that was nevertheless tender.

He was a man used to having his own way, however, and he didn't intend to give in to me in this matter of the rooms. So this is how he finally arranged things: I was to have the little room, and he would take the suite in front. When he was in Chicago, he would use these rooms; but when he was not, I was to have the use of them, and he made me promise that I would use the big room for writing.

This arrangement satisfied Mrs. Kingston and delighted me, but mama was inclined to grumble. She wanted to know just why he should maintain rooms in the house, anyway, and just what he was "after" me for. She was in a perverse and cranky mood. She talked so that I put my hand over her mouth and said she had a bad mind.

Roger explained to Margaret—he pretended to ignore mama, but he was talking for her especially—that they need have no anxiety in regard to his intentions toward me; that they were purely disinterested; in fact, he felt toward me pretty much as they did themselves. I was an exceptional girl who ought to be helped and befriended; that he had never made love to me, and, he added grimly, that he never would. My! how I hated mama at that moment for causing him to say that. In fact he talked so plausibly that Margaret and I threw black looks at mama for her gratuitous interference, and Margaret whispered to me that it should not happen again. Mama "stuck to her guns," however, and finally said:

"Well, let me ask you a question, Mr. Hamilton. Are you in love with Nora?"

He looked over my head and said:

"No."

That was the first time he had directly denied that he cared for me, and my heart sank. I wouldn't look at him, I felt so badly, nor did I feel any better when, after a moment, he added:

"I'm old enough to be Nora's father, and at my time of life I'm not likely to make a fool of myself even for Nora."

"Hm!" snorted mama, "that all sounds very fine, but what about Nora? Do you pretend that she is not in love with you?"

His stiff expression softened, but he said very bitterly, I thought: "Nora is seventeen."

Then he laughed shortly, and added: "I don't see how it can hurt her to have me for a friend, do you? As far as that goes, even if she does imagine herself in love with me, a closer acquaintance might lead to a complete cure and disillusionment, a consummation, I presume, much to be desired."

He said this with so much bitterness, and even pain, that I ran over to him and put my face against his hand.

"Wait a bit, Nora. We'd better get this matter settled once and for all," he said. "Either I am to come here, with the understanding and consent of these ladies, whenever I choose and without interference of any sort, or I will not come at all."

"Then I won't stay, either," I cried. "Margaret, *you* know that if he never comes to see me again, I'll jump into Lake Michigan."

They all laughed at that, and it broke up the strained conversation. Margaret said in her big, gay way:

"Of course you can come and go as you please. The rooms are yours, and I shouldn't presume to dictate to you." And then she said to mama: "Amy, you've had too much wine. Let it alone."

XXVII

Everything being made clear, Roger and I went up to his rooms. He shut the door, and said that "the two old ones" were all right enough, but he had come over 250 miles to see me, and he didn't care a hang what they or any one else thought, and that if they'd made any more fuss, he'd have taken me away from there without further parley. Then he asked me something suddenly that made me laugh. He wanted to know if I was afraid of him, and I asked:

"Why should I be?"

"You're right," he replied, "and you need never be, Nora. You can always trust me."

I said mischievously:

"It's the other way. I think *you're* afraid of me."

He frowned me down at that, and demanded to know what I meant, but I couldn't explain.

He lighted the logs in the fireplace, and pulled up the big Morris chair and a footstool before it. He made me sit on the stool at his knee. Then we talked till it was pretty late, and mama popped her head in and said I ought to go to bed. I protested that as I didn't have to go to work next day, I need not get up early. Roger said she was right, and that he must be going.

I had thought he was going to spend Christmas with me, and I was so dreadfully disappointed that I nearly cried, and he tried to cheer me up. He said he wouldn't go if he could help it, but that his people expected him home at least at Christmas. That was the first time he had ever referred to his "people," and I felt a vague sense of jealousy that they meant more to him than I did. But I did not tell him that, for he suddenly leaned over me and said:

"I'd rather be here with you, Nora, than anywhere else in the world."

I sat up at that, and said triumphantly:

"Then you *must* care for me if that's so."

"Have I ever pretended not to?" he asked.

"You told them down-stairs—"

He snapped his fingers as though what he had said there didn't count.

"Well, but you must be more than merely interested in me," I said.

"Interest is a pretty big thing, isn't it?" he said slowly.

"Not as big as love," I said.

"We're not going to talk about love," he replied. "We'll have to cut that out entirely, Nora."

"But I thought you said you wanted me to go on loving you, and that I was not to stop, no matter what happened."

He stirred uneasily at that, and then, after a moment, he said:

"That's true. Never stop doing that, will you, sweetheart?"

You see, I was succeeding beautifully with him when he called me *that*. He regretted it a moment later, for he rose and began fussing with his bag. I followed him across the room. I always followed him everywhere, just like a little dog. He took a little package out of his bag, and he asked me if I remembered the day in the carriage, when he told me to open my mouth and shut my eyes. Of course I did. He said that I was to shut my eyes now, but I need not open my mouth. He'd give me the real prize now.

So then I did, and he put something about my neck. Then he led me over to the mirror, and I saw it was a pearl necklace.

At that time I had not the remotest idea of the value of jewelry. I had never possessed any except the ring Dick had given me. In a vague sort of way I knew that gold and diamonds were costly things, and of course I supposed that pearls were, too. It was not, therefore, the value of his present that impressed me, for I frankly looked upon it merely as a "pretty necklace"; but I was enchanted to think he had remembered me, and when I opened my eyes and saw them, they looked so creamy and lovely on my neck that I wanted to hug him for them. However, he held me off at arm's length, to "see how they looked" on me.

He said I was not to wear them to work, but only on special occasions, when he was there and took me to places, and that he was going to get me a little safe in which to keep them. I thought that ridiculous, to get a safe just to keep a string of beads in; and then he laughed and said that the "beads" were to be only the forerunner of other beautiful things he was going to give me.

I had never cared particularly about jewelry or such things. I had never had any, and never had wanted any. I liked pretty clothes and things like that—but I had never thought about the subject of jewelry. I told this to Roger and he said he would change all that.

He was, in fact, going to cultivate in me a taste for the best in everything, he said. I asked him why. It seemed to me that nothing was to be gained by acquiring a taste for luxurious things—for a girl in my position, and he replied in a grim sort of way:

"All the same, you're going to have them. By and by you won't be able to do without them."

"Jewels and such things?"

"Yes—jewels and such things." Then he added:

"There need never be a time in your life when I won't be able to gratify your least wish, if you will let me."

When he was putting on his coat, he asked me what sort of position I had, and I told him it was pretty bad. He said he wished me to go down to see Mr. Forman, the president of a large wholesale dry-goods firm. He added that he had heard of a good position there—short hours and good salary. I was delighted, and asked him if he thought I'd get the position, and he smiled and said he thought I would.

He was drawing on his gloves and was nearly ready to go when he asked his next question, and that was whether I had made any new acquaintances; what men I had met, and whether I had been out anywhere with any particular man. He usually asked me those questions first of all, and then would keep on about them all through his visit. I hesitated, for I was reluctant to tell him about Bennet. He roughly took me by the shoulder when I did not answer him at once, and he said:

"Well, with whom have you been going out?"

I told him about Bennet, but only about his coming to see me, his reading to me, and of my going to his and Butler's rooms, and to Hull House. He stared at me so peculiarly while I was speaking that I thought he was angry with me, and he suddenly took off his coat and hat and sat down again.

"Why didn't you tell me about this chap before?" he asked me suddenly.

"I thought you wouldn't be interested," I quibbled.

"That is not true, Nora," he said. "You knew very well I would."

He leaned forward in the chair, with his hands gripped together, and stared at the fire, and then he said almost as if to himself:

"If I had come on, this wouldn't have happened."

"Nothing has happened," I insisted.

"Oh, yes, this—er—Bennet is undoubtedly in love with you."

"Well, suppose he is?" I said. "What does it matter to you? If you don't care for me, why shouldn't other men?"

He turned around and looked at me hard a moment. Then he got up, walked up and down a while, and then came over and took my face up in his hand.

"Nora, will you give up this chap if I ask you to?"

I was piling up proof that he cared for me more than he would admit. I said flippantly:

"Old 'Dog in the Manger,' will *you* love me if I do?"

He said in a low voice:

"I *can't*."

I said sadly:

"Is it so hard, then?"

"Yes, harder than you know," he replied.

Then he wanted to know what Bennet looked like. I painted a flattering picture. When was he coming? To Christmas dinner, I told him.

It was now very late, and I heard the clock in the hall strike twelve, and I asked him if he heard the reindeer bells on the roof.

"Nora, I don't hear or see anything in the world but you," he replied.

"If that's so, you must be as much in love with me as I am with you," I told him.

He said, "Nonsense," and looked around, as if he were going to put his things on again.

"Stay over Christmas!" I begged, and after staring at me a moment, he said:

"Very well, I will, then."

That made me tremendously excited. Mama came down the hall and called:

"Nora, aren't you in bed yet?" I called out:

"I'm going now." Then I seized his hand quickly, kissed it, and ran out of the room to my own.

XXVIII

Early next morning while we were at breakfast, a huge box of flowers and a Christmas package from Bennet came for me. It was fun to see Roger's face when I was unwrapping the flowers. I think he would have liked to trample upon them, he who did not love me! They were chrysanthemums, and the other present was a beautiful little painting. Mama asked Hamilton to hang it for us, and he said curtly that he didn't know anything about such things.

Christmas morning thus started off rather badly, for any one could see he was cross as a sore bear, which, I don't mind admitting, gave me a feeling of wicked joy. To make matters worse, mama began to talk about Dick. I tried to change the subject, but she persisted, and wanted to know when I had heard from him last and whether he was still as much in love with me as ever. There was no switching her from the subject, so I left the table, and pretended to fool with the books in the library. He followed me out there, and his face was just as black!

"So," he said, with an unpleasant laugh, "you've been having little affairs and flirtations right along, have you? You're not the naïve, innocent baby child you would like me to think, eh?"

"Now, Roger, look here," I said. "Didn't you tell me you weren't going to scold me any more, and you said I could do as I pleased, and be independent and—"

"I supposed you would be candid and truthful with me; I didn't suppose you'd be carrying on cheap little liaisons—"

When he got that far, I turned my back on him and walked out of the room.

I adored him, but I was not a worm.

I went back to the kitchen, and watched Margaret clean the turkey and make the stuffing. I thought I was much interested in that proceeding, but all the time I was wondering what he was doing, and soon I couldn't stand it any longer, and I went back to the living-room, which was also our library, but he was not there. I went up-stairs, with "my heart in my mouth," fearing he had gone. I found him, if you please, in my room. He was looking at the photographs on my bureau.

I came up behind him, slipped my hand through his arm, and rubbed my cheek against his sleeve. I could see his face in the mirror opposite us slowly softening.

ONOTO WATANNA

"Are you still angry with me for nothing, Roger?" I asked.

"Was this fellow Lawrence in love with you, too?"

I nodded.

"All men aren't like you," I said slyly. "Some few of them do like me."

He took that in as if it hurt him.

"He's in Cuba, you say?"

I nodded.

"You hear from him?"

"Yes."

"Where are his letters?"

I couldn't show him the letters, I said. So then he tried to free himself from my hand, but he couldn't; I held so tightly.

"It wouldn't be square to Dick to show you his letters," I said.

"So it's 'Dick,' is it?" he sneered.

I nodded.

"Yes, just as it was 'Fred' with O'Brien."

"O'Brien wasn't in love with you."

"Oh, well, maybe Dick isn't. He just thinks he is."

"Any understanding between you?"

I hesitated. I really think he would have taken pleasure in hurting me then for that long pause. I said at last:

"He asked me to wait for him, but I'm not going to, if you'll come lots to see me."

"Did you promise to?"

Again I paused, and this time he caught up my face, but savagely, by the chin.

"Well?"

I lied. I was afraid of him now.

"No," I said.

For a man who did not love a girl he was the most violently jealous person I have ever known. When he got through questioning me about Dick, he started in all over again about Robert Bennet. I foresaw that we were to have a pretty quarrelsome Christmas, so I tried my best to change the subject.

I showed him all the photographs on my bureau, of my father, my mother, and my thirteen brothers and sisters, and told him about each of them. He listened with seeming politeness, and then swept the whole matter aside with:

"Hang your family! I'm not interested in them. Now, about this Bennet—" and he started in all over again.

Finally, thoroughly exasperated, I turned on him and said:

"You have no right to question or accuse me like this. No man has that right unless I specially give it to him."

He said roughly:

"Give me the right then, Nora."

"Not unless you care for me," I said. "You say you are only interested in me. Well, say you love me, and then I'll do anything you wish. I won't look at or speak to or think of any other man in the world."

"Well, suppose I admit that. Suppose I were to tell you that I do love you, what would you want then, Nora?"

"Why, nothing," I said. "That would be everything to me, don't you see? I'd go to school then, just as you want me to, and I'd study so hard, and try to pull myself up till I was on your level—"

"Oh, good God!" he said, "you are miles above me now."

"Not socially," I said. "In the eyes of the world I'm not. I'm just a working-girl, and you're a man in—in—fashionable society, rich and important. I guess you could be President if you wanted to, couldn't you?"

"Oh, Nora!" he said, and I went on:

"Yes, you might. You can't tell. Suppose you got into politics. You said your grandfather was governor of your State. Well, why shouldn't you be, too? So don't you see, to be your wife, I'd have to—"

"To be—what?" he interrupted me, and then he said sharply and quickly:

"That's out of the question. Put all thought of anything like that out of your head. Suppose we change the subject right now. What do you say to a little sleigh-ride?"

I nodded and I tried to smile, but he had hurt me as hard as it is possible for a man to hurt a woman.

It was not that I looked upon marriage as such a desirable goal; but it was at least a test of the man's sincerity. As he had blundered on with his senseless jealousy of men who did want to marry me, I had dreamed a little dream.

We had our ride, and then dinner in the middle of the afternoon. Bennet was there for dinner. He thought Mr. Hamilton was our new lodger, and before him at least I did conceal my real feelings. Anyhow, I confess that I felt none too warmly toward Roger now. He had descended upon me on this Christmas day, and while putting his gifts on my neck with one hand, he had struck me with the other. Do not suppose, however, that my love for him lessened. You can soothe a fever by a cooling drink; you cannot cure it.

Bennet had to go immediately after dinner, and I went with him as far as the door. All our rooms on the ground floor ran into one another, so that from the dining-room one could see directly into the reception-hall. Bob—for I always called him that—led me along by the arm, and suddenly mama clapped her hands loudly, and he seized me and kissed me! I was under the mistletoe. Roger knocked over his chair, and I heard him swear. Bob also heard, but neither of us cared.

XXIX

That Christmas visit of Roger's was the first of many in that house. From that time he came very frequently to see me, sometimes three or four times a month; in fact, a week rarely passed without his appearing. All of his visits were not so tempestuous as the one I have described, but he was a man used to ruling people, and he wished to govern and absorb me utterly. Well, I made a feeble enough resistance, goodness knows. I was really incredibly happy. I always used to come home from work with the excited hope of finding him there, and very often he was, indeed.

Of course he was exacting and at times even cruel to me. He really didn't want me to have any friends at all, and he not only chose all my clothes, but he tried to sway my tastes in everything. For instance, Bennet had cultivated in me a taste for poetry. Roger pretended that he didn't care for poetry. He said I would get more good from the books he had chosen for me, and just because, I suppose, Bennet had read aloud to me, he made me read aloud to him, sometimes my own stories, sometimes books he would select; but never poetry.

The first thing he would always say when he came in, after he had examined my face, was:

"What's my wonderful girl been reading?"

Then I'd tell him, and after that I'd have to tell him in detail everything that had happened through the week, several times sometimes. He knew, of course, that Bennet came regularly to see me, and he used to ask me a thousand questions about those visits; and I had a hard time answering them all, particularly as I did not dare to tell him that every day Bennet showed by his attitude that he was caring more for me. He asked me so many questions that I once asked him seriously if he was a lawyer, and he threw back his head and laughed.

I had secured a very good position through his influence, for I was private secretary to the president of one of the largest wholesale dry-goods firms in Chicago. I had easy hours, from ten till about four. I had no type-writing at all to do, for another girl took my dictation. What is more, I received twenty-five dollars a week.

Besides my good position, Fortune was smiling upon me in other ways. The Western magazine began to run my stories. I was the most excited girl in Chicago when the first one came out, and I telegraphed to Roger to get the magazine.

And now I must record something about Robert Bennet. He had been pushed from my pages, just as he was from my life, by Roger, and yet during all this time I really saw more of him than of Roger himself. The day I paid him back the money he lent me he told me he loved me. Now, I had for him something the same feeling I had for Fred O'Brien—a blind sort of fondness rather than love, and overwhelming gratitude. It was not so much because of the money he had lent me, but for the many things he was always trying to do for me. In a way he and Mr. Butler tried to educate me. They planned a regular course of reading for me, and helped me in my study of English. I should not have dared to admit it to Roger, but those boys were really doing more for me than he was, and they wished me to enter Cornell, and wrote to certain professors there about me.

It's a fact that nearly every man (and some women) who became interested in me during this period of my career seemed to think himself called upon to contribute to my education. I must have been truly a pathetic and crude little object; else why did I inspire my friends with this desire to help me? And everybody gave me books. Why, that Western editor, after he had met me only once, sent me all sorts of books, and wrote me long letters of advice, too.

But about Bennet. When he told me he loved me—and it is impossible for me to say in what a manly way he declared himself—I was too overwhelmed with mingled feelings, and I was such a sentimental, impressionable little fool, that I did not have the strength to refuse him. The first thing I knew, there I was engaged to him, too!

It was a cruel, dishonest thing for me to accept him. I see that now; but somehow, then, I was simply too weak to tell him the truth—that I loved another man. Well, then, as I've said, I was engaged to Bennet.

In a psychological way it might be interesting to note my feelings at this time toward both Hamilton and Bennet. I truly was more afraid for Bennet to find out about Hamilton than for the latter to find out about Bennet. To Roger I could have defended my engagement; but how could I have justified myself to Robert Bennet, whose respect and liking I desired very much? Indeed, they were now a potent influence in my life, a clean, uplifting influence.

Robert Bennet had unconsciously given me a new ideal of life. My own crude, passionate views were being adjusted. It was slowly dawning upon me that, after all, this thing we call convention, which I had previously so scouted, is in fact a necessary and blessed thing, and that the code which governs one's conduct through life is controlled by certain laws we cannot wilfully break. I had just grown, not like a flower, but like an unwieldy weed. Robert Bennet and George Butler were taking me out and showing me a new world. I was meeting people who were doing things worth while, sweet women and big men, and there were times in my life when I realized that the spell under which Roger held me was an enchantment that in the end could lead only to degradation or tragedy.

Nevertheless, I could no more break away from his influence than the poor victim of the hypnotist can from the master mind that controls him. What is love, anyhow, but a form of hypnotism? It's an obsession, a true madness.

Yet Roger Hamilton, in his way, had not deceived me. He had never once professed to love me. On the contrary, he had denied that very thing in the presence of Mrs. Kingston and Mrs. Owens. Perhaps if he had cared for me, if he had given me even some slight return, my own passion for him, from its very force, would have spent itself. But he did not. He kept consistently to his original stand. I was his special protégé, his wonderful girl, his discovery, his oasis, and compensation for everything else in life, which he said was sordid, nasty, and wrong. But that was all I was, it seems, despite his incomprehensible jealousy, and his occasional unaccountable moods of almost fierce tenderness toward me.

There were few times that he called me by endearing terms. Twice, I think, I was his "sweetheart," and several times I was his "precious girl." Once I was his "poor little darling," and I was always his "wonderful girl."

Nor was he a man given to demonstrations of affection. My place was always on the stool at his knee. I used to put my head there, and look with him into the fire. He never took me in his arms during those days, though I was always clinging to his hand and arm. He kissed my hands, my hair, and once my arms when I was in a new evening gown that he had chosen for me; but he never kissed my lips.

I loved him blindly and passionately. I used to save things that he had touched—absurd things, like his cigar-butts, a piece of soap he had used, his gloves, and a cap he wore on the train. He hunted everywhere for it, but I did not give it up. I was like a well-fed person, with an inner craving for something impossible to possess.

ONOTO WATANNA

On my eighteenth birthday Roger gave me a piano. He had already given me many jewels, some of them magnificent pieces that I never wore except when he was there. I kept them locked up in the little safe. The piano, however, troubled me more than the jewels. It was big and, therefore, impressed me. When I protested to him about accepting it, he declared that he had bought it for himself as much as for me, but he arranged with a German named Heinrach to give me vocal lessons, and with a Miss Stern to teach me the piano. Heinrach said I had an exceptionally fine contralto voice, but I think Roger told him to say that. However, I enjoyed the lessons, though I soon realized that my voice was just an ordinarily good contralto. Roger said it was good enough for him, and that he wanted me to sing to him only. He chose all my songs, French, German, and English.

If I stop here to tell of the attentions and proposals I received from other men at this time, I'm afraid you will agree with Lolly that my head was a bit turned. But, no, I assure you it was not. I realized that almost any girl, thrown among men as I was, half-way good-looking, interesting, and bright, was bound to have a great many proposals. So I'll just heap all mine together, and tell of them briefly.

One of the chief men in the firm where I worked asked me to marry him. He was a divorcé, a man of forty-five, but looked younger. He said he made fifteen thousand dollars a year. He wanted me to marry him and accompany him on a trip he was to make to England to buy goods. I refused him, but—away from Roger, I confess there were the germs of a flirt in me—I told him to ask me again as soon as he got back. I might change my mind. Before sailing, he brought his young son, a youth of twenty, to see me. Papa had scarcely reached the English shores before the son also proposed to me! He was a dear child.

An insurance agent offered himself to me as a life policy.

An engineer, a politician (Irish), and two clerks in our office were willing to take "chances" on me.

A plumber who mended our kitchen sink proposed to me just because I made him a cup of tea.

I had a proposal from a Japanese tea merchant who years before had been my father's courier in Japan. Now he was a Japanese magnate, and papa had told me to look him up. He made a list of every person he had ever heard me say I did not like, and he told me if I would marry him, he would do something to every one of them.

A poet wrote lovely verse to me, and the Chicago papers actually published it. Finally, that Western editor proposed to me upon his fourth visit to Chicago, and I am ashamed to confess that I accepted him, too. You see, he had accepted my stories, and how could I reject him? He lived far from Chicago, and the contemplated marriage was set for a distant date, so I thought I was safe for the present.

I was now, as you perceive, actually engaged to three men, and I was in love with one who had flatly stated he would never marry me. I lived a life of not unjoyous deceit. I had only a few qualms about deceiving Roger, for with all these other men proposing to me, I resented his not doing so, too. However, I was by no means unhappy. I had a good position, a charming home, good friends, a devoted admirer in Bennet, and was not only writing, but selling, stories, with quite astonishing facility. Add to this my secret attachment to Roger, and one may perceive that mine was not such a bad lot. But I was dancing over a volcano, and even dead volcanos sometimes unexpectedly erupt.

Bob was not an exacting fiancé. As he worked at night, he could not often come to see me; but he wrote me the most beautiful letters—letters that filled me with emotion and made me feel like a mean criminal, for all the time I knew I could never be more to him than I was then.

Like me, he was an idealist and hero-worshiper, and in both our cases our idols' feet were of clay. I deliberately blinded myself to every little fault and flaw in Roger. His selfishness and tyranny I passed over. It was enough for me that for at least a few days in the month he descended like a god into my life and permitted himself to be worshiped.

I made all sorts of sacrifices and concessions to his wishes. Time and again I broke engagements with my friends, with Bob and with others, because unexpectedly he would turn up. He never told me when he was coming. I think he expected some time to surprise me in doing some of the things he often accused me of doing, for he was very suspicious of me, and never wholly trusted me.

XXX

It was Bennet's letters that finally got me into trouble with Roger. I had been engaged to him only a little more than two weeks, and I must have dropped one of his letters in Roger's sitting-room, for on arriving home from work one afternoon I found that he had come in my absence, and, as Margaret warned me before I went up-stairs, seemed to be in a "towering rage" about something.

He was walking up and down, and he swung around and glared at me savagely as I stood in the doorway. He had a paper in his hand (Bennet's letter), and his face was so convulsed and ugly and accusing that involuntarily I shrank back as he came toward me. I have never seen a man in such an ungovernable rage. He did not give me a chance to say anything. There was nothing of which he did not accuse me. I was a thing whose meaning I did not even know. He, so he said, had been a deluded fool, and had let himself be led along by a girl he had supposed too good to take advantage of him. Yet all the while, while I was taking gifts—yes, the clothes on my back—and other favors, even my position, which I kept only because of Mr. Forman's obligations to him, I had, it seems, given myself to another man!

The accusations were so gross and monstrous and black that I could not answer him. I knew what was in Bennet's letter—terms of endearment, expressions of undying love, *and* (this is where I came under the judgment of Roger) the desire to see me soon again and hold me in his arms.

Yes, Bob had held me in his arms,—he believed I was to be his wife,—but I was not the thing Roger accused me of being. My relations with Bennet were as pure as a girl's can be. It would have been impossible for a girl to have any other kind of relations with a man like Bennet. I stood bewildered under the storm of his accusations and cruel reproaches, and the revelation of the things he had done for me without my knowledge or consent. At first, as he denounced me, I had flinched before him, because I was aware of having really deceived him, in a way; but as he continued to heap abuse upon me, some rebellious spirit arose in me to defy him. I had not had an Irish grandmother for nothing.

I waited till he was through, and then I said:

"You think you are a man, but I declare you are a brute and a coward. Yes, it is true, I am engaged to Mr. Bennet, and I defy you to say to him what you have said to me."

Then I fled from his room to my own. I locked myself in there. He came knocking at my door, and rattling at the handle, but I would not open it, and then he called out:

"Nora, I am going away now—forever—never to come back, you understand. You will never see my face again unless you come out and speak to me now."

But I would not open my door. I heard him going down-stairs and the slam of the front door. Now I realized what had happened. He had actually gone! Never before had he left me like this. I opened my door, went down-stairs, and then I saw him waiting for me in the living-room. I tried to run back, but he was too quick for me. He sprang after me, caught me in his arms, and half carried me up to his room. There he locked the door, and put the key into his pocket. I wouldn't look at him, I wouldn't speak to him. He came over, and tried to put his arms about me, but I shoved him away, and he said in a voice I had never heard from him before:

"So I've lost you, have I, Nora?" And then, as I would not answer him: "So Bennet cut me out. That's it, is it?"

I said:

"No; no one cut you out but yourself. You've shown yourself to me just as you are, and you're ugly. I *hate* you!" and I burst into tears.

He knelt down beside me. I was sitting on the edge of the big Morris chair, and all the while he talked to me I had my face covered with my hands.

"Listen to me, Nora. I know I've said things to you for which I ought to be horsewhipped; but I was nearly insane. I am still. I don't know what to think of you, what to do to you. The thought that *you*, whom I have cherished as something precious and different from every one else in my life, have been deceiving me all these months drives me distracted. I could *kill* you without the slightest compunction."

I looked at him at that, and I said:

"Roger, you don't think I've done anything wrong, do you?"

"I don't know what to think," he said. "It is a revelation to me that you were capable of deceiving me at all."

"But I am only *engaged* to Bob; that's all."

"Only *engaged*! In heaven's name! what do you mean? Do you intend to marry this man?"

"No, I never did; but—"

I was beginning to soften a bit to him. I could see his point of view. He was holding me by the arms so I couldn't get away from him, and when you are very close like that to a man you love (almost in his arms) you cannot help being moved. I was, anyway, and I said:

"I'll try and explain everything to you, if you won't be too angry with me."

"Go on."

"Well, you know when I got that fifty dollars, and gave up my position? Well, I spent it all and got down to ten cents, and I couldn't get work, and I was nearly starving—honestly I was. That last day I didn't have any dinner and hardly any luncheon or breakfast. Well then, I met Bob, and I told him—that very first night—and he lent me ten dollars, and insisted that I should take something from him each week till I got a position."

"In God's name, why did you not ask *me*?"

"I *couldn't*, Roger; I couldn't."

"Why not? Why not?"

"Because—because—I *loved you*. I could take help from a man I didn't love, but not from one I did."

I began to sob, and he sat down in the Morris chair, and lifted me up on his knee, but he held me off, so I could continue with my story.

"Go on now."

So then I told him everything: how, later, when I at last returned the money to Bennet, he had proposed to me, and how I couldn't help accepting him. "And, anyway," I finished, "engagements are nothing. I'm engaged to two other men as well."

I thought this was my chance to make a reckless clean breast of everything.

He tumbled me out of his lap at that, stared at me, gasped, threw back his head, and burst into a sort of wild laughter, almost of relief. Then suddenly he pulled me up into his arms, and held me hard against his breast for the longest time, just as if he were never going to let me go again, and then I knew just as well as anything that he did love me, even though he wouldn't admit it. So, with that knowledge, I was ready to forgive him for anything or everything.

You see, things were all turned about now, and I was in the position of the accuser and not of the accused, and that despite the attitude he pretended to assume. He wanted to know if all three of my friends had kissed me, and I had to admit that they had, and tell him just how many times. Dick had kissed me just that one time, Bob four times, and the Western editor just once. It was a bitter pill for Roger to swallow, and he said:

"And I have been afraid to touch you."

"That's not my fault," I said. "You can kiss me any time you wish."

He didn't accept my hint or invitation. He was walking up and down now, pulling at his lip, and at last he said:

"Nora, get your things all packed. I'll have to take you with me."

"Where?"

"I'm obliged to go abroad on a certain pressing matter. I came here to-day specially to be with you before leaving. I see I can't leave you behind."

"Do you mean—" I said, and for one delirious moment I imagined something that was impossible.

"I mean simply that, though it will be devilishly inconvenient, I shall be obliged to take you with me. I can't trust you here."

That thought still persisted in my foolish head, and I said:

"Roger, do you mean that we are going to be married?"

He stared at me a moment, and then said shortly:

"No. That's impossible."

I swallowed a lump that came up hard in my throat, and I could not speak. Then after a moment I said:

"You want to take me, then, because you are afraid some other man might get me, not because you want me yourself."

He said, with a slight smile:

"The first part of your statement is certainly true; the second part is questionable."

"I'm not going," I told him.

"Oh, yes, you are."

"Oh, no, I'm not."

"Are we to have another combat?"

"I'm not going."

"Can't leave your fiancé?" he asked.

"I'm just not going, that's all."

"What do you intend to do, then, while I'm gone?"

"Just what I'm doing now."

"You intend to continue your—er—engagement?"

"No; I'll break that off." I looked at Roger. "I owe that to *him*."

"H-m! Owe nothing to me, eh?"

My eyes filled up. I did owe much to him. He came over, picked my face up by the chin, and then drew me back to the seat by the fireplace, seating himself in the Morris chair, with me on the stool. He talked very gently to me now, and as if he were speaking to a child; but I could think only of one thing—that he was going away and I *could* not go with him. Why, he had not even told me he loved me, and though a few moments before I had believed he did, now the torturing doubts came up again. If he loved me, would he not want to marry me? Other men, like Bob and Dick, did.

"Roger, tell me this," I said. "Suppose I went to school and then to college, would I be like—other girls—I mean society girls—girls in your class?"

"You're better than they are now. You are in a class all by yourself, Nora."

"Don't answer me like that. You know what I want to know. Would I be socially their equal, for instance?"

"Why, naturally. That's a foolish question, Nora."

"No, it isn't. I just want to know. Now, supposing I got all that—that—culture—and everything, and I had nice manners, and dressed so I looked pretty and everything—and you wouldn't be a bit ashamed of me, and we could say my people were all sorts of grand folks,—they really are in England—my father's people,—well, suppose all this, and then suppose that you really loved me, just as I do you, then wouldn't I be good enough to be your wife?"

"Nora, why do you persist about that? I tell you once and for all that that is absolutely out of the question. I'm not going to marry you. In fact, I can't."

"Why?"

"I won't go into details. Let it suffice that there are reasons, and put the idea out of your head."

So, after that, there was nothing more for me to say; but he realized I would not go with him. When he at last resigned himself to this, he made me promise that while he was gone I would not only break my engagements with Bennet and the Western editor and Dick, but that I would in no circumstances let any man kiss or touch me, or make love to me in any way. He said if I'd promise him that, he'd be able to make his trip to Europe without undue anxiety, and that he would come back just as soon as he could.

"All right, then," I said; "I cross my neck."

I wrote three letters that night, all of which he read. If he had had his way, I would have rewritten them and worded them differently. He thought I ought to say: "Dear Mr. Bennet," "Dear Mr. Lawrence," etc., instead of "Dear Bob," "Dear Dick." My letters were virtually the same in each case. I asked to be released from my engagement; but I begged Bob to forgive me, and I said I should never forget him as long as I lived. Roger argued with me a whole half-hour to take that out. But I didn't, and I even cried at the thought of how I was hurting this boy who loved me. I was so miserable, in fact, that Roger said we'd go out and hear some music, and that would cheer me up.

Conscience is a peculiar thing. We can shut it up tightly, and delude ourselves with diversions that infatuate and blind us. I did not think of Bob while Roger was with me. I put on my prettiest dress, one of the dresses I now knew that he had paid for! It was a shimmering, Oriental-looking thing that had the stamp of Paquin upon it, and I had a wonderful emerald necklace, and a wreath of green leaves, with little diamonds sprinkled like dew over it, in my hair. Roger said that there was no one in the world like me. I suppose there was not. I certainly hope there was not. I was a fine sort of person!

I think it was the Thomas Orchestra we heard. I forget. I should have enjoyed it, I suppose, in ordinary circumstances, but I could not think of anything that night except that Roger was going away and that I might never see him again. And I thought of all the accidents that occurred at sea, and even though he was holding my hand under the program, I felt that I was the most unhappy girl in the world.

We couldn't stop to have even a little supper after the theater, for he was taking a train to New York, whence he was to sail.

His man Holmes (it was the first time I had ever seen him) was at the house when we got back, and had his bag and everything ready, waiting for him. I thought as he was going away on such a long trip he would at least kiss me good-by, and I could not keep from crying when, after we got in, he said right before Holmes, who *wouldn't* leave the room:

"I'll have to rush now. Be a good girl."

Then he said I was to go down to Mr. Townsend's (his lawyer's) office, and he would tell me about some arrangements he himself had made for me, and I was to write to him every day, though he said nothing about writing to me. He wrote down an address in London where I was to send my letters. The only thing he did that approached a caress was that, when his man went ahead of him down the stairs, he stopped in the upper hall, lifted my face, and gave me a long, searching look. Then he said:

"I'm not likely to think about anything but you, darling." Then he went quickly down the stairs, leaving me sobbing up there.

XXXI

I had enough to occupy my thoughts now without thinking of Bennet. Passionately as I loved Roger, I perceived that night, in a dim sort of way and with a burning remembrance of his brutality to me, that I was fast becoming the infatuated victim of one who was utterly unworthy. He had not hesitated to denounce and accuse me of things of which I was certainly incapable of being guilty. Though he had said I was his cherished and precious girl, and he knew I was a good girl (in the sense the world calls good), yet he did not consider me worthy of being his wife. It irritated him, that poor aspiration of mine. Yet other men, better men than he, men who, I do not doubt, though not possessing his great wealth, were his social equals,—Bennet and my editor,—had not thought me beneath them. I puzzled and tortured myself over it, but I could find no answer.

No one could deny that I was a clever girl. I was not the genius O'Brien and perhaps Roger believed, but I certainly was above the average girl in intelligence. Not many girls of eighteen are writing stories and having them accepted by the magazines. And yet, queerly enough, beyond my one precocious talent, I was in many ways peculiarly gullible and stupid. Why, the girls at the Y. W. C. A. teased me in all sorts of ways because of this, and Estelle used to say a blind beggar could sell me a gold brick at any street corner, and I would believe every word he said. This peculiar streak of credulousness in me was, I suppose, the reason I never found out anything about Mr. Hamilton.

He never talked to me about his business or home affairs. I knew he was president of half a dozen big firms, because I saw his name on stationery. Sometimes he talked to me about his horses and dogs,—he had many of these,—but he always said my little dog Verley, which he had never given back to me, and which was not, after all, a thoroughbred, was his inseparable companion. Even Mrs. Kingston and Mama Owens and Lolly knew more about this man than I did.

Love, it seems, is not only blind, but deaf, dumb, and paralyzed. I heard nothing, I knew nothing, and, what is more, I would have believed nothing that was not good of him. Surely a faith like that is deserving of some reward!

There is an adage of my mother's land something like this, "Our actions are followed by their consequences as surely as a body by its shadow." That proverb recurred to me in the days that followed.

The morning after Roger went, our bell rang before I was up. Our servant "slept out," and had not yet arrived. So Margaret went down, grumbling about the girl, supposing she had lost her key. As I didn't have to be at my office till ten, and as I had been up late, I turned over to go to sleep again, when I heard Margaret at my door. She came in in her bath-robe. She said Mr. Butler was down-stairs, and wanted to see me at once.

I don't know what I thought. I know I felt panic-stricken and afraid. Roger had sent my note to Bob by messenger the previous evening, so he had had it over night. I slipped on a dressing-gown quickly and went down-stairs.

Butler was sitting stiffly in the middle of the reception-hall, and as I came down he stood up, though he did not touch the hand I held out to him. He said abruptly:

"What did you do to Bennet?"

I felt like an overtaken criminal. I could not say a word. I could not look at the face of Bennet's friend. He said:

"Bob had a dinner engagement with me at a friend's house last night. He didn't turn up. I feared something was wrong. In fact, I've feared for Bob ever since he became infatuated with you." Butler did not mince his words; he just stabbed me with them. "He has been walking about the city like a madman all night long. What did you do to him?"

"Oh, George," I said falteringly, "I had to break it off."

As if distinctly to cut me for calling him "George" (I had always called him that), he addressed me as "Miss Ascough."

"Miss Ascough, were you ever really engaged to Bennet?"

He asked that as if the thought of it was something not at all to his liking. I nodded.

"And you broke it off, you say?"

Again I nodded.

"Why?"

"Because I didn't love him," I said truthfully.

I was so nervous and conscience-smitten and unhappy, and the room was so cold, that I was seized with a shivering fit, and could hardly keep my teeth from chattering; but Butler did not seem at all moved by my condition.

"May I ask if you were 'in love,' as you call it, with him when you accepted him?"

I shook my head. I could not trust myself to speak.

"Why did you accept him, then?"

"He had been good to me," I faltered.

"Oh, I see. It was his reward, eh?" He sneered in my face. "I came here," he said, "with some idea of patching up things. I wanted to help Bennet. He's in a bad way."

What could I say? After a while he said:

"Will you go back with me? I have him at our rooms."

"It would do no good."

"You mean you could not be made to reconsider the thing? You may be mistaken. You may care for him, after all. There are few like him, I assure you. You're dead lucky to have a man like poor Bennet care for you. He's of the salt of the earth."

"I know; but—I can't deceive him any longer. I'm—in love—with another man."

There was a long silence after that, Butler just staring at me. Then he asked:

"Been in love long?"

I nodded.

"Before you met Bennet?"

Again I nodded.

He laughed bitterly.

"Personally I suspected you from the first. I had an intuitive feeling that there was something under cover about you. I never could see what Bennet saw in you. He was head and shoulders above you in every way. You're not in his class at all. I don't mean that in the cheap social sense— simply morally. Bennet's been my friend for years. I know him. There's no one like him. It's damned hard luck, I can tell you, for me to see him come up against a proposition like you. According to your own story, you must have deceived him from the first. Women like you—"

He stopped there, for I was crying so bitterly that mama came in to see what the trouble was. Margaret was listening all the time at the head of the stairs. Butler then just clapped his hat on his head, picked up his stick, and went.

And that was the opinion of me of one of the brightest men in the United States, a man who subsequently became internationally famous. Nothing could have equaled the contempt of his looks or his cutting words. He had stripped me bare. For one startling moment the scales dropped from my eyes. I *saw* myself! And I shrank before what I saw— shrank as only a weak coward can.

O'Brien had called me a "dead-game sport"; Roger once said I was a "mongrel by blood, but a thoroughbred by instinct"; Lolly had called me a "snake"; but George Butler, that keen-sighted, clear-headed man, knew me for something to be despised! What did I think of myself? Like every one else, I was capable of staring wide-eyed at my own shortcomings only for a little while, and then, like every one else, I charitably and hastily and in fear drew the curtains before me, and tried to hide myself behind them.

I pitied Bennet, whom I had hurt; but I had a vaster pity for myself, whom Roger had hurt.

Perhaps it will not be out of place for me to say here that Bennet achieved all that I tried to do. Such fame (if fame I may call it) as came to me later was not of a solid or enduring kind. My work showed always the effect of my life—my lack of training, my poor preparation for the business of writing, my dense ignorance. I can truly say of my novels that they are strangely like myself, unfulfilled promises. But Bennet! He climbed to the top despite me, and there he will always be.

It may well be believed that the days that followed were unhappy ones for me. Not only had I lost my two best friends, Bennet and Lolly, but Roger had disappeared, as it were, completely from my life.

I went to Mr. Townsend's office, as he had told me to do, but I did not accept the "arrangements" that Roger had made for me, and this despite the very earnest exhortations of his lawyer. I did not want, and I would not touch, the money that Roger had directed should be put in banks for me. He ought to have known I would not do that.

All day long my face burned. Something within me, too, was burning like a wild-fire. A thousand thoughts and ideas came rushing upon me. Everything that Roger had ever done for or said to me recurred to my mind, and jumbled with these thoughts came others of Bennet.

His was the most honest heart in the world. The little he had done for me had all been open and above board. He had not even declared his love for me until the day I was out of his debt, and free, therefore, to give him an honest answer.

But Roger! When I would not take what he tried to force upon me, he had found tricky channels through which they would fall upon me, anyway, and then had taunted me with their possession!

When I got home from work that night I asked Margaret if she knew that Roger had been paying for most of my clothes. She answered, with a chuckle:

"Naturally."

"What made you think that?" I asked.

"Because no girl working as you are could afford such things. That Paquin gown alone is easily worth two hundred dollars, if not more."

"I paid twenty for it," I said.

She laughed. I told her about the shop where there were "bargains," and she, as Lolly had done, laughed in my face.

"No shop," she said, "could give you a bargain in sables such as you have."

I had a brown fur set. I did not know they were sables. I had been less than a year in America. I was just eighteen. I came from a large, poor family. I did not know the value of clothes or jewels any more than poor, green Irish or Polish immigrant girls would know it in that time. What could I know of sables?

We lived very quietly now. I had to stay at home, as I had promised Roger to go out with no one till he returned. And then, of course, Bennet and Butler no longer came, and I abandoned my music lessons. I had never taken more than a half-hearted interest in them.

A restless spirit possessed me at this time, and I could not settle my mind to anything. I used to wander about Roger's rooms, with my thoughts disjointed and jumbled. I thought I was brooding over his absence, and then again I thought I was worrying about Bob. Then one day as I stood staring into the leaping flames of that fireplace, almost like an inspiration there came to me a great idea for a story.

For an hour I sat staring into the flames, the story slowly taking root in my mind, and the fascinating plot and characters unraveling before me. It was ten o'clock at night when I began to write, and I worked without stopping till the dawn.

That was how I began to write my first novel. I lived now with only one avid thought in my mind—the story I was writing. It infatuated me as nothing I had ever done before had infatuated me.

I resigned my position, and took a half-day place. I had a little over a hundred dollars saved, and the new position paid me seven dollars a week. As I supplied my own type-writer, I had the privilege of taking outside work in the afternoons.

I think Mr. Forman was really relieved when I told him I had decided to go, though he asked me anxiously whether I had consulted Mr. Hamilton about it. I said that I had written and told him. I had done my work there adequately (he gave me an excellent reference), but he had dismissed a faithful secretary, to whom he was attached, to make a place for me at Mr. Hamilton's request. I never knew this when I took that position, else I would not have taken it.

I left because of what Roger had said, for one thing. I preferred not to be under obligations to him for my position. Besides, I wanted a little more time in which to write my novel. The seven a week just paid for my board, and I had enough saved to carry me along otherwise.

My new position was in a school, a sort of dramatic school where calisthenics, fencing, and other things were also taught. I had a chance to see something of the young men and women who were studying there, mostly of wealthy families. The courses were very expensive. A great many Chicago society women took fencing lessons there, and one of them was kind enough to offer to pay for lessons for me. I would have liked to learn, but I could not afford the time. Every minute that I had away from the school I gave to my precious novel. I used to get home about two. I'd have a glass of milk and a cracker for my luncheon, and then I would write until six. Then came dinner, and then again I wrote, sometimes till as late as midnight. I wrote my novel in twenty-two days. It is impossible for me to describe my delight and satisfaction when I put the last word to my manuscript.

Then for a long time I sat by the fire and re-read my story, and it seemed to me I had created a treasure. Roger, who professed to know something about palmistry, had averred there was a gold-mine in my hand, and he said that it was he who was going to put it there; but when I read my story that night I had a prophetic feeling that my mine would be of my own creating.

I now had to revise and type-write my story, no light task.

Outside of the work I did for the school, I had secured bits of copying for a few people in the building; but I had made very little above my salary. The head of the school was an imposing and majestic woman of about fifty, very handsome and charming and gracious in her manner, though I always resented the difference between her tone to me and that she assumed to her pupils and the people who frequented her studios—she called them studios. She had a little salon in a way. Nearly all Chicago's important people, and especially the celebrities, came to her "afternoons." I had a chance to see authors who had "arrived."

There was one very tall woman who wore glasses and talked through her nose. She was very well known at that time, having had a witty serial published in the very magazine that bought my first little story. She was much sought after, and was suffering from a bad case of what O'Brien always called "the big head." She looked and talked as if she were a personage of great superiority, and her sharp retorts and witty comments, always a bit malicious, were quoted everywhere in Chicago. I think she believed me to be one of her many silent admirers. I was not. I knew that when one has reached a stage of complete satisfaction with oneself, one has reached one's limitation. Chicago's popular writer at the zenith of her fame was not to me a particularly attractive object.

Then there was a celebrated Western author who was a giant in size and a giant in heart. I secretly adored him both as a writer and as a man. He wore his straight hair rather long, and though his face was becoming florid and full, he had a fine, almost Indian-like, profile. He was tremendously popular in Chicago, and Mrs. Martin, my employer, flattered and courted him despite his careless and rather grimy clothes and utterly unmanicured nails. Behold the measure of my sophistication! I who knew not the meaning of the word "manicure" less than a year before, took pride in my own shining nails now, and remarked the condition of those of a great author!

There was another less famous, but more exclusive, author who fascinated me chiefly because he had a glass eye. I had never before seen a glass eye.

I have mentioned the authors because they interested me more than the artists, sculptors, musicians, and actors and actresses who also came to these studios where I worked. The building itself was full of artists' studios.

Do not think of me as being one of this distinguished "set." I was, in fact, simply on the outskirts, a rather wistful, perhaps envious, and sometimes amused observer of these great people who had obviously "arrived."

Few of these celebrities noticed me. Several of the artists asked me to pose for them. I did not pose, because I had no time. I did go up to the studio of a hunchback artist who painted divinely and had a pretty wife and an adorable baby. I became very friendly with that lovely family, and even shyly confessed to them that I wrote. Just fancy! I, who only a few months before had forced every one to listen to my poems, now when I was in contact with people who did the very things I wished to do, experienced a panic at the thought of their finding out about it or of revealing myself to them!

Even Mrs. Martin never suspected me. I was simply a stenographer who had come to her from a mercantile firm. The only thing about me that ever appealed to her was my looks. Think of that! She said to me one day as I was going out:

"Miss Ascough, you look like a poster girl. Where did you get your hat?"

I told her, and she raised her eyebrows.

"Well," she said, studying me through her lorgnon, "your hair looks astonishingly well against that silver fur. Have you ever thought of going on the stage?"

I replied that I had not.

She regarded me speculatively a moment, and then said:

"There are worse-looking girls than you in the choruses."

I told her I could sing a little. Whereupon she said:

"Oh, I don't mean sing or act. However, you'd better stick to what you're doing until my season closes, and then, if you're a good girl"— she smiled very graciously—"I'll see what I can do for you."

Her season ended in June. You perceive I had something to look forward to!

And now I come to the author who was the cause of my discharge from this place.

Mrs. Martin herself had brought him to my desk and introduced him to me. He had with him a thick manuscript when he asked me, with a very charming smile, if I would type-write for him. You may be sure I was glad to get this extra work, as my funds were running low. So I put aside the copying of my own novel, and went hard to work upon the play of this Chicago author. It was a closely written manuscript, a play in six acts. He required eight copies, only four of which were to be carbons. In order to get the work done as soon as possible and resume the copying of my own story, I went down to the office three nights and worked till eleven.

As I have said, there were six acts, and each was of forty pages. So, you see, it was a fairly big manuscript. A public stenographer would have charged at the rate of five cents a folio,—that is, one hundred words,—and there were about two hundred and eighty words to a page. She would also have charged about two cents a page for the carbon copies. I made out my bill for five cents a page, and did not charge for the carbon copies.

The author had been coming every day and going over the work as I did it, and he had me not only bind his play, but rule parts of it in red ink—the descriptive parts. I felt mightily pleased when I handed him the completed manuscript. Rather apologetically I proffered him my bill.

He took the latter, and looked at it as if much surprised and pained, and then said:

"Why, Miss Ascough, I brought this to you as a friend of Mrs. Martin."

I said:

"Yes, that's why I did not charge for the carbons, and made you just a half-rate."

"There seems to be some mistake," he replied. "I understood from Mrs. Martin that you would do this work just as if it were for her."

"Do you mean," I said, "for nothing?"

He made a gesture with his hands, as much as to say, "Don't put it so baldly."

I stared at him. I could not believe that any one would be mean enough to let me do all that work for nothing. He was a greatly admired author. His play seemed, in my youthful judgment, a fine thing, and yet was it possible that he would impose upon a poor working-girl? Could he really believe that I, who was being paid only seven dollars a week for my morning services, would have worked afternoons and evenings to type-write his play without charge?

He put his play in a large envelop, and then he said:

"I appreciate very much what you have done, and I am pleased with your work. I shall make a point of recommending you to friends of mine." He cleared his throat. "I've also brought you a little present in token of my appreciation." He took from his coat pocket a book, one of his own. "It's autographed," he said, smiling, and gave it to me.

I held his book with a thumb and forefinger, as if it were something unclean, and then I deliberately dropped it into the waste-paper-basket.

He turned violently red and walked into Mrs. Martin's studio.

I had started in aimlessly to change the ribbon,—I had worn out one for his play,—when Mrs. Martin sailed majestically from her room and up to my desk.

"Miss Ascough," she said, "I won't require your services any further. You may leave at once."

I shrugged my shoulders, sneered, and laughed right up in her face, as if the loss of such a job as that was a matter of supreme indifference to me. She became as red as her friend, and walked haughtily back to her private quarters.

XXXII

I carried my machine home. Machines are heavy things. A sort of rainy snow was falling, and though it was only four in the afternoon, it was beginning to grow dark. The streets were in a bad state with slush and mud and ice, and I got very wet on my way to the car, for I couldn't put up an umbrella, as I had to carry my machine under one arm and my manuscript under the other.

As soon as I walked into our house, Margaret called out from the dining-room:

"Mr. Hamilton is here." Then he got up—he was having tea with them—and came over to me. I had the type-writer in my hand, and I don't know whether I dropped it or set it down on the floor.

I hadn't had any luncheon, I was soaked through. I had worked for weeks on my novel, and, besides the office work, I had type-written that long play. I had been working day and night, and I had been insulted and discharged. I was tired out, cold, and wet. Add to this the sudden shock of seeing Mr. Hamilton, and you will understand why even a healthy girl of eighteen may sometimes faint.

It was only a little faint, and I came to while Roger was carrying me up-stairs; but I did not move, for his face was against mine.

Mama had come up with us, and when Roger set me on the couch, she said she'd take charge of me. She told him to go down-stairs and have Margaret make me a toddy, and to bring it up on a tray with my dinner. I felt like a big baby to have her fussing over me and taking off all my wet things. I had a lovely pink eider-down dressing-gown that she had made me, and she forced me to get into that and into dry stockings and slippers.

By this time Roger and Margaret came up with the tray, and all three were doing things for me. Roger himself mixed me a drink. It was hot, with brandy and lemon in it. As soon as I drank it, it went right to my head, for I had eaten nothing since morning, and I tried to tell them about Mrs. Martin's discharging me, and how that author had not paid me for all my work.

Cloudy as my head was and stumblingly as I talked, I won their sympathies. Roger said that the author was a mean little sneak, a cursed small cur, and that he'd like to kick him all over the town.

Then, because I started to cry, they tried to make me eat something and drink some coffee; but I was so sleepy I could not keep my eyes open. The first thing I knew, I was in my bed.

I slept and slept; I slept till ten o'clock the next day. The first thought I had was that Roger must have gone. I never dressed so quickly, and I ran to his room and knocked; but he was not there.

Margaret also had departed for work, but I found mama in the kitchen. She was making me an oyster stew, a thing for which I had acquired a liking. As soon as I appeared, she cried:

"You bad girl, what did you get up for? Here's a note for you."

With hands trembling with excitement, I read Roger's first letter to me. It was like him, those two brief, laconic sentences:

Back by noon. Stay in bed.

ROGER

Stay in bed! I never felt better in my life. I had my stew, and then I went up-stairs and finished copying my novel.

At noon to the minute Roger returned. He had all sorts of things for me: flowers,—orchids, mind you!—squab, fruit, jelly, and magazines. One would think I was an invalid, and I had to laugh at his look of disapproval when he discovered me busy at work. He said I was incorrigible.

He made no effort that day to conceal his feelings from me. It was not that he petted or caressed me; but he fussed over me all day, kept me right by the fire, and brought up my luncheon to me, as he said the lower floor was draughty. He kept feeling my head to see if I was feverish. I think I gave him a good fright the night before. He said he ought to have returned to Richmond the previous night, as there was important business there that needed his attention. He'd been obliged to keep the wires scorching all the morning. He would have to get away that night, however; but he wanted to make absolutely certain that I had recovered.

He said that he had been obliged to hasten his return, neglecting certain business in Europe, because I had not written to him as I promised to do. I did write him once, but the letter must have miscarried. However, he was not in a scolding mood that day, and every minute I thought he was going to pick me up in his arms.

He wanted to know if I had missed him, and I tried to pretend that I hadn't, that I had been absorbed in my writing. He looked so solemn over that and so far, far away from me that I wanted instantly to put my arms about his neck, and I debated with myself how I could reach him. I pulled up the stool in front of him, stood on it, and in that way reached his face. I gave him a quick kiss, and then jumped down. I thought he would laugh at that, but he didn't. I did though; but while I was laughing I suddenly thought of something that frightened me, and I asked him if he had had a fine time in Europe, and added that I supposed he had seen many lovely women.

I had a vague idea that France was simply brimming with fascinating, irresistible, and beautiful sirens whom no man could possibly resist, and the thought that Roger had been there made my heart almost stop beating; but not for long, for he said very gravely:

"I never noticed anything nor any one. My mind was engrossed with one thought only—my *own* little girl in Chicago."

Then he asked me if I realized that he had spent fewer than ten days in Europe, and that he had come here to me before even going to his home.

"Goodness!" I said slyly, "you *are* interested in me, aren't you?"

He looked at me queerly then, and he said:

"Nora, I'm 'dippy' about you."

"Is that slang for love, Roger?" I asked, which made him laugh, and then he tried to frown at me; but he could not. So he changed the subject abruptly, and made me tell him about all the things that had happened to me while he was away.

He said I was a "precious angel" for giving up Bennet, and that Butler was a "conceited pup," and I was a "little idiot" to mind anything he said. He wished *he* had been there. He said Mrs. Martin was a sycophant and a kowtowing old snob, and that he knew her well; and as for my going on the stage! One would think I was considering jumping off the face of the earth.

I told him he was pretty nearly as bad as the little Japanese, and he laughed and said:

"That Jap's all right. By George! I like his idea. It would give me peculiar satisfaction to wring the necks of one or two people we know," and he clapped his fist into his hand.

I said mischievously:

"Well, you know that Jap hated those enemies of mine because he loved me."

Roger chuckled, and said I might sit on that stool and hint till doomsday, but he was not going to tell me he loved me till he was good and ready.

"When will that be?" I asked, and he said solemnly, with mock gravity:

> "*I'm sure I don't know,*
> *Said the great bell of Bow.*"

"My father always said that there was no time like the present," I replied.

He laughed, but said seriously:

"Nora, if you play with fire, you'll be burned. Burns leave scars. Scars are ugly things, and I love only pretty things, like my precious little girl."

"Aha!" I said triumphantly, "then you admit it at last."

He burst out laughing and said:

"Trapped! Help!"

After a while he wanted to hear my novel. So then I read it to him, my beautiful story.

I read it well, as only an author can read his own work—not well in the sense of elocution, but with every important point brought out. It took me two and a half hours to read it, and when I was through, twilight had settled. I had read the last words chiefly by the light of the blazing fire. Roger got up, and walked up and down the room. I watched him from my seat on the stool by the fire. Then he suddenly came back to me, seized my manuscript, and made a motion as if he would consign it to the flames. At that I screamed, like an outraged mother, and caught at it, and he stood towering over me, watching me curiously.

"I wanted to try you then, Nora," he said. "Now I know that I have a bigger rival in your work than any man. What am I to do?"

I held my novel out to him.

"Burn it if you wish to, then. It represents only the product of my fancy; but *you* are my life," I said.

"Do you mean that?" he asked me, and I replied:

"Oh, yes, I do, I do."

"If I asked you to give up your writing, as I asked you to give up Bennet, would you do it for me?"

"Yes, everything and every one, Roger," I replied, "if only you will love me. Won't you?" In a voice full of emotion, he then said:

"Can you doubt it?"

A moment later he seemed to regret having revealed himself like that, and he swiftly made ready to go. He was taking an early train for

Richmond. His man was waiting for him at some hotel. I wanted to go down to the door with him, but he would not let me, and we said good-by before mama, who had come up to say dinner was ready. He didn't kiss me, but I kissed him right before mama, on his hand and sleeve. If I could have reached his face, I would have kissed him there. He kept smoothing my hair. He said he would be back very soon, that he would never stay away from me long now.

I watched him from the window. The rain of the previous day had frozen on the trees, and everything was glistening and slippery. A wind was coming from the north, and the people went along the street as if blown against their will.

Roger looked up before getting into the cab and waved to me at the window, and I thought, as once before I had thought, as I watched his carriage disappear, that perhaps it would always be like this. He would always go. Would there ever come a day when he would not come again?

That was on the twenty-sixth of February. He could not have stayed in Richmond more than a few hours, for at ten o'clock the following night he came back to me.

I was running over some new pieces at the piano when I heard the bell ring; but I had no idea it was he until he came into the room without knocking. There was something about his whole appearance and attitude that startled me. His face had a grayish, haggard look, as if he had not slept. I ran up to him, but he held me back and began to speak rapidly:

"Nora, I've only a few minutes in Chicago. I must catch the 11:09 back to Richmond. It's after ten now. My cab's at the door. This is what I've come for. I want you to go to-morrow, on as early a train as you can get, to a little hunting-lodge of mine in the Wisconsin woods. Holmes [his valet] will come and take you, and I want you to stay there for a week or ten days."

The oddness of his request naturally puzzled me, and of course I exclaimed about it, and wanted to know why he wished me to go there. He said irritably:

"What does it matter why? I want you to go. I insist upon it, in fact."

"But what will I do up there?" I asked.

"Anything you wish. Write, if you like. I've a man and woman there. You'll not be entirely alone. The change will do you good."

"Aren't you going to be there, too?"

"I'm afraid not. I'll try to get there for the weekend if I possibly can."

"But I don't want to go to a place all alone, Roger."

"I tell you, you won't be alone. I have a man and a woman there, and Holmes will take you."

"But I don't see the sense in going away out there in the middle of winter."

"I particularly want you to go. Are my wishes nothing to you, then? I want you out of Chicago for a few days. You've not been well and—"

"I never felt better in my life."

"Nora, I want you to go. You must go. Do this thing to please me."

As, puzzled, I still hesitated, he began to promise that he would join me there the next day, and when I still did not assent, he tried coaxing me in another way. He said he'd bring Verley and a hunting-dog, and he'd teach me how to ride horseback and to shoot. He had horses, too, somewhere near there; a big stock farm, I think. I told him I didn't want to shoot or kill things.

By this time he had worked himself up to a state of exasperation at my stubbornness, and his request really seemed to me so ridiculous and capricious that I began to laugh at him, saying jokingly:

"You're worse than a dog in a manger: you're a Turk. You want to shut me up in a box."

"That's true enough," he replied. "I wish I'd done it long ago."

He was standing very tall and stiff by the door, with his coat still on, and his arms folded grimly across his breast. I looked at him, and a half-mischievous, half-tender impulse overwhelmed me. I went closer to him, and put my hands on his folded arms as I said:

"I'll go, Roger, if you'll take me in your arms and kiss me."

He gave me *such* a look at that, and then his face broke, and he opened his arms. I went into them. I don't know how long I was in his arms. I never wanted to leave them again.

I presently heard his voice, low and husky, and felt he was trying to release himself from my hands. He said:

"I must go. I'll miss my train."

"O Roger, please don't leave me now!" I begged.

"I must," he replied, and then he went quickly out of the room. I followed him into the hall, though he was striding along so swiftly I could not keep pace with him. Just where the stairs began, I caught at his arm and held him.

"O Roger, you do love me, don't you?" I asked sobbingly, and he said hoarsely:

"Yes, I *do*."

Then he went down the stairs, and I after him. At the door he said I must go back; but I was still clinging to his hand, and when he opened the door I, too, went out.

Snow was falling densely, and the great north wind had brought on its wing a blizzard and storm such as Chicago had seldom known; but Roger and I, in that porch, saw nothing but each other.

He kept urging me to go in, saying I would catch my death of cold, and stooping down, and without my asking him this time, he took me in his arms and kissed me again and again.

"I love you, Nora," he said. "You're the only thing in the world I have ever loved. I swear that to you, darling."

Then he kissed me again, opened the door, and turned me back.

"Roger, tell me just this, at least," I pleaded. "Is there any other woman in your life?"

The question was out now. Like a haunting shadow that I dared not face there had always been that horrible thought in my mind, and now for the first time I had voiced it. With his arms still about me, looking down into my face, he said:

"No; no one that counts. I swear that, too, Nora."

Then I went in. I was like one in a beautiful trance. That room seemed to me the loveliest place on earth. Everything about it spoke of him. He had chosen the softly tinted Oriental rugs, the fine paintings,—there were paintings by great masters there,—my piano, and the great long table where I wrote. He had chosen all these things for me, and now I knew why he had done it. He loved me; he had said so at last.

I went about the room touching everything, and gathering up little things of his—papers and books; I went into his bedroom, and found his bath-robe. I put it on, and for the first time—though he had said the rooms were mine, I had not used them—I threw myself down there in the room where he had slept and all night long I lay dreaming of him.

XXXIII

The next day found Chicago enveloped in one of the worst snow-storms that had ever come out of the north. Of course the idea of my going to the Wisconsin woods was out of the question. It was impossible even to leave the house. All the trains were stalled, and many wires were down. I could not have gone, even had I tried. So I was obliged to remain at home, and even Holmes did not appear at the house, though he telephoned to say he would be up as soon as the storm stopped.

Shut in as we were in a great city caught in the paralyzing grip of a snow-storm, I did not come out of my exalted mood of intense happiness. All through that long day, when I had nothing to do but to watch the blinding snow and the vehicles and people that had dared to venture out, I was with Roger, alone, this time, never to be parted again. All the barriers were down between us. All we knew was that we loved each other. What did anything else matter? My work? Ah, it was a poor, feeble little spark that had fluttered out before this vast flame in my heart. I had no room, no thought, for anything else.

I loved. I had loved for many months in hunger and work and pain, and now at last the gods had rewarded me. My love was returned; Roger loved me. That was the most wonderful, the most beautiful, the most miraculous thing that had ever occurred in the world.

The telephone was ringing all day, and so was the door-bell. Mama, who wandered in and out to chat with me about the storm or other things, kept grumbling. She said some one had been trying to get Margaret on the long-distance telephone all day, but Margaret had to go out on a case. Whoever it was, he would leave no message.

Once I answered the telephone myself, and though the voice sounded as if it was far away, I fancied the voice was Roger's. Oh, I had only him on my mind! It was some one for Margaret, and when I said:

"I'm Miss Ascough. Can't I take a message?" he replied:

"No," and rang off.

Margaret came in about five, and when we told her about the telephone, she seemed much mystified, and called up the information bureau and asked who had called her, and the bureau said Richmond had been calling.

Naturally, we were surprised that the calls were really from Richmond, and we were sure it must be Roger. Mama said he was probably anxious about me, but I could not help wondering why, if it was he on the telephone, he had not spoken to me. Margaret said it was probably his secretary or a clerk, and when I spoke of the voice, she said all Southern voices were alike.

She was called out again as soon as she had changed her clothes; but it was only in the neighborhood, and she had only thrown a shawl about her and run out, saying I was to take any messages that came.

So when a telegram came, I signed for it, and then, though it was addressed to Margaret, I opened and read it, thinking it might be important. I couldn't for the life of me understand it, and I handed it to mama. She read it, glanced at me, and then said that Margaret would probably understand.

It was really from Roger, but why he should telegraph Margaret not to let me see some papers, I could not understand. This was the telegram:

On no account let Nora see the papers.

While I was puzzling over this, Margaret came in, and I gave her the telegram. She took a long time to read it, and then she said carelessly that he referred to some papers,—deeds and things like that,—and he probably wished to surprise me.

It was a poor sort of explanation, but it satisfied me. I was too far up in the clouds to give the matter much thought, so Margaret and mama and I had dinner together. I prepared spaghetti, a dish of which they were fond, and which I made better than any one else. However, I burned the spaghetti,—let it go dry,—and mama said:

"You're a nice cook, with your mind away off in Richmond."

Margaret was in the pantry, but I knew she was listening. I said, after giving mama a squeeze for forgiving me about the spaghetti:

"You're going to find out a thing or two about him soon. You don't know what a beautiful character he has, and you know very well no man ever had a nicer smile than Roger."

Mama nodded, and went on stirring what she was cooking.

"You're a foolish old angel," I went on. "You just don't like him because you're fond of me. Well, if it weren't for me, you would like him, wouldn't you, Mama?"

She said:

"It may be a case of prejudice, dearie, but he's got to 'show' me first, though."

"Oh, he will," I assured her. "You'll see." Then I added: "Anyhow, you'll admit that he does care for me, won't you?"

"Any one can see with half an eye that he's head over heels in love with you; but—"

Margaret had come out of the pantry, and she banged some things down so noisily that we both jumped.

"For heavens' sake! don't talk about that man!" she said.

Then mama and I laughed, and we had dinner. I had been up-stairs only a few minutes after dinner when I heard Margaret at the telephone again. I went down to learn what the trouble was. As I was going down I heard her say:

"It's impossible. A dog couldn't go out in a storm like this." Then after a moment, she added, "I said I'd do what I could," and then: "You needn't thank me. It's not on your account, d—— you!" She hung up the receiver.

"Who was that?" I asked. She answered savagely—she she had never spoken so crossly to me before:

"None of your business!" and slammed out into the kitchen.

The storm abated during the night, and by morning it had ceased; but the city was still snow-bound, though workers were out all night clearing the streets, and an army of snow-shovelers went from house to house as soon as daylight came. They began ringing our door-bell as early as six o'clock, and that awoke me; so I dressed and went down-stairs. Margaret was ahead of me. I went to the porch to get the papers, but she was irritable because I opened the door and let in the cold. She said she wished to goodness I'd stay in my own room.

At breakfast we were without the papers, and Margaret told mama they had not come. The storm had probably prevented their delivery. I said I didn't mind running out to the nearest newsstand, but she said:

"For heaven's sake! Nora, find something to amuse yourself with without chasing wildly round! Now the storm's over, that man Holmes will be here, and you'd better get ready."

So, though I thought we'd have some difficulty in getting a train,— none was running on time,—I packed the few things I intended to take with me.

If any one sees anything particularly immoral in my calmly preparing to go on a trip with this man, I beg him to recall all of my previous experiences with him. He had never done anything that caused me to fear him, and now he could do nothing that would have been wrong in my eyes.

I was love's passionate pilgrim. I could not look ahead; I turned not a glance back; I only thrilled in the warmth of the dear present.

About ten, Holmes arrived. He said we could get a train at eleven and one at four. The four o'clock one would be better, as by that time the snow would be cleared off; but Mr. Hamilton had telephoned and telegraphed instructions that we should take the very first train.

So, then, with my bag packed, I came down-stairs, and went to the kitchen to say good-by to Margaret and mama. When I opened the door, they sprang apart, and I saw the morning paper in their hands; mama was crying. All of a sudden I had a horrible fear that something had happened to Roger, and I sprang over and tried to take the paper from mama. She tried to put it behind her, and we struggled for the sheet, but Margaret cried out:

"For God's sake! let her have it! We may as well end this."

And then I had the paper.

It was on the front page, so important was he, that vile story. I saw his face looking up at me from that sheet, and beside him was a woman, and under her picture was another woman. The type danced before me, but I read on and on and on.

And this was my love, my hero, my god—this married man whose wife was divorcing him because of another woman; whose husband in turn had divorced her because of him, Roger Avery Hamilton. I read the sordid story; I read the woman's tale in court, of his many infidelities, which had begun soon after their marriage, of the fast life he had led, and of his being named as co-respondent by his best friend in Richmond, whose wife had admitted the truth of the charge, and had been cast out by her husband.

This wife of his, of whose existence I had never even dreamed, said in an interview that although she did not believe in divorce and had endured her husband's infidelities for years, she was now setting him free for the sake of the other woman, whom he was in honor bound to marry. They had all been friends, they were of the same social set, and the relations between this woman and Hamilton, his wife declared, had existed for three years, and still continued.

If one's body were dead, and the mind still alive, how might that vital, mysterious organ find utterance through the paralyzed body? I have often wondered. Now I was like one dead. There was no feeling in any part of my body but my poor head, and through it surged, oh, such a long, long, weird procession of all the scenes of my life since I had left my home! It seemed as if every one I had ever known danced like fantastic shades across my memory, each one in turn beckoning to me or beating me back. And through that throng of faces, blotting out the black one of Burbank, the sensual one of Dr. Manning, the kind, grotesque face of O'Brien, and the rough, honest mask of Bennet, like a snake *his* bitter face rose, and stared at me with his half-closed, cruel eyes.

I was before the fireplace where I had often sat with him. Some one, mama or Margaret, had brought me there. They fluttered in and out of the room like ghosts, and they spoke to me and cried over me, but I do not know what they said. I had lost the power of hearing and of speech. I tell you I was dead—dead.

Then that little valet of his came up to the room and asked me if I was ready!

"Go away! Go away!" I murmured peevishly when he came around in front of me and looked at me curiously. Then Margaret came in and called shrilly at him:

"You get out of here—you and your d—— master!"

That commotion, I think, roused me slightly, for I went to my room, and I took from my lower drawer all of the foolish little things of his that I had collected at various times and treasured. I gathered them up in a large newspaper, carried them into his room, and dumped them into the fire.

Then I took that newspaper and spread it out on the desk, and I read the story all over again, slowly, because my brain worked like a clock that has run down and pulls itself to time only in spasmodic jerks. I found myself studying the picture of that woman who was not his wife. I cared nothing about the wife, but only of that other one, the woman his wife said he still loved.

She was all the things that I was not, a statuesque beauty, with a form like Juno and a face like that of a great sleepy ox. Beside her, what was I? Women like her were the kind men loved. I knew that. Women like me merely teased their fancy and curiosity. We were the small tin toys with which they paused to play.

I crushed that accursed sheet. No, no, she was not better than I. Strip her of her glittering clothes, put her in rags over a wash-tub, and she would have been transformed into a common thing. But I? If you put *me* over a wash-tub, I tell you *I* would have woven a romance, aye, from the very suds. God had planted in *me* the fairy germs; that I knew.

But rage! What has it ever done to heal even the slightest hurt or wound? Oh, I could tramp up and down, up and down, and wring my hands till they were bruised, but, alas! would that bring me any comfort?

I went back to my own room, and I packed not my clothes—those clothes he had paid for, but my manuscripts. They at least were all my own. They filled my little old black bag—the bag I had brought from Canada.

Margaret came to my door, and when she knocked I controlled my voice and said:

"I am busy. Go away."

"O Nora dear, Mr. Hamilton is on the 'phone," she said. "He is calling from Richmond. He wants to speak to you, dearie."

"I will never speak to him again," I declared.

"O Nora," she said, "he is coming to you now. He is taking a special train. I am sure he can explain everything. He says that he can, dear."

"Everything is explained. I know *now*," I replied. Yes, that was true. I did know now.

I went stealing down the stairs on tiptoe. They had relaxed their guard, and I had watched for this moment as craftily as only one can who is insane, as indeed I was.

Outside the cold wind smote me. Snow was piled high on all sides. I passed along through great banks of it, and I climbed over sodden drifts and gigantic balls that children had rolled, and with my little black bag I went down to the beach. Where it began, I do not know, for I thought the white caps on the water, breaking against the shore, were great drifts of snow; and I went plodding on and on till I came to the water.

A policeman who had spoken to me when I turned down toward the lake must have followed me, for suddenly he came behind me and said roughly:

"Now, none of that," and I turned around and looked at him stupidly, only half seeing him.

He took me by the arm and led me away, and he asked me what was my trouble, and when I did not answer (how could I, who could scarcely speak at all?) he said:

"Some fellow ruin you?"

Ruin!

That word has only one meaning when applied to a woman. I had not been ruined in the sense that Chicago policeman meant, but, oh, deeper than that sort of ruin had been the damnatory effects of the blow that he had dealt me! He had destroyed something precious and fine; he had crushed my beautiful faith, my ideals, my dreams, my spirit, the charming visions that had danced like fairies in my brain. Worse, he had ruthlessly destroyed Me! I was dead. This was another person who stood there in the snow staring at the waters of Lake Michigan.

Where was the heroic little girl who only a little more than a year before, penniless and alone, had fearlessly stepped out into the smiling, golden world, and boldly challenged Fate? I was afraid of that world now. It was a black, monstrous thing, a thief in the dark that had hid to entrap me.

O Roger, Roger! I loved you even as my little dog had loved me. If you but glanced in my direction, I was awake, alert. If you smiled at me or called my name, my heart leaped within me. I would have kissed your hand, your feet; and when you were displeased with me, ah me! how miserable I was! There was nothing you touched I did not love. The very clothes you wore, the paper you had read and crushed, the most insignificant of your personal belongings were sacred to me. I gathered them up like precious treasures, and I hoarded them even as a miser does his gold. I was to you nothing but a queer little object that had caught your weary interest and flattered your vanity. You saw me only through the cold eyes of a cynic—a connoisseur, who, seeking for something new and rare in woman, had stumbled upon a freak.

The policeman said:

"I could run you in for this, but I'm sorry for you. I guess you went 'dotty' for a while. Now you go home, and you'll feel better soon."

"I have no home," I said.

"That's tough," he replied. "And you look nothing but a kid. Are you broke, too?"

"No," I said, though I really was.

"Have you any friends?"

I thought painfully. Mama and Margaret were my friends, but I could not go back there. *He* was coming by a special train. O'Brien? O'Brien was in New York. Bennet? I had stabbed Bennet even as Roger had stabbed me.

Who, then, was there?

Lolly; there was Lolly.

Drifts of feathery snow kept flying down from the housetops as the policeman and I passed along, and as icicles came crashing down upon the sidewalks he led me out into the middle of the road.

We came to Lolly's door, and the policeman rang the bell. I don't know what he said to the woman when she answered the door, but I ran by her and up the stairs to Lolly's room, and I knocked twice before she answered. I heard her moving inside, and then she opened the door and stood there with her blue eyes looking like glass beads, and a cigarette stuck out between her fingers. And I said:

"O Lolly! *Lolly!*" She stood aside, and I went in and fell down on my knees by the table, and threw out my arms upon it and my head upon them.

I felt her standing silently beside me for a long time, and then her hand touched my head, and she did a strange thing: she went down on her knees beside me, lifted up my face with her hand, just as Roger used to do, and stared at me. Then she threw her arms about me and drew me up close, and I knew that at last Lolly had forgiven me.

She could cry, but not I. I had reached that stage where tears are beyond us. They precede the rainbow in our lives, and my rainbow had been wiped away. I was out in the dark, blindly groping my way, and it seemed to me that though there were a thousand doors, they were all closed to me.

I was now sitting on a chair opposite Lolly. I had the feeling that I was crumpled up, crushed, and beaten. My mind was clear enough. I knew what had befallen me, but I could not see beyond the fog.

"I could have told you about him long ago," said Lolly, after a while.

I said mechanically:

"You spared me. I did not you."

"No, you did the right thing," Lolly replied. "If I had told you then what I knew—that Hamilton was a married man—I might have saved you this."

There was silence between us for a time, and then Lolly said:

"Did you know that Marshall Chambers is married? He married a rich society girl—a girl of his own class, Nora."

"Lolly, I don't know what to do. I think I am going to die," I said.

Lolly threw down her cigarette, and came and stood over me.

"Listen to me," she said. "I'll tell you what *you* are going to do, Nora Ascough. You are going to brace up like a man. You're going to be a dead-game sport, as O'Brien said you were. *You* have something to *live* for. You can start all over again. I wish that I could, but *I* have cashed *my* checks all in."

I looked up at her. There was something in her ringing voice that had a revivifying effect upon me. It aroused as the bugle that calls a soldier to arms.

"What have I to live for that you have not?" I asked her.

"You can *write*," she said. "You have a letter in your pocket addressed to posterity. Deliver it, Nora! Deliver it!"

"Tell me how! O Lolly, tell me how!"

"Get away from this city; go to New York. Cut that man out of your brain as if he were a malignant cancerous growth. Use the knife of a surgeon, and do it yourself. Soldiers have amputated their own legs and arms upon the battle-field. You can do the same."

She had worked herself up to a state of excitement, and she had carried me along with her. We were both standing up now, our flashing eyes meeting. Then I remembered.

"I have no money."

She dipped into her stocking, and brought up a little roll.

"There, take it! I'll not need it where I'm going."

Then I told her I had no clothes, and she filled her suitcase for me.

"Now," she said, "you are all ready. There's a train leaving about seven. You'll get to New York to-morrow morning. O'Brien will be there to meet you. I'll telegraph to him after I've put you on the train."

"Come with me, Lolly."

"I can't, Nora. I'm going far away."

O Lolly! Lolly! little did I dream how far. Two weeks later, riding in an elevated train, I chanced to pick up a newspaper, and there I learned of Lolly's suicide. She had shot herself through the heart in a Chicago hotel, leaving a "humorous" note to the coroner, giving instructions as to her body and "estate."

I was in the Chicago train whirling along at the rate of sixty miles an hour. I lay awake in my berth and stared out at a black night; but in the sky above I saw a single star. It was bright, alive; and suddenly I thought of the Star of Bethlehem, and for the first time in many days, like a child, I said my prayers.

ONOTO WATANNA

A Note About the Author

Winnifred Eaton, (1875–1954) better known by her penname, Onoto Watanna was a Canadian author and screenwriter of Chinese-British ancestry. First published at the age of fourteen, Watanna worked a variety of jobs, each utilizing her talent for writing. She worked for newspapers while she wrote her novels, becoming known for her romantic fiction and short stories. Later, Watanna became involved in the world of theater and film. She wrote screenplays in New York, and founded the Little Theatre Movement, which aimed to produced artistic content independent of commercial standards. After her death in 1954, the Reeve Theater in Alberta, Canada was built in her honor.

A Note from the Publisher

Spanning many genres, from non-fiction essays to literature classics to children's books and lyric poetry, Mint Edition books showcase the master works of our time in a modern new package. The text is freshly typeset, is clean and easy to read, and features a new note about the author in each volume. Many books also include exclusive new introductory material. Every book boasts a striking new cover, which makes it as appropriate for collecting as it is for gift giving. Mint Edition books are only printed when a reader orders them, so natural resources are not wasted. We're proud that our books are never manufactured in excess and exist only in the exact quantity they need to be read and enjoyed. To learn more and view our library, go to minteditionbooks.com